WAR'S EDGE

METAL FURY

RYAN W. ASLESEN

Cover Illustration Copyright © 2021 Ryan Aslesen
Cover design by Marc Lee www.marcwashere.com
Cover layout by Shawn T. King www.stkkreations.com
Editing by Tyler Mathis and Jason Letts
Interior design by FormattedBooks

ISBN 978-1-7375457-0-5 – Ebook
ISBN 978-1-7375457-1-2– Paperback

www.ryanaslesen.com

FLOATING DEATH...

**THE EVOLUTION OF A THOUSAND YEARS OF AR-
mored combat, grav-tanks are fusion-powered fortresses
weighing over 120 tons and equipped with the latest in high-
tech sensors, plasteel armor, and deadly weaponry. They are
humanity's ultimate war machines.**

Samuel Rutger was out of options and out of luck. Broke and
jobless, he turned to the only option that could provide for his
wife and sick daughter. He became a mercenary. When he joined
Breacher's Berserkers, the galaxy's most elite private military
force, he was initially designated as a logistics specialist. Far from
the front lines, Rutger never thought war would reach him, but
when he is reassigned as a gunner on a grav-tank he finds himself
at the tip of the spear in a bloody planetary civil war.

Rutger must learn to kill and do it well to survive the high
stakes of mechanized warfare. Fighting on the frozen fields and
congested urban streets of Scandova-4, staying alive becomes a
daily battle. But the grind of intense combat is only one of his
worries. He's also waging a war on the home front, trying desperately to keep his family intact, and the only ticket home is to fight
through a gauntlet of enemy forces. Haunted by the horrors of
war, hoping to save his family against all odds, Rutger discovers
that the toughest fight is not on the battlefield—but within.

In memory of Marine Lance Cpl. Joseph T. Welke,
who died November 20, 2004, serving
during Operation Iraqi Freedom.

ACKNOWLEDGMENTS

WRITING A NOVEL IS NOT AN EASY ENDEAVOR, AND as always, I would like to thank those that helped make this book possible. They are the talented people who work tirelessly behind the scenes to make me look good or at least do what they can to minimize the damage.

Special thanks to Tyler Mathis, a fellow Marine and brother-in-arms, for all his help with this story. You have been both a mentor and a friend. My stories wouldn't be what they are without your input and guidance.

I would also like to thank Jason Letts for the final edit of my manuscript. Any mistakes or shortcomings that remain in this book are mine and mine alone.

A big thanks to Marc Lee for the amazing cover art. Thanks to Shawn King for the great cover layout.

A heartfelt thanks also goes out to my readers. I appreciate you purchasing my books and taking the time to experience my stories. And a very special thanks to all of you who have extended kind words of positive support or left reviews and recommendations. It truly means a lot to me. I continue to enjoy this amazing journey, and I'll keep writing these books as long as you keep buying them or pay me to stop.

Last, and most importantly, I want to thank my family for all their continued love and support.

"Only the dead have seen the end of war."
–Plato

CORPORAL SAMUEL RUTGER PEERED FROM THE gunner's hatch at shapes moving in the night as he nervously waited. The rings of Scandova-4 and its several small moons provided enough ambient light for excellent night vision through the visor on his commo helmet. A cool breeze swayed tree branches overhead, and flashes of heat lightning flared silently from clouds on the horizon, hinting at a coming winter storm.

He watched logistics personnel and fellow grav-tank crewmen working in silent haste to resupply their M3A7 Patton tanks. The tanks' active camouflage systems had turned the squat, angular hulls of the grounded machines black to match the shadows in the forest of towering, fir-like trees around them. The transformation made them appear like dark specters scattered amongst the trees.

Second platoon had reached the bivouac site just before dusk, bringing with them the telltale signs of an army on the move. The moss-covered ground had been churned up by both wheeled and anti-gravity vehicles. Discarded ammo crates and ration packages littered the ground, and the smell of human waste and vehicle lubricants permeated the air in the once-pristine area.

Past the grove of trees, rolling fields of genetically modified purple corn rustled in the distance, the harvest delayed due to the protracted and bloody planetary civil war. The only other sounds were scuffs of boots on armored hulls and the soft chirps of fall crickets which would soon succumb to the planet's brutal winter season. Like humans, the crickets weren't native to Scandova-4. Both species were a pestilential presence to the natural order of things on the planet.

At the approach of a 25-ton Mk 98 Bear wheeled heavy logistics vehicle, Rutger pulled himself from the gunner's hatch and crouched on the rear deck beside the turret of his tank, *Bounty Hunter*. A tanker truck had topped off the tank's fusion reactor with liquid deuterium half an hour earlier. A specialized ammo tender would normally have resupplied the tank with 150mm cobalt rounds for the main gun using a special feed mechanism that mated with a recessed panel atop the turret, but the tenders were priority targets and in scarce supply at the front, so a flatbed Bear had been dispatched. *Great*, Rutger thought. The Bear had no feed mechanism; each main gun round would have to be loaded by hand, a laborious and time-consuming process. *Meanwhile, we're sitting ducks out here.*

The eight-wheeled truck pulled parallel to the tank. A trooper riding the bed threw back a section of plastic tarp and began to open a thick green polymer ammo crate. The heads-up display (HUD) on Rutger's visor identified the man wrestling with the crate as Corporal Yen.

"Reckon it'll rain?" Yen asked through the proximity net.

"Likely snow if it gets any colder," Rutger responded. "What's the word in the rear?" Rutger didn't personally know Yen, yet he recognized him from Headquarters & Services Battalion, where he worked before being transferred to tanks. Hopefully Yen knew something; REMF troops always had the gouge. Rutger briefly smiled to himself at the reference, Rear Echelon Mother Fucker, since he'd been one just a few months prior. The men and women on the front lines always seemed left in the dark, though in the logistic corporal's defense there really hadn't been a safe rear area in this conflict. The Repub support forces they'd caught with their pants down in the last breakthrough could attest to that. Rutger could still see the destroyed trucks and burning bodies in his mind.

"Oh, you know, another day in the suck," Yen replied, handing Rutger a 150mm plasma round. Wrapped in a thick gray polyurethane protective layer, the fat, cylinder-shaped shell contained molecularly aligned cobalt atoms.

Rutger quietly slid the round into the tank's reserve magazine at the back of the turret. If an enemy sniper hit them handling one of the rounds with a plasma rifle, he knew there wouldn't be anything left of him to ship back to his home planet of New Helena.

"C'mon. Don't bullshit me, gimme the scoop."

The corporal paused for a second, studying Rutger as though seeing him for the first time. Though they were likely the same age, Yen looked older than Rutger's twenty-three standard years and stood half a head taller. Rutger had a broad nose and thatch of black hair that suited his shorter stature. He'd been told he had his father's gray eyes, but Rutger had no idea. He'd been a kid when his father abandoned the family.

"You didn't hear this from me," Yen said, "but it looks like we're gearing up for another push. Talks of a cease-fire have fallen through." He handed Rutger another round.

Damn it! Not the news he'd wanted to hear. *I shouldn't have gotten my hopes up.*

The loading seemed to take forever. His back began to ache from being hunched over.

"That's the last round," Yen finally announced. He waved and then returned to the Bear's cab. The driver activated its hydrogen-injected engine and pulled out of the grove, heading back down the road. Though the engine emitted only a whiny hum, the sound of its acceleration seemed to echo through the night air.

Rutger depressed the button to close the armored magazine hatch. Standing up, he glimpsed the faint shimmer of a nearby Berserker tank from his platoon in the trees, but only because he knew where to look. The tank's active camouflage made it almost invisible. The platoon's four tanks were spread fifty meters apart in a defensive coil, with *Bounty Hunter* on the far left of the crescent formation. A paved road bisected the platoon and proceeded on, between trees, hedgerows, and open fields toward a forested ridge straight ahead.

Rutger's eyes followed the road to the ridge, where the storm clouds darkened the horizon. Forces from the Free Norden Republic awaited them somewhere out there, the enemy in a civil war that had gripped the planet for several months. The planetary government, the Scandovan Federation, had hired the Berserkers to help quell the renegade Republic's military coup. Rutger didn't consider either side good or evil. He had no real hatred for the enemy; he just wanted to survive the conflict. It didn't matter who they fought for, since the pay was the same, but experience had taught him that the money came easier when you fought for the winning side.

They'd arrived on Scandova nearly three months ago after roughly ninety days in transit, and now the troopers of Second Platoon, B Company, call sign "Bruiser," were deep inside Republic territory. The Berserkers had helped turn the tide of the conflict, but the outcome remained undecided.

Though numerically inferior to the Federation, the Repub forces showed more faith in their cause and a fiercer fighting spirit, especially since the conflict had moved into their territory. Federation and Berserker gains had come meter by bloody meter, yet much progress had been made. Civil wars were never civil, and the likely outcome would be a cease-fire and subsequent treaty, but Rutger couldn't predict the winning side. That was all above his pay grade. He only knew that somebody was getting rich one way or another, while the people of Scandova suffered. The Berserkers would keep pushing forward regardless. Second platoon would soon be underway again from the sound of things. *Enjoy the quiet while it lasts...*

For now they'd been tasked to hold the road and the line while Fed forces consolidated the rapid gains of the last two days. Their orders from the company commander, Captain Hensley, were clear: engage and destroy anything that came down the road.

It wasn't supposed to be like this. He'd been working as a driver in H&S Battalion, stationed in the rear. That had changed after a resupply trip, however, when his platoon sergeant informed him of his transfer to 1st Battalion as a replacement tank driver in a line company—tip of the spear. That was four days into the deployment.

After his recent promotion to corporal, Rutger had been reassigned from driver to gunner. He'd dreaded the promotion despite the bump in pay, because he would be replacing the tank's prior gunner and his brief best friend Tyrone Banks, who had been killed by a sniper. Though driver was the lowest-ranking man in the tank, he had enjoyed the position. Despite the virtual reality training and some brief hands-on experience, he considered himself ill-suited for the gunner's job. He lacked the killer instincts.

Over the past months, his crew had become his family away from home, surrogates for his wife and daughter back on New Helena, and losing Tyrone had hurt. Tyrone had acted as his mentor and was one of the best tankers in the company. *If he couldn't make it, what chance do I have?*

Even if he did survive, Rutger wondered if he would still have a family to return to.

Rutger stole one last look at the ridge ahead before lowering himself through the gunner's hatch. He settled into the bio-form seat, and the hatch closed automatically with a heavy thud above him. His cockpit-like console sat left of the main gun. The commander's station was to his right, on the opposite side of the gun's autoloading mechanism. Despite the 120-ton tank's massive footprint, there wasn't much room for the crew, their workstations shoehorned in almost as an afterthought.

"Any issues?" Staff Sergeant Todd Duran asked from the commander's station. He lay back thirty degrees in his reclining seat, eyes closed. Thirty-two standard years old, Duran was also the platoon sergeant, respected by all for his technical and tactical knowledge and extensive experience. Rutger knew he'd lucked out in being assigned to Duran's tank.

"No, Sarge," said Rutger.

"Good. Wake me up when it's my watch."

"Roger that." By the time Rutger strapped himself into his ejection seat, Duran was already asleep. He wished he would have remembered to piss outside before slipping into the turret, but in his haste to get back inside he forgot. The tank had a built-in relief tube for that purpose. His armored skins could allow him to urinate without that device if he needed to, but nobody liked soiling themselves if they could avoid it. Besides, the cabin smelled bad enough already.

Rutger pulled out a ration bar and stared at his station as he chewed the rubbery, tasteless stick of whey protein fortified with vitamins and minerals. His turret exterior holo displays remained as he left them. The three large holographic screens wrapped around, providing a panoramic view of the world outside in a host of enhanced spectra including magnification, infrared, thermal, millimetric radar, and sonic imaging. The screens could be further split or overlaid to show additional data. He could also project images directly onto his HUD, and virtually peer through the tank in any direction.

The control console below the screens featured a series of built-in multifunction displays and digital gauges that showed the vehicle's load out, weapons systems, power plant status, damage assessment, and threat detection. For enhanced viewing, this information could also be displayed on the larger holo-screens.

The weapons systems controls and the primary fire control joystick were positioned to his right, which allowed him to traverse the turret and fire the tank's weapons. The joystick also contained an emergency override switch, which would allow him to pilot the tank in an emergency or if short crewed. To his left, the secondary fire control joystick allowed him to operate secondary weaponry independent of the turret, such as the turret's remote weapon station or the port and starboard weapons pods that contained the tank's dual particle cannons and 30mm rotary plasma cannons. Further left along the console a currently inactive backup throttle provided control of the repulsors.

Each crewman performed specific duties—driver, gunner, commander—however, redundancies had been built into all control stations. If a man died or went missing, the other crewmen could perform his job from their positions. One trooper could operate the tank, yet if it came to that, his best move would be to drive off the battlefield. *If that's even an option.* Rutger had come a long way since joining the tankers but doubted he could control the entire beast on his own with his limited training. Hopefully it would never come to that.

The tank also contained a powerful AI computer, usually given ubiquitous names like George or Mary, that helped control and monitor the complex gravitational drive components plus the numerous sensors and weapons systems. It could respond to verbal as well as thought commands relayed via the microchip embedded in the base of each trooper's skull.

Behind the armored door to the driver's compartment, located beneath the main gun where the turret basket faced forward, the driver, Lance Corporal Zack Aubrey, likely lay fully reclined in his seat asleep. Unlike the other seats, the driver's reclined all the way to horizontal to facilitate egress out of the compartment, and was thus a hell of a lot more comfortable to sleep on. The driver also had privacy within his compartment, which Rutger missed even more than the fully reclining seat.

I wonder what Serena and Callie are doing right now? Holo-vids of his little girl Callie kept Rutger's morale up, yet he hadn't heard from them in several weeks. Serena usually sent one every week, but digital mail transfers often took considerable time reaching the front lines. With all the electronic interference and enemy jamming, units right next to each other had difficulty communicating. The last few videos she'd sent had been short. Rutger sensed resentment from her and a growing distance between them. The videos appeared to have become a chore for her, just a box to check on her to-do list. Rutger had joined the Berserkers for the excellent dependent medical care that Callie needed. Serena had agreed with the decision at the time, but now she acted resentful, as if he'd made the choice alone. *She resents me, but she sure as hell doesn't resent the money.*

Bathed in the soft blue interior lighting, Rutger stared at the holo-screens for the next two hours. The screens utilized a complex algorithm to provide a full-color view from outside, even in total darkness. The colors weren't quite as vivid as in full daylight but came damn close to it. Zooming in on the ridge, he could make out individual leaves and needles on the trees buffeted by the wind.

The tank's environmental control system normally kept the interior at a comfortable temperature when stationary. Rutger turned on the cooling vents above his seat to keep himself alert. The crew had gotten little rest over the last couple of days. Despite the cabin air filters, the environmental system didn't do much to combat the odor of unwashed bodies and stale breath. Rutger was used to it. He just wished Duran would allow him to keep his hatch cracked open a hair while on watch, as other commanders did despite regulations. Alas, Duran operated strictly by the book in that regard.

An alert chimed on the threat display. *Bounty Hunter's* passive electronic sensors detected an unidentified electronic signature from the tank's six o'clock. They'd been ordered to keep active sensors off and maintain radio discipline to avoid detection. Only the tank's passive sensors and essential equipment were online, which coupled with the tank's stealth features further reduced their electronic footprint. The signal detected was faint and intermittent, and the AI reported the source as unknown.

Rutger's mind raced. *Is that the logistics platoon returning with additional supplies, or Repub forces at our rear?* There was no other scheduled traffic for the night. He checked the tank's communication system, finding no new messages. The last one received several hours earlier reported that a recon drone had been shot down four kilometers to the northwest, well ahead of them.

George, he thought, *provide more data on bogie.*

"Due to electronic interference and current range, an accurate determination is unavailable at this time," the synthesized male voice replied smoothly.

Great. The unknown contact continued to move up the range bars toward their position. Rutger looked over at Staff Sergeant Duran and hesitated. He didn't want to wake the man unnecessarily, and he had nothing definitive to report. *You're a corporal now—start thinking like one. What would Banks do?*

Rutger watched and waited as the intermittent signal grew closer. Another contact appeared, followed by a third, all about two klicks away and closing. They appeared to be following the tree-lined road bisecting second platoon. Rutger relaxed somewhat, thinking that only friendlies would follow the road. *Maybe some Fed troops that wandered out of their AO.* This area was allegedly clear, yet he had to consider that some Repub forces might have been bypassed during their last rapid advance. He needed to know more, and quickly.

AI could be tricky; sometimes how you phrased the question influenced the answer. "George, what's your best ID estimate on approaching bogies? Friendlies or enemies?"

A microsecond later, the computer replied. "Based on electronic signature, speed, and pattern of movement, I estimate there is a 53.1 percent chance that the contact is hostile."

Shit, that's greater than half. He decided to wake Duran. Before he could, a more urgent alert tone suddenly sounded in his headset, signaling that George had positively identified the closing signatures as hostile. Rutger's face paled as he looked at the schematic on the threat display. *Enemy tanks.*

CHAPTER

RUTGER STARED IN DISBELIEF AS FOUR—*MAKE IT six!*—bright red squares suddenly appeared on the threat display, glowing and growing nearer. Occupying the center multifunction screen on his console, the threat display constituted the detection hub of the tank's sophisticated electronic sensor suite, able to pick up radar, electromagnetic, sonic, and radio signals. He knew the enemy tanks had a similar sensor suite.

"Staff Sergeant!" Rutger called.

Duran sprang awake. "What is it?"

"Repub tanks."

"On the ridge?"

"No, behind us on the hardball."

Duran's eyes widened as he focused on the displays. The AI had identified the six red icons as four Repub HBT-6 tanks and two Type 98 armored personnel carriers (APCs). Schematics of the enemy vehicles rotated on Rutger's righthand display. He watched in rapt fascination as the formation closed on the platoon's rear, now about a klick away and in perfect firing position.

"Should I alert the others?" Rutger asked.

"No, they may have detected them as well," Duran said. "If we radio them, we may alert the enemy. Aubrey, wake up! We have enemy tanks behind us, don't do *anything* unless I say."

"Roger that," Aubrey replied in a hoarse whisper from the driver's compartment. The most junior member of the crew, Rutger could only imagine what was going through his mind having to wake up to this shit storm.

Do they know we're here? If not, then perhaps they would drive past them. No such luck. Rutger watched the icons turn off the road and finally got visual on the green and gray camouflaged machines in the rear-view display as they moved into the grove of trees. They saw the open field ahead and the ridge beyond and had probably stopped to ensure all was clear before proceeding.

Adrenaline coursed through Rutger's veins, heightening his senses as he watched the vehicles grow larger in his rear displays. *Fuck! Fuck! Fuck!* The six vehicles pulled in amongst the Berserker formation, their blower fans audible in the fighting compartment without the aid of audio sensors. *Maybe they're just pausing for a moment before moving on.* No dice—the Repub vehicles grounded and turned off their blowers, and the area fell quiet again. *So much for that idea.*

Rutger found himself reflexively squeezing the turret joystick. Fortunately, the automatic defense weapon atop the turret had been set to air defense mode, not that the 15mm plasma machine gun would do much against the Repub tanks' armored bulk. The HBT-6 weighed 145 tons, and rode on a cushion of air instead of a gravitational field, powerful blower fans providing the lift. Though not quite as fast or maneuverable as the Berserker's Patton tanks, they matched them in armor and overall firepower.

Rutger and Duran watched and listened with strained eyes and ears. Sweat began to bead on Rutger's face. A tank had grounded a mere twenty meters to their right, its bulbous hull partially obscured by a tree. An APC behind them at five o'clock sat only fifty meters away.

Rutger's quickened pulse hammered in his ears. They hadn't been detected *yet* it seemed, but perhaps the enemy had realized their error and were waiting for the right moment to fire. He flicked the weapons-arming switch on the righthand console to ON. He didn't dare move the turret until given the order.

He hated this and wished he were a driver again. Locked in the forward compartment, drivers had the benefit of blissful ignorance, not privy to the decision making and more detailed threat displays in the main cabin. They simply awaited the next command to move out or follow an ordered course. Junior men, the drivers performed most of the grunt work, but they didn't do much of the fighting. As his stomach twisted in knots, Rutger mused that the bump in pay as a gunner wasn't worth it.

Bounty Hunter's audio sensors picked up the audible whine of a rear ramp dropping on one of the APCs. Rutger exchanged glances with Duran. If the troops deployed, they were bound to notice at least one of the Berserker tanks. Their infantry might be armed with missile launchers or heavy lasers, both serious threats to armor.

"Rutger, target that APC on my command," Duran said softly. "Aubrey, when I give the command to fire, power up and pivot so we face the turret, and be prepared to scoot."

Aubrey and Rutger responded with a soft affirmative. *I hope the other tanks are on the same page.* If they weren't, this was going to be a short fight. The turret motor wasn't loud, but it could still alert the enemy.

"Execute," Duran said.

Rutger jammed the fire control joystick hard to the right, rotating the turret on precision magnetic bearings at over seventy degrees per second. The screen panned rapidly, but an eternity seemed to pass before the rectangular shape of the Repub APC filled his screen. He settled the orange pipper of the main gun's targeting reticle just below the APC's turret. The troop deployment ramp had fully dropped, and a pair of uniformed figures in power armor emerged from the APC. Rutger's finger hovered over the trigger on the joystick in his trembling hand.

"Fire!" Duran ordered.

Rutger mashed down the trigger. Night morphed into day as a crimson bolt of super-heated plasma violated the darkness with a thunderous crack. *Bounty Hunter* jolted from the recoil. The APC turned into an expanding ball of flames, the close quarters shot fully illuminating *Bounty Hunter* to the enemy.

"Target de—" Rutger began.

"The tank!" shouted Duran.

Everything seemed to slow down as Rutger traversed the turret left onto the new target. The main gun's autoloader chambered another round with a *thunk*. *Bounty Hunter* rose from the deck as Aubrey engaged the repulsors and pivoted the tank underneath the turret.

The Repub tank's broad circular turret spun toward them. *Shit!* It had a shorter distance to rotate to fire. Out of his peripheral vision, he saw the tank's thick barrel swing toward them, he wasn't going to be quick enough. Only a small portion of the enemy tank's rear hull protruded from behind the thick tree, but that particular section housed the fusion bottle. As soon as his reticle covered it, he fired.

The holo displays automatically dimmed the brilliant flash of crimson lightning and remained dark as the target exploded in a mini supernova. A powerful shockwave rolled over *Bounty Hunter*, rocking it like a boat on a storm-tossed sea. Metal shards sprayed outward in a shotgun blast of shrapnel that peppered the hull.

"Aubrey, move!" shouted Duran.

Rutger saw the urgency in the order—the blast had shattered the trunk of the massive tree and set its branches aflame. It started to slowly tilt toward *Bounty Hunter*. Aubrey gunned the repulsors and reversed, banking the tank hard to the left. Rutger's head snapped forward at the reverse lunge. The tree crashed down where *Bounty Hunter* had been just a moment before.

Several other explosions flashed in the grove, followed by concussive shockwaves. Then it was over, and silence hung like a stifling pall.

"You see anything else?" Duran asked, eyes glued to his screen.

Rutger looked at his holos. The map display now showed six cross-hatched enemy icons. The AI reported no further threats. "Negative, Staff Sergeant."

"George," Duran said, "damage assessment."

"No damage sustained," George replied. "Tank is—"

"George, switch to active sensors, sweep for threats."

The platoon commander's voice crackled in Rutger's headset, "All units report in."

"Blue 1, this is Blue 4," Duran said. "We're undamaged, two bogies destroyed."

The radio came to life with relieved voices as the platoon checked in, all tanks undamaged and fully operational.

"Good work," Lieutenant Mosley said. "But I'd say we've blown our cover. We're going to displace to this location." The new position flashed on the terrain map, half a klick away and parallel to the road with a good field of view. "But first I want a solid damage assessment and a sweep for enemy intel. Give me a body from each tank. We have ten mikes."

"Aubrey—" Duran said.

"I'll go, Staff Sergeant," Rutger said, unbuckling himself. Aubrey was new to the platoon and had only been on the planet a couple of weeks. Rutger felt responsible for him, just as Tyrone had been like an older brother to Rutger when he'd joined the crew. Rutger grabbed the plasma submachine gun from the cradle next to his seat and stood. He extended its telescoping stock and ensured it was loaded. The gunner's hatch opened with a hiss from the crew compartment's over-pressurization.

"I'll cover you," Duran said. He opened the commander's hatch and swiveled the 15mm plasma machine gun mounted on the commander's cupola.

Rain began to fall. Rutger activated night vision on his visor and slid off the turret. He crouched on the vehicle's deck for a second before dropping to the ground with a soft thud. His legs almost gave out underneath him in the soft soil. Nothing moved near the destroyed vehicles. Raindrops hissing on *Bounty Hunter's* still hot main gun barrel and the soft crackle of nearby flames were the only sounds. He checked his rear—nothing.

Rutger sweated profusely inside his armored tanker skins as he approached the burning husk that had been a Repub tank. Little remained of the hull, and the turret, knocked askew, still glowed faintly red with intense heat. Rutger halted ten meters from the wreckage, the heat barring him from proceeding any further. The tank's main gun pointed lifelessly toward the ground. Rutger followed the intended trajectory of the muzzle—it had come to rest only a few degrees shy of where *Bounty Hunter* had sat. Perhaps half a second had decided the fate of both crews, victors and vanquished. *That might have easily been us.*

He tried to push the thought from his mind as he moved cautiously toward the APC. Falling harder now, the rain had extinguished the flaming wreckage, but acrid smoke and steam still rose from the hull. Black singed the camo pattern on the flank where the 150mm plasma bolt had struck and entered. He warily approached the rear of the vehicle and paused near the lowered ramp. He took a deep breath and whirled around, ready to face whatever, or whoever, might be inside.

Nothing but carnage—burnt, blackened pieces of at least half a dozen human beings. He could make out a boot, a part of a face, a hand still clutching a weapon. The rest was just melted armor and seared meat. The stench overpowered his helmet's filters and assaulted his nose. The main gun bolt had punched a massive exit hole as well. Metal fragments had flown about the troop compartment at high velocity, dicing the occupants. Searing hot plasma had simultaneously sucked the oxygen out of the troops while superheating their bodily fluids, causing them to explode.

Rutger felt ill and fought back the urge to vomit. *Don't fucking lose it! You've seen this shit before.* True enough, but he'd never witnessed his own handiwork up close. He reflexively took a step back.

A hand slapped him on the shoulder, startling him. "Minced meat!" said Lance Corporal Okada, the driver from Blue 3.

"Yeah," sighed Rutger as he bent to search the charred remains of a Repub soldier in power armor lying beside the ramp. Intel wise, he found nothing of value in any of the pouches on the man's gear. He captured a picture of the deceased solider and the vehicle's hull number with his built-in helmet camera before jogging back to the safety of his tank.

Back aboard *Bounty Hunter*, Rutger relayed the information to Duran, though he knew the platoon sergeant had likely been monitoring his helmet's camera feed. Rutger plopped down into his seat and threw up his visor, taking a few ragged breaths before sucking down some water from his condenser canteen.

Duran transmitted the captured images to Lieutenant Mosley, then said, "Good shooting back there, Rutger."

Rutger nodded at the older man's comment as he buckled in, his hands trembling.

Duran stared at Rutger for a few silent seconds. "You okay, kid?"

"I wonder if they knew what killed them," Rutger said, his voice sounding far away in his mind.

"You can't dwell on it. It's just a job."

"Yeah, I know," Rutger said, trying to convince himself. "Just a job."

He wondered if the dead had thought the same thing.

★ ★ ★

3

CHAPTER

BOUNTY HUNTER AND THE REST OF SECOND PLA-
toon were on the move again before first light.

Despite the previous night's action, they and the rest of
Bruiser Company were no worse for wear. Other units in First
Battalion hadn't been so fortunate. Constant electronic jamming
made communication difficult, but a laser burst transmission had
gotten through early that morning, relaying that Anvil Company
to the south had faced a fierce counterattack late last night by
sizable Repub forces. They'd held, but at the cost of two destroyed
tanks and over a dozen casualties.

Shortly after receiving the message, Lieutenant Mosley had
relayed that second platoon and the rest of Bruiser would continue their advance southeast per orders from battalion. Their
mission: locate and destroy the Repub force that had attacked
Anvil, whose exact whereabouts were now unknown after breaking contact.

Bruiser Company was a combined arms unit consisting of
two tank and two infantry platoons, the latter equipped with
one-man skimmers and infantry fighting vehicles (IFVs). To
prevent the enemy from slipping past their sweep, the company

had spread out in a broad arc covering nearly ten kilometers. This separated the platoon's tanks by over a thousand meters at times. Though Rutger could see the other tanks' blue icons moving on the tactical display, visual contact proved impossible in the thick morning mist.

The tank rolled and yawed as Aubrey guided the 120-ton behemoth over rolling terrain. The Patton had a top speed of 250 kph under ideal conditions, but at present *Bounty Hunter* moved forward at a steady 25 kph, the top speed at which ground-penetrating radar and electromagnetic sensors could effectively sweep for antitank mines given the local terrain.

The fusion reactor whirred nonstop; Rutger could feel its enormous power through the ejection seat. The reactor's only drawback was that it created immense amounts of radiant heat when operated at high capacity. Heat levels had to be constantly managed, otherwise the crew risked damaging the reactor containment bottle or, even worse, causing a core meltdown, the latter a death sentence.

Rutger monitored the tactical display and neighboring tanks on the three-dimensional terrain map, though not much changed as the company moved through the area, a patchwork of fields, forests, and hills crisscrossed by small creeks and hedgerows three meters high. Fire support was available assuming comms worked, but he couldn't help feeling alone as the sweep progressed. He kept his eyes glued to the 120-degree arc in front of them on the exterior holos, switching frequently between different scans, careful not to miss even the most minuscule detail. Every tree, bush, or ditch could hide a deadly threat. The enemy had proven adept at fighting defensively, and their familiarity with the terrain only enhanced their capabilities.

Staff Sergeant Duran had launched *Bounty Hunter's* last remaining recon drone an hour earlier, splitting his attention between scanning around the tank with the commander's periscope and monitoring the drone's feed from above. The drones were useful in scouting ahead without risking anyone's life but were easily spotted and betrayed the presence of nearby Berserker forces. They were also easy targets. Two of *Bounty Hunter's* three surveillance drones had already been destroyed; replacements had yet to arrive.

While the human crew stayed vigilant, the tank's AI continued to analyze data from its host of sensors, identifying and displaying potential threats and recommending routes to their next waypoint.

Initially upon joining the tankers, learning his new duties had completely occupied Rutger's mind. But it was all old hat now, and as he monitored their progress his mind began to wander toward home and family, and the reasons he'd landed on another godforsaken world with the Berserkers, his third deployment in two years.

The first two had been with H&S Battalions participating in non-violent peacekeeping missions that had nevertheless given him his first taste of combat on Gaston-3 during an impromptu counter-insurgency operation. His unit covered over 1100 kilometers in three days to reach the capital city and wrest it from guerrilla forces. The fighting brief yet intense. He would never forget the corpses lining the road during the approach to the city, the blackened bodies nothing more than withered charcoal caricatures.

Rutger had been fighting, literally and figuratively, all his life. He'd been booted from several public schools. He had a mild temper—at least back then—and never liked to fight, but he didn't back down from anyone.

Academics weren't his strongpoint, but he worked well with his hands and understood machines. After serving as a truck driver during his compulsory eighteen months of service in New Helena's planetary defense force, he got an apprenticeship and earned a two-year certificate as a machinist from a trade union school.

Through the trade union he found a rare job in an agri-mech manufacturing company. Things were good for a spell. He met Serena, another worker at the plant, and they married a few months later. With two incomes, they were able to get a decent government-subsidized apartment. Two years later they decided to start a family. Callie came, their beautiful baby girl. Rutger couldn't have been prouder, and the next few years were pure bliss.

Like all good things, Rutger's period of contentment didn't last. Yet another outbreak of the wellow virus closed the plant for several months. The company decided to downsize in the uncertain economic environment. Rutger and Serena lost their jobs and medical benefits. It couldn't have happened at a worse time, because six months later Callie was diagnosed with a rare form of leukemia. She could be cured through gene therapy, but that wasn't covered under the Standard Benefits Act, which only provided treatment for her symptoms.

Advanced medical treatments, such as gene therapy, were only authorized for citizens. As residents, Rutger and Serena weren't eligible, and they couldn't afford the out-of-pocket expense. It would take a minimum of ten years of public or military service to earn citizenship.

Rutger desperately searched for options to treat Callie, who had only months to live unless she received proper therapy. When several private military contractor companies began recruiting on New Helena, he made his decision. His prior military service and technical training made him a solid candidate. Other less-reputable outfits paid slightly more than the Berserkers, offered shorter contracts and no compulsory boot camp, but he chose the Berserkers for the outstanding dependent medical benefits they offered. Callie could begin treatment immediately.

His technical scores and training as a driver landed him a job in logistics, making his mom and Serena so proud. Rutger caught a transport off planet two weeks later, surviving the grueling boot camp and schoolhouse training to become a logistical support specialist. He felt immensely confident in himself upon graduating, sure he could endure anything. *I was wrong.*

He returned to New Helena nine months later for thirty days of leave. Things went great and instilled Rutger with the belief that things were going to work out just as they'd hoped. Callie had begun gene therapy, and the money he'd earned during boot camp and training kept his family in their apartment.

But he found a different situation upon returning from his second deployment. His thoughts kept drifting to his platoon mates on Gaston, the burnt bodies and firefights appearing constantly in his head. Life on New Helena had gone by without him. Callie barely recognized him, his relationship with Serena had deteriorated, and he found himself irritable and quick to anger. Serena's problems seemed insignificant and unreal to him. They only made love twice in the three weeks he was home, and it felt forced each time. They fought a lot, Serena blaming him for becoming a merc and leaving them alone. She hardly spoke to Rutger when she took him to the space port.

Now on Scandova, the separation and estrangement from his family ate away at him. The romance of being a merc had worn off. It was just a paycheck, and he needed the money and benefits. Being on the front lines, with about three years remaining on his five-year contract, compounded his feelings of frustration and helplessness. He'd initially thought becoming a Berserker was the hard part, since the elite unit had high standards. Now he knew better.

Sure he could always opt out of his contract, but a large percentage of his salary was kept in an escrow account; he would lose it all and be blacklisted by the Mercenary Guild. And he would need to find a job on New Helena, where he would be just another number in the massive queue of people seeking work on the depressed planet. *I should have kept my mouth shut and paid more attention in school, gotten an advanced university degree. Those guys were never out of work.*

"Approaching Objective Taurus," Aubrey announced over the intercom when they reached another waypoint on their pre-determined course.

They moved into a clearing on a wooded hill with a good view of the surrounding area. "Hold here, Aubrey," Duran said. Rutger noticed on the tactical display that some of the neighboring company vehicles had fallen behind from having to sweep through or circumvent thicker terrain and wait for grunts to ensure it was clear. Though they'd traveled only fifteen klicks on the map, they'd covered twice that distance at their position on the end of the long, arcing sweep. The entire morning had been a series of starts and stops.

Duran radioed a sitrep to Lieutenant Mosley, while Rutger examined the terrain below. Fields of knee-high pasture grass lined with hedgerows stretched down the slope ahead. To their left, a wood line ran down the hill and intersected with a tree-lined road 1.6 klicks away, the dirt road running perpendicular to their present position.

As they waited, Duran studied the holographic map and awaited guidance from higher command on how long they should sit tight. Rutger watched the exterior holos, pulling up the drone feed on a lower quadrant for a bird's-eye view of the terrain and zooming in with powerful optics. Movement on the tree-lined road caught his eye for a moment. The feed suddenly turned to static.

"Shit, we lost the drone," Rutger said. He nervously eyed the exterior feeds and zoomed in on the road with the forward external cameras.

"Just stay sharp," Duran said, checking the map. "I just got off the radio with higher. There have been multiple reports of enemy contact to the northeast of us. We are to hold here until a squad from third platoon links up." Several loud reports came from the valley, reverberating through the tank's audio sensors, as if to punctuate the enemy threat nearby.

Rutger had heard Duran's conversation over the company net. *Not good.* He checked weapons and ammo status again out of habit. All weapons showed green status, fully operational. They were topped off with ammo, minus the two main gun rounds they'd expended last night and a few dozen rounds from the automatic defense weapon fired to counter some harassing artillery fire received during their move.

The air defense sensor pinged, and icons of three Berserker aircraft appeared on the radar screen. On exterior holos, Rutger watched the Dragon gunships roar by at treetop level to their right, banking hard and disappearing behind the hills. He hoped they sought whatever forces were in front of them. *Less for us to fight.*

Duran briefed them while they waited: "Rutger, cover the left-hand sector. Keep an eye on those woods. I'll cover the fields and hedges to the right. Aubrey, ground us to minimize our signature, but keep the reactor powered up just in case, and watch our six."

"Roger that, Sarge," they both responded.

They began a relatively silent vigil. Rutger put a caffeine tab in an aluminum thermos full of water and waited a few seconds for the instant coffee to heat up. He offered Duran some as they sat and stared at their displays. As Scandova's blood-red sun dipped in the sky, the shadows in the trees grew darker and more ominous. *Wish the damn grunts would hurry up and get here.*

Rutger raised his visor, rubbed his eyes, and cracked his neck, fatigue setting in. He switched to passive infrared view for a moment, then tried to get a feed from one of the few remaining Berserker reconnaissance satellites in high orbit. The feed came through, but Rutger wasn't surprised to find it wasn't oriented to their AO.

"Contact two o'clock, nine hundred meters. Looks like infantry," Duran announced.

Rutger bolted upright and almost dumped coffee in his lap. He slapped down his visor and expanded the holos, seeing faint silhouettes of numerous men cautiously moving along the hedgerow to their right. They wore sensor-scattering cloaks to conceal their thermal signatures, appearing as black shadows against the hedges, so Rutger switched to normal full-spectrum display. Zooming in, he saw the green and gray speckled camouflage of Repub infantry, helmet visors concealing their faces. About sixty troops had emerged, roughly two platoons moving parallel to the open field in a long column. Seeing the fat tubes of guided missile launchers slung over some of their shoulders disquieted Rutger.

Rutger tilted the joystick right slightly and slowly traversed the turret, putting the orange targeting pipper on the vanguard of the troop formation. Duran tracked them as well, taking manual control of the automatic defense weapon atop the turret and putting the pipper on the approaching men, still over 800 meters away.

"Enemy infantry, main gun plasma, 30 mike mike. On my command," Duran ordered.

The command meant to open fire with the main gun and then follow with dual 30mm rotary plasma autocannons, located in the right and left weapons mounted on the side of the turret beneath the 100mm particle cannons.

Rutger's mouth suddenly felt dry. "Identified," he said, signaling he had the target and understood the order. Sweat from his armpits trickled down his sides as a wave of icy fear washed over him. The figures slowly marched closer. In magnified view,

Rutger clearly saw the slings on their weapons and the pouches on their load-bearing harnesses. One of the soldiers paused, raising his visor to wipe sweat from his brow. Rutger could make out the stubble on the young man's face as his eyes darted around nervously. He could sense the man's apprehension. The fear and uncertainty. *He's no different than me.*

"Fire!" Duran said.

Rutger squeezed the trigger. A bolt of plasma leapt from the main gun with a thunderous crack, rocking the tank and impacting dead-center in the column of advancing troops. The blinding ball of fire annihilated men in the direct blast radius, sending nearby troops flying like flaming bowling pins. Uniforms and armor on men up to twenty-five meters away began to melt, and the hedges burst into flames.

The blinding flash momentarily blacked out *Bounty Hunter's* holos. Rutger fired the 30mm cannons when the screens cleared, working the heavy automatic weapons across the column as the troops dove for cover. The gatling-type cannons whirred with a throaty roar, spitting streaks of deadly crimson that cut down everything in their path, as spent matrix cases dropped to the hull below. The thumping grenade launcher on the automatic defense weapon added to the deadly thunder as Duran sent rapid bursts of 40mm high-explosive (HE) grenades into the field. The whizzing shrapnel cut down several Repub soldiers as they attempted to flee into non-burning sections of the hedgerow.

A handful of Repub soldiers returned fire. Streaks of blue plasma began snapping around *Bounty Hunter*, a few striking home. The rifle fire wasn't a dire threat to the massive tank, though the bolts could damage external optics and sensors. It was the shoulder-mounted weapons that were the real threat.

To the left, a Repub solider popped up at the tree line with a tube on her shoulder. Rutger swerved the turret rapidly toward her and fired the 30mm cannons but shot high and to the right in his haste. The woman seized the opportunity and loosed a guided missile at the tank. The flaming projectile appeared to launch in slow motion before whooshing toward them. *Bounty Hunter's* active protection system (APS) engaged. A small pod on the turret rotated and fired a handful of miniature self-forging projectiles that slashed through the hyper-velocity missile with an echoing bang. Fragments of the missile's exploding warhead plinked against the armor.

The woman began to duck down into the tall grass. *Too late!* Rutger already had her in his sights and stroked the trigger. A stream of bolts cut through the grass into her crouching form until her body exploded in a cloud of red mist. It was all a blur to Rutger as he sought out running figures and flashes of weapons, cutting down troops and sending body parts spinning through the air.

Several more missiles launched from the edge of the field, their accuracy hampered by the blistering incoming fire. Two of them were so off target that the APS didn't perceive them as threats, letting them sail overhead. Rutger poured bursts of fire toward the launch sources, the AI identifying the direction of each threat and providing a reverse azimuth. Sometimes he witnessed the grizzly results of his efforts, but most of his targets simply fell in a crimson flash, never to rise again. Soon the return fired slackened as the remaining handful of Repub soldiers reached the relative safety of the hedgerow and nearby ditches, many dragging or carrying wounded men.

"Cease fire!" Duran said.

Rutger released the trigger and suddenly remembered to breath; the muscles in his hand hurt from squeezing the joystick. The compartment had grown stiflingly hot and smelled of ozone from the weapons. For a moment, it was quiet, the breathing of the two men in the turret the only sound.

Rutger gazed upon the field ahead—pocked with scores of blackened craters, the grass scythed down and burning in several places. Dozens of Repub corpses littered the slope, many still writhing in blazing uniforms and melted armor. Several crawled through the grass, hoping to reach cover. *Like an open-air abattoir.* The images assaulted his mind and he fought back the urge to scream. He shook his head at the carnage he'd wrought, and wished he could just throw open the hatch and run from the tank. To be anywhere but here.

After a couple deep breaths, he got hold of himself. *Calm down, you've seen it before. And it could be worse. Could be one of those poor bastards out in that field.* He might have been a burning corpse himself had one of the missiles gotten through.

Duran broke the silence. "George, enemy damage assessment."

"On screen two," the AI replied.

Duran stared at the enemy casualty estimate. "This was a sizable element, I gotta try to call this in." He paused before adding, "Rutger, check our ammo and keep your eyes peeled. They may come again."

Pray to God they don't.

CHAPTER 4

SERGEANT TULMAN'S VOICE CRACKLED OVER THE
company net. "Blue 4, this is White 1 actual. We're coming up
on your pos."

Corporal Joseph Bukar heard the transmission through his
headset over the drone of his skimmer. The one-man vehicle
looked like a commercial grav-bike but was equipped with an
armored cowling and a weapons mount and could be operated
from both sitting and prone positions. He and the rest of first
squad, third platoon, Bruiser Company were cruising toward
the wooded hillock marked on the map. They had been tasked
with clearing the wooded area adjacent to Blue 4's position. The
tactical display under the skimmer's armored cowling identified
Blue 4 as *Bounty Hunter.*

"Copy, White 1. Glad to see you," replied the tense voice of
Staff Sergeant Duran. "We're just over the crest. Be advised, we
just repelled a sizable Repub force, and more hostiles may be in
the area."

"Copy, Blue 4," said Sergeant Tulman. Over the squad net
he said, "You heard the man. Stay sharp. Deploy below the rise."

Always, Bukar thought, following Tulman to a clearing near the woods. They jumped from the vehicles as they decelerated, seeking cover as the skimmers grounded and slid to a halt.

The ten-member squad wore power armor dirty and scarred from hard use. They moved with cat-like silence despite being encased in plasteel. The myofibril layer beneath their armor acted as an exoskeleton and an additional layer of muscle, amplifying neural signals and granting them enhanced strength and speed. Their suits' active camouflage blended them into their surroundings with chameleon ease.

Corporal Bukar led the second fire team in first squad. He'd deployed all over the galaxy during his twelve years with the Berserkers, yet was still surprised to find himself on Scandova. He'd come a long way from the jungles and slums of his home planet Beninia, a dangerous environment that had honed his keen senses at an early age.

"Squad, wedge formation," Tulman said. "Preacher, take point."

"Roger," said Bukar, already moving up. The small Christian cross affixed to his chest plate, blackened for light discipline, had earned him the nickname Preacher.

After forming the wedge, the squad advanced cautiously toward the dark shadows within the tree line. Bukar took the lead, snaking through thick, towering pines and patches of dense ferns with the cat-like ease of a panther.

They started over the rise and entered an even denser area of fern undergrowth, so thick that the squad members lost sight of one another, forcing them to rely on HUD to identify their squad mates. Vision through their visors adjusted, turning the shadows into day, but no sort of visual aid could pierce the dense vegetation itself. The veteran troopers' highly tuned instincts—which technology could never replicate—kicked in.

The dark forest reminded Bukar of the Beninian jungles of his youth and of the hunts he'd led for genetically modified tigers. Rich folks from all over would travel to Beninia for a chance to kill the deadly and formerly extinct animals, whose pelts were still highly prized in certain corners of the galaxy. He recalled how quickly the hunter could be become the hunted. *A worthy and cunning adversary. Unlike men, who can kill with the simple pull of a three-pound trigger.*

Periodically, the squad would stop and listen as they worked their way down the slope toward the road over a kilometer away. When they did, Bukar's eyes would continually dart around, peering between the trees and into the undergrowth, almost feeling the environment with an ingrained sixth sense. He didn't like what his gut told him. *This doesn't feel right.*

He stopped for a moment and took a pull of water from his hydration tube to cool his throat. Despite their suits' built-in cooling function, they still sweated and had to be wary of dehydration. The squad said nothing as they waited; they trusted Bukar's instincts as much as he did.

Realizing there was nothing more to perceive, Bukar moved on, still unable to see more than three meters ahead through the ferns as he descended the slope. He paused, again sensing something that turned out to be nothing, though he swore to himself that he'd heard a noise. He stepped off again. His helmet featured advanced audio sensors, but Bukar felt separated from nature within its armored confines. A part of him wanted to rip it off, to let his ears hear without the mechanical divide.

He heard a twig snap and froze, the squad following suit. *No doubt about that.* They stood silently for at least a minute. No other sounds came. Bukar held up his hand, signaling them to wait as he cautiously advanced. He again thought of tigers in the jungle. Back then he could sense when one was stalking him, and he had the same feeling now. His mind flashed to his sister Adeze. *Focus. You can't think of her now.*

He pushed through the ferns, slipped around a tree trunk and saw something move in the distance, losing sight of it behind a fern branch. Unsure of what he'd seen, he took another step forward, all of his senses now screaming at him. Holding his breath, he slowly swept the branch aside.

A white streak punched the ground in front him and erupted in a blinding orange flash of flaming, flying steel. The explosion blasted him backwards into a tree and peppered his suit with pieces of shrapnel. Another streak flashed through the forest and exploded in a shockwave laced with flying metal, followed by yet another. Concussive force knocked the wind from Bukar. He looked up in a state of shock and saw a mech moving between the trees. The bipedal armored colossus stood over five meters tall and bristled with an array of weaponry.

Bukar struggled to his feet and dove behind a tree trunk as another blast struck just behind him. The forest exploded into a maelstrom of fire as energy beams and flying steel whizzed past. Severed leaves and branches floated down all around him.

"Contact!" Bukar heard in his earpiece. Perhaps he had screamed it—difficult to say.

Bukar stumbled to his feet and ran about ten meters before diving behind another tree trunk. Insufficient cover against 60mm explosive shells, he realized. Glancing around the tree, he saw three of the green and gray mechs charging through the forest toward him, followed by at least 40 Repub infantrymen.

"Fall back!" Sergeant Tulman shouted over the explosive cacophony.

Controlled by a human pilot, each mech carried a chain-fed 60mm autocannon in its right hand and a 20mm plasma cannon in the other. A pod containing four rockets sat atop each shoulder. Flashes of light danced from their weapons as they laid down a withering curtain of fire.

Bukar sprayed the closest mech with his M-17 plasma rifle before turning to bolt. Smoke and vegetation limited his vision. The ground seemed to heave and sway beneath him from the explosions all around. Blue plasma bolts snapped past him. Though just as deadly, the concentrated plasma streams of energy seemed insignificant compared to the erupting shells. Shrapnel and massive wood splinters plinked off his armor.

He saw his squad mates ahead, two men already hit and stumbling as they fled. He threaded through the trees, bracing for the round that would strike at any moment. His HUD identified Sergeant Tulman straight ahead. Bukar had almost caught up to Tulman when a shell landed next to him. Lifted off his feet, Bukar tumbled through the air like a leaf in a breeze. He landed hard on his back. A lightning bolt of pain shot up his spine. *Pain is good. Means you aren't dead yet.*

He rolled over, trying to clear his head, and heard a load moan off to his right. He crawled a few meters and found Sergeant Tulman covered in blood, lying in a bush. The blast had blown off his left leg below the knee. His left arm looked shattered and part of his hand was missing. Bukar stared for a moment in dumbstruck horror. *Shit!*

"I got you, Sergeant," Bukar said, his mind functioning again.

"Leave me, Preacher! Go, damn it, that's an order!"

"I'm not leaving you." Bukar hefted Tulman and slung him over his shoulder.

"You stubborn bas—" A grunt of pain cut Tulman off. Bukar ran for the clearing, pulse pounding in his ears as his armored boots churned up the dark soil. The noise of the mechs smashing through the forest grew distant. Finally he reached the clearing and caught up with his squad, all panting as they crouched among the bushes atop the hill.

Bukar eased Tulman down behind a fallen log and looked around. Only seven of them remained. He remembered the tank. *Bounty Hunter.* His hands trembled as he tried to recall the tank's call sign.

"Blue 4, this is White 1 Bravo," Bukar said through ragged breaths. "We made contact with three Repub mechs and a platoon of infantry. We need immediate fire support, over."

"White 1 Bravo, this is Blue 4, say again, you're breaking up, over."

"Blue 4, enemy mechs in trees we need fucking support, over!"

Bukar felt the ground tremble beneath him as the 60-ton mechs strode toward them through the forest. *We can't fight them here!* Not enough cover, and the squad was bunched together. How would he take down a stalking tiger? *I need bait.* He scanned the troopers around him. Though not officially in charge, Corporal Rivers was his senior as second fire team leader, and the other troopers looked to him for leadership. Noticing the missile launcher strapped over Lance Corporal Hector's shoulder, Bukar formed a hasty plan.

"Rivers, take your team and set up to the left with Orell's machine gun," Bukar said. "Hector, everyone else, move to the far side of this clearing and prepare your missile launchers." The men nodded and scrambled to their feet, grabbing Tulman and taking him along. Bukar stared at the forest. "Rivers, when the mechs burst through, have your team unload on them. Aim for their cockpit and optics, try to draw them toward you."

"Are you fucking serious?" Rivers asked.

"Yes. We want them to expose their rear so we can take them out with missiles."

"Sure, put our necks on the line," Rivers said. "What the fuck will you be doing during all this?"

"I'm the bait. I'm going back in there."

CHAPTER 5

INFANTRY REINFORCEMENTS FROM THIRD PLATOON had finally arrived. *About fucking time.* Not the whole platoon, unfortunately, just a squad, but troopers in power armor could be quite formidable, and it was reassuring to have more eyes and ears patrolling the woods to their left.

Rutger panned the forward screens upward slightly to focus on the wood line at the slope's far end and felt relieved when the dead and dying Repub soldiers littering the burning field disappeared from view. The continued moans and cries from the wounded caused him to turn down the tank's external audio sensors. Despite the one-sided outcome, the recent engagement with the Repub troops had left him shaken.

"Can we pull further back?" Rutger asked. Their position was tactically sound, but the enemy now knew their location. He wanted to be on the move again. *Anywhere but sitting here.*

"Our orders are to hold here. You know that," Duran replied. "Once the grunts get the other side of this slope cleared, we should be able to displace again."

Rutger was about to check on the grunts' status when George announced, "Enemy mechanized forces detected." The threat alert flashed on screen, accompanied by an audible tone. He acknowledged the alert and saw three red enemy icons to their left.

"Mechs!" shouted Rutger. "In the woods, just under a thousand meters to our 10 o'clock."

"Where the fuck did they come from?" Duran asked.

"I don't know! They weren't—"

"Warning, missile launch," George said with electronic urgency.

A threat warning wailed in Rutger's ear, and the telltale signs of multiple missile launches appeared on the forward screens. George projected their estimated launch points. Rutger watched in horror as the wave of flaming hypersonic missiles darted toward *Bounty Hunter*, swirling vortices in their wake. The automatic defense weapon swung into action half a second later. The whirling 15mm machine gun spat crimson streaks at the missiles, detonating them in orange flashes. Fragments of the exploded missile casings rained against the tank's plasteel armor with sharp plinking noises.

"Enemy troops direct font!" yelled Staff Sergeant Duran as scores of Repub soldiers opened fire with automatic weapons from positions along the tree-lined road. "Hit 'em with the thirty mike mike."

Rutger was already swinging the turret over as blue plasma bolts struck the sloped forward armor, erupting in showers of sparks and slag. He put the reticle on troops dashing from the far-left ditch before the tree line. The Repub soldiers advanced in bounds and hit the deck every few meters. They had plenty of cover fire from additional troops in the tree line. *They're gonna try to flank us!* Rutger squeezed the trigger. The 30mm plasma cannons burped bolts of ionized death toward the enemy.

Rutger swept a stream of red bolts across the advancing troops. Dark green shadows darted about below him as the auto cannons, able to fire over 600 rounds a minute, snarled murderous glowing streaks at them. On the forward screens, Repub soldiers burst apart in puffs of red mist, the bolts blasting them into pieces. The bursts of plasma exploded the ground in great clods as he walked the rounds across the rushing Repub troops. He caught another group, too ambitious with their rush, out in the open and scythed them down. A white haze from energy bolts, burning grass, and flaming corpses began to form over the battlefield.

But the enemy had learned from their previous failed assault. This time they dispersed across the slope, using the micro terrain for cover and forcing Rutger to traverse fire over an ever-widening front. Finger mashed on the trigger, Rutger divided his attention between the enemy and the ammo counter, which inexorably counted down toward zero. *Shit, we'll have to switch to the coaxial weapon.* The tank had a smaller coaxial 15mm plasma gun and a plasma flame thrower, both effective against troops up close, but they couldn't match the awesome firepower of the dual 30mm cannons.

Repub troops responded with heavy plasma machine gun fire from the road, first from the right and then from the far left. Positioned at opposite corners of the slope, they pinned down *Bounty Hunter* in a hail of crackling crossfire. The tank could withstand such bolts initially, but the heavy stream of fire would eventually peck through the tank's plasteel armor and disable critical weapons and systems.

Panicked screams from the grunts erupted on the command net as they engaged the mechs in the forest. They weren't faring well from the sound of things. Duran had noticed as well. "The grunts are in trouble, and it looks like those mechs are trying to flank us," he shouted. "See if you can engage them through the trees. I'll handle the infantry."

"Roger that." Rutger's stomach twisted into tighter knots. There was something primal and intimidating about a 60-ton walking killing machine that struck fear in his heart. Grav-tanks could handle most mechs in a straight-up fight, even a couple of them, given their heavier armor and greater maneuverability. But most fights weren't fair. If the mechs flanked them and struck from the rear or above on the turret, where the armor was thinnest, they could turn the tank into a kiln. He cringed at the thought.

He swung *Bounty Hunter's* turret over to face the mech threat. He caught glimpses of the mechs' silhouettes as they ran through the trees, the flash of their weapons the only thing giving away their position. They were almost at the top of the hill.

Rutger put the main gun's orange pipper on the lead mech's silhouette and fired. A brilliant flash disintegrated a tree in front of it, sending flaming splinters in all directions. Rutger adjusted his aim and fired two more times in quick succession, the main gun's recoil rocking the tank and causing the temperature in the fighting compartment to jump fifteen degrees. The lead mech's torso exploded in a shower of sparks and flames, taking another step before it plowed into the ground.

Rutger scanned frantically for the other two mechs. The tank's AI provided targeting squares where it detected the mechs' reactor signatures, but Rutger still couldn't get a good visual through the trees.

"George," Rutger said, "predict mechs' course through the woods."

The AI put glowing course paths on the holos before Rutger completed his sentence. Flashes from the corner of the screen—another swarm of anti-tank missiles had launched from the tree line. A series of nearby explosions rained shrapnel on the tank, then the automatic defense weapon suddenly ceased firing.

"ADW is down!" Duran said. "Keep engaging those mechs! I'm gonna man the commander's weapon."

Duran stood on his seat and opened the commander's hatch. Sounds of explosions and plasma weapon fire immediately intensified, the battle seemingly closer now, more real to Rutger. He tore his gaze from Duran standing on his seat in the open hatch and returned to hunting the mechs. The rapid hiss-crack staccato of the commander's 15mm plasma gun soon roared from above. The automatic protection system pods fired as well in sharp booms, louder still.

Rutger trained the main gun on the mechs' predicted path, trying to get a lead on the sprinting machines. He fired two quick main gun rounds at what appeared to be the mech's outline in the trees. He missed again and watched the hulking green and gray machine cross over the rise, illuminated for barely an instant by a flaming tree. *They're getting behind us!* And the main gun had gotten dangerously hot; he would have to moderate his fire and make every shot count. No more shooting at shadows.

Rutger heard the whoosh of incoming antitank missiles, followed by a series of explosions that rocked the tank and hit it with a hailstorm of shrapnel that pinged angrily off the turret. The commander's weapon suddenly fell silent. *What the fuck?* The ammo counter showed it had plenty of rounds remaining.

Rutger looked up just as Duran dropped into the fighting compartment and slumped toward him, his helmet and half of his face missing. The AI in Rutger's helmet computer scrolled an unnecessary message in red letters on HUD—STAFF SERGEANT DURAN KIA. Rutger screamed in horror and reflexively shoved away the grizzly sight. Duran's body drooped over the side of his seat, blood and brain matter dripping onto the housing for the autoloader and trickling onto the floor of the fighting compartment.

This can't be fucking happening!

Rutger's blood turned to ice in his veins as he frantically keyed the company net and hysterically babbled, "Help us! We need a medic!"

"Who is this?" a distant voice replied. "Slow down. Identify yourself."

Blue plasma bolts snapped overhead, loud through the open hatch. Rutger turned back to the holos as advancing dark silhouettes poured across the slope.

"Dismounts are everywhere. They're starting to encircle us," Aubrey said over the intercom, his voice cracking and betraying fear and uncertainty at notification of Duran's death.

The world closed in on Rutger like a vice. Tears filled his eyes. *I'm in charge… What the fuck do I do?* He fought back the bile in his throat. His thoughts raced, a tidal wave of fear overriding any logical, coherent thoughts.

"They're getting closer! What do you want me to do?" Aubrey pleaded. "Rutger? Rutger?"

"Shut the fuck up! I don't know," Rutger snapped, a feeling of helplessness tearing at his sanity. He tried to think, to act. He began traversing the main gun, firing bolts at the infantry every few degrees, transfixed as he watched bodies disappear in the apocalyptic fire storm.

An amped voice crackled in Rutger's ear. One of the grunts, though he couldn't understand the man. He consulted the comm display for their callsign, and fought to speak into his helmet's microphone. "White 1 Bravo, this is Blue 4, say again, you're breaking up, over."

"Blue 4, enemy mechs in tree. We need fucking support, over!"

The mechs! Rutger's mind raced. The enemy seemed to be everywhere. He needed to prioritize. The infantry was a threat, but the mechs would surely destroy *Bounty Hunter* if they flanked around and got behind. Rutger felt a new sensation, a burning emotion welling up inside to guide his thoughts and actions—hate.

Bukar crouched behind a massive trunk and waited for the mechs, their armored legs crashing through the brush and snapping massive limbs. His heart pounded, and it suddenly occurred to him that he was very much alone. He began to pray. *Our father, who art in heaven...*

He stepped from behind the tree, the lead mech to his right only twenty meters away, and fired his rifle's M-28 grenade launcher. The high explosive round struck its torso but only scored the surface, doing little else. The mech's torso turned to face him and fired its 20mm plasma cannons just as he dove back behind the trunk. The bolts splintered the thick bark and ignited nearby ferns. Bukar felt the bolts' searing heat as they streaked past him.

The mech continued to approach as his heart hammered in his chest. *Good, come to daddy. Now the tricky part.* He spun to the other side of the trunk and emptied his rifle's magazine. He then turned and ran like hell. *Sister wouldn't be happy if she knew what an idiot I'm being right now.*

His lithe legs and enhanced neuromuscular strength carried him through the woods. Bukar recalled the feeling of being chased by a tiger once through the jungles of Beninia. He dodged tree trunks and crashed through ferns as bolts zipped by. He came tearing into the clearing and bolted right, diving behind a fallen tree where the squad's other half lay in cover.

He heard a loud report, followed by two more. Peering over the log, his visor dimmed when the first mech exploded in a dazzling orange ball of flames just as it crested the hill. The mech's momentum carried it forward another step before it spun and plowed into the ground. Only a grav-tank's main gun could have wreaked such havoc on a mech with a single hit. *Hope he can get the other two.*

Snapping branches on approach, the second mech sprinted up the rise. *Shit! Guess we do it the hard way.* He wished he were encased in a 120-ton tank right about now.

"Stay down!" Bukar said. "Rivers," he called over the squad net, "hold fire until it reaches the clearing."

The mech slowed slightly as it stepped into the open, the earth trembling beneath its footfalls.

"Now!" Bukar shouted.

Rivers's fire team opened up from the far side of the clearing. A stream of red plasma bolts from Orell's M-361 machine gun pecked at the mech's torso. Simultaneously, Lance Corporal Hector rose up with a guided-missile launcher. The weapon's triple tubes could fire all three missiles in rapid succession. Another trooper further to Bukar's left did the same.

The first launcher fired with a *whoosh*, sending three hypersonic missiles screaming toward the mech's back. The mech's active protection system engaged and detonated the first salvo of missiles in a chorus of cracking flashes. The second trooper fired his launcher a split second later, scoring two hits. The missiles' dual warheads, consisting of a shaped charge and depleted uranium penetrator, blew glowing orange holes in the mech's back. A series of internal explosions rippled through the mech; smoke poured from its seams as the machine took another uncertain step and toppled sideways in a motionless heap. Bukar thought he heard the pilot scream for an instant over the cacophony of secondary explosions and sparking circuits.

Bukar's men roared and raised fists, but their elation quickly faded at the heavy thuds of more earth-shaking footsteps. Bukar turned and stared at the mechanical behemoth that had emerged from the tree line behind them, the machine towering above them with weapons poised to spit death.

God save us.

"Aubrey!" Rutger said as bolts smacked into *Bounty Hunter's* front turret armor, leaving tiny glowing dimples in its surface. "Back us the fuck up!"

"Aye, Sarge, I mean, Corporal!" Aubrey said.

Aubrey threw *Bounty Hunter* hard into reverse, pitching Rutger forward against his harness. The tank quickly accelerated to 90 kph up the hill. Rutger felt the tank hit something, likely the grunts' skimmers. He checked the forward holos and saw the bikes knocked aside like toys discarded by bored children.

Rutger didn't care—only the mechs mattered at the moment. One of them went down in flames, apparently from the grunt's missile fire, before he could put his sight on it. He then spotted the final one as it reached the zenith of the hill. It stood towering in the open, Berserker troops scampering away from it. *Bounty Hunter* was still moving, rapidly approaching the tree line to their rear. "Ground us!" shouted Rutger.

Aubrey immediately dumped the gravitational lift from the repulsors. Rutger bit his tongue when the tank dropped like a stone. He didn't notice the pain as his screen filled with the mech that slid into his sight picture. *Got you now, you bastard!*

He jammed down the trigger; the main gun fired with a jolt. The bolt struck the side of the mech's torso, blowing off its arm armament and sending pieces of armor and inner machinery flying. He noticed the red warning light on the barrel temperature gauge when he went to fire a second bolt, the tube still critically hot from the furious fusillade of main gun bolts he'd previously fired.

"Dammit!" Rutger couldn't wait for the barrel to cool, so he reflexively followed up with a center-mass salvo from *Bounty Hunter's* dual 100mm particle cannons. Nearly at the weapon's minimum standoff distance, the dual streams of concentrated protons lit up the hillside like lightning bolts, vaporizing centimeters of armor plating and lancing into the mech's internal ammo storage compartments. The torso disintegrated in a massive secondary explosion as the ammo cooked off, showering the area with shards of flaming steel. *Hope the grunts there are all right.*

Rutger turned his attention back to the Repub troops beginning to come over the rise.

"Aubrey, get us airborne again!" Rutger said.

Bounty Hunter rose to a half-meter hover on its repulsors, clots of mud still hanging from the armored skirting. "Advance, 20 kph."

Rutger swung the turret onto the enemy troops, his finger hovering above the trigger as he zoomed in on them through the haze. He could make out their light-absorbing ponchos, visored helmets and muddy boots. Many appeared injured, blood staining their armor plates and uniforms, and some assisted wounded comrades. He was about to squeeze the trigger when he noticed all had raised their hands in the air.

"They're surrendering," Rutger mumbled in disbelief, but it made sense. The mech assault had been stopped and the Repub grunts had failed to destroy *Bounty Hunter.* To continue the assault would be suicidal, as would retreat over the open field. The Berserker's rules of engagement for this campaign stated that retreating troops were still fair game...but Rutger figured the men before him were simply tired of war.

Feelings of hate and pity warred inside Rutger. He removed his finger from the trigger, not even considering killing the surrendering men. He raised his visor. The stale, stinking odor of the cabin felt like a breath of fresh air, his first since beginning the engagement.

Reluctantly, Rutger tore his gaze away from the holos to look over at Duran's body, and quickly wiped burning tears from his eyes. Thankfully he couldn't see the remains of Duran's face, not that he needed to. That gruesome image of his face had been permanently seared into his mind with only one glance.

Rutger needed no more self-convincing—Duran's fate had confirmed his decision. *The Berserkers can keep my fucking escrow money. I'm going home when this war's over.*

Looking up at the mech, Bukar turned reflectively away as brilliant blue-white beams from the tank struck the metal beast. His visor automatically dimmed to save his eyesight as a wave of heat slapped him. He stood to run, but a shockwave from a secondary explosion immediately knocked him flat. Now an angry fireball, the disintegrating mech hurled jagged pieces of flaming metal at him and his squad.

Dazed for a second, Bukar slowly sat up, along with his squad mates. They'd taken no further casualties dueling the last two mechs. He watched as the grav tank that had saved them glided back toward the top of the hill. *Good shooting.* He then realized that the sounds of battle had ceased.

"Anyone else wounded?" asked Corporal Rivers, reasserting himself in charge.

Bukar didn't care; he was just happy to still be alive. *Praise God!* He stood and swayed a bit on rubbery legs. The last concussive blast had left him with a dull, throbbing headache. Out of the corner of his eye, he detected movement to his left in the trees and reflexively raised his rifle.

"Don't shoot! Don't shoot!" several Repub soldiers shouted in accented Standard as they stepped from the woods with raised hands. One of them waved what had once been a white undershirt. "We surrender!"

Bukar stared at them for a second, then removed his finger from the trigger. "This way," he said hoarsely, motioning with his rifle barrel toward the clearing. He felt no ill-will toward the haggard and scared-looking men and women who had tried to kill him. They had only been doing their job, their duty, just like him. They had almost succeeded.

Adeze wouldn't have been happy at the chances he'd taken today. *Necessary risks.* He stared over the darkening woods to where Scandova's sun sunk slowly toward the distant hills. Gazing at the flaming red sky, he wondered how long his luck would hold out. He crossed himself. *God willing, all the way to New Oslo!*

CHAPTER

RUTGER AND AUBREY SAT IN *BOUNTY HUNTER*, bathed in the light of their displays. They had drawn first watch after arriving at the company assembly area. Bruiser Company had stood up a third of its tanks as a static guard in the relatively safe area, which the command still considered unsecured. Despite his fatigue, Rutger didn't mind, always happy to draw first or last watch instead of a middle one. When they were done, he and Aubrey would have eight hours of uninterrupted rest.

Bruiser Company's ten grav tanks sat grounded in the dark amongst houses on the outskirts of Oacoma, their guns pointed outboard in a rough defensive laager. The eight company IFVs were parked amongst them. The night air had grown colder lately as winter descended on this part of Scandova. Clattering tools and cursing voices outside the tank couldn't quite silence the trickling of a small stream nearby.

The company had been rotated to the rest area after yesterday's fighting. The front lay about six klicks to the east, at the rim of the valley they were in. Occasional reports of weapons could be heard, and flashes of light seen in the distance as Cyclone Company and Federation forces kept pressure on the Repub forces. Rutger listened intently to the traffic on the battalion net as the action unfolded. A part of him felt guilty for being glad that he wasn't at the front.

Bruiser Company had been tip of the spear the past two weeks, and this rotation to the rear provided the troops a chance to rest and perform repairs on their equipment. Men and machines alike had been pushed to their breaking points, and sometimes beyond, during the last offensive.

The command had good reason to consider this rear area unsecured. Snipers and harassing artillery were still a threat, and there had been reports of partisan activity as well. Fearing that their unwilling hosts might be Repub sympathizers, the troopers had forcibly removed civilians from their makeshift camp.

"Blue 4, this is Blue 2. You stand relieved," the tired voice of Sergeant Willard said in Rutger's headset.

"Copy, Blue 2," Rutger responded over the company net. He switched to the intercom. "You heard the man, Aubrey. Let's find someplace to crash."

Rutger popped open the gunner's hatch, grabbed the submachine gun from the cradle by his seat and lifted himself onto the turret. He took one last peek inside at the dark blood stains on the commander's station before closing the hatch. Rutger, Aubrey and one of the infantry troopers had extracted Duran's body from the cabin and placed it in a body bag. They'd secured Duran and two dead grunts to the tank's rear deck, and had left the bodies with a logistics unit while traveling to the bivouac site. *Fuck if I'm going home in a rubber bag,* Rutger had thought as he watched them carry Duran away.

Aubrey awaited him on the ground, holding his own submachine gun and a small assault pack. "Man, I'm fucking beat," Aubrey said. "You think we'll be here long, Corporal?"

How the fuck would I know? Rutger believed that the Feds and Berserkers had the upper hand, but the Republic seemed to dictate the pace of war by springing surprise offensives and forcing them to react. "No idea, just rest whenever you can. Let's go. Keep your head down."

Staying low behind a brick wall, they darted to a nearby house and joined other resting crews from second platoon. Six troopers lay about the house, sitting in kitchen chairs or sprawled out on living room furniture. Everyone sat well clear of the windows. A dim electric lantern cast soft blue light over the room. Each platoon had claimed a house or two close to their vehicles. The elderly couple who owned this particular house had been forced to vacate and stay with neighbors down the street.

Only a couple of tankers raised their heads when the pair entered. The house didn't offer much in the way of cover but was a welcome break from the tight confines of the Pattons. No one spoke. All were dirty and tired. A few ate from ration trays while others slept. Rutger knew he needed to eat, but the thought of food made him nauseated.

"Sorry to hear about Duran," said Corporal Hinton.

Aubrey nodded in return.

"Thanks," Rutger said, eager to change the subject. "Any word on when the LT will return?" Lieutenant Mosley had left a few hours ago to link up with a nearby maintenance unit and lead them back to the rest area.

"He should be back shortly." Hinton pointed to a ration pack on the table. "You want some of this? I won't be able to eat it all."

"You want any, Aubrey?" Rutger asked.

"No, thanks. I ate a nutrient bar on watch. I'm gonna find a place to wash up and lay down for a bit, if you don't mind, Corporal."

"Go right ahead. Just keep your weapon and helmet in arms reach."

"Aye, Corporal" Aubrey said. He disappeared into the adjacent room.

Rutger warily eyed the food, knowing he wouldn't be able to sleep with hunger pangs. "Yeah, I should probably try to eat." He pulled up a chair next to Hinton. "What do you got?"

"Beef brisket and rice."

"Thanks," Rutger said, relieved it wasn't dreaded tuna mac.

Hinton scooped some of the synthetic beef chunks and white rice onto a kitchen plate and pushed it over to him. Rutger pulled a plastic spoon from his armored vest and wiped it off on his uniform. He mechanically shoveled the food into his mouth, and soon felt better as the calories entered his body and settled his stomach. He couldn't recall the last time he'd eaten. *Sometime before Duran died.*

Berserker ration kits were actually pretty good except for a couple of menu items, though the nutrient bars were notoriously disgusting. All of it seemed to plug him up, not in a constipated way, but seemed to keep the body from wanting to shit, which was an added benefit in the field. Eating on the elderly couple's glass plates in the quaint yet well-furnished house reminded Rutger of the small living room table in his old apartment back home, eating with his mom and sister while they watched the latest reality vid. The food their ration cards could buy always tasted bland, but his mom did her best to prepare and season it. Each family member received only two thousand calories per day, just enough to get a person through a workday if they were fortunate enough to have a job. But Rutger had always been overly active growing up, playing various sports and hustling a living on the streets at times. He remembered always being hungry. Something he didn't have to worry about as much since he joined the Berserkers. The Berserkers fed their troops well—staying alive to enjoy the next meal was the hard part. *And staying sane...*

Rutger finished eating and stood with his plate. He noticed that most of the troopers had simply stacked their dirty dishes on the counter. Rutger walked to the sink and tried the tap. The water still flowed, though electricity had either been cut to the town or disabled by an EMP weapon. He washed his plate and dried it with a nearby towel, then placed it in what appeared to be the appropriate cabinet. He filled his canteen with water that was probably filtered; if not, the canteen automatically filtered it for impurities. He sat again at the table and immediately felt his eyelids grow heavy. He let them droop and dozed off.

The sound of several vehicles pulling up outside startled Rutger back to consciousness. Rutger checked his watch. He'd slept for over two hours. It had felt like a minute, his body still heavy with fatigue.

Voices and footsteps sounded from outside, approaching the front door. Lieutenant Mosley entered, followed by a female staff sergeant carrying a worn rucksack. Troopers not sleeping stood out of respect but did not come to attention.

Mosley surveyed the room. "Where is Sergeant Willard?"

"He's on watch, sir." Rutger said.

Mosley focused his chameleon green eyes on him. "Rutger, this is Staff Sergeant Faora. She'll be taking over as platoon sergeant. Show her where our tanks are located. I have to go and talk to the company commander."

Rutger stood and grabbed his helmet. "Yes, sir."

Mosley turned to Faora. "Staff Sergeant, get yourself situated and see to it that repairs and maintenance are completed in a timely fashion."

"Yes, sir," Faora replied, all business. Mosley wheeled and walked out of the house.

Faora gave Rutger a cursory glance as he stared at her in the dim light. She was of average height, sharp featured, and fair skinned with steely eyes and dark hair peeking out from beneath her commo helmet. She seemed to radiate intensity, like a coiled snake ready to strike.

"I'm Corporal Rutger." He offered her his hand.

She ignored his hand and stared past him at the other tankers lying around the room. Rutger dropped his hand. *Okay, so much for formalities.*

"Show me where our tank is located," Faora ordered, turning toward the door.

"Yes, Staff Sergeant."

Rutger led her toward *Bounty Hunter*. Upon reaching the grounded tank she conducted a walk around, her eyes scanning over the hull. Now and then she would run a finger over a scarred section of missing reactive armor, or inspect a sensor.

"How long you been a gunner, Corporal?" Faora asked, not looking at him.

"A few weeks," Rutger said. "I was recently promoted from driver."

"And you were about to be promoted to tank commander," she said, her voice trailing off. "You any good as a gunner?"

He hadn't considered himself a tank commander during the short period after Duran's death. *Hell, I didn't even sit in the commander's chair.* To do so had seemed blasphemous, and he'd never considered that the command might officially promote him. That he'd lost the opportunity just now occurred to him. *Probably for the best.*

"I've done okay," Rutger replied, choosing his words carefully.

"How many kills do you have?"

"Kills?"

"How many enemy tanks and combat vehicles have you destroyed?" she said, plainly annoyed at having to explain herself.

Put on the spot, Rutger hesitated, but his mind finally computed the math. "One tank, an APC and two mechs."

She studied him for a moment in the ambient starlight. "Good. I hate popping newbie's cherries." She turned back to her inspection.

Rutger didn't know what to make of the new platoon sergeant. He didn't care for martinet types, and her demeanor was nothing like Duran's easy-going manner.

Faora handed Rutger her ruck and climbed onto *Bounty Hunter's* deck, using the spring hatches on the armored skirting with practiced ease. She walked to the bustle rack behind the turret and opened one of the empty ammo containers the crew used to store personal gear, the one marked DURAN. Rummaging inside, she put a few items in the pack that had been stowed within, then tossed it at Rutger's feet.

"This is Duran's stuff. You and the driver can pick through it and keep what issued gear you want. Turn over any personal effects you find so they can be given to graves registration."

Rutger stared down for a second at the pack, the name DURAN stenciled on it.

"You just gonna stand there with your thumb up your ass, or are you gonna toss me my ruck?" Faora said.

Rutger tossed it up to her. She shoved it into the ammo container and turned her attention toward the turret. Eying the automatic defense weapon, she peered into where the actuator had been damaged by a large-caliber bolt. "Has this been reported to maintenance?"

"Yes, Staff Sergeant."

"How long has the barrel on the left particle cannon been damaged?"

Rutger hadn't noticed the damage until several hours after Duran's death. *Good thing I didn't fire it a second time during the battle.* The gash in the outer barrel might have disrupted the bore's containment field and caused the barrel to explode. "It happened the other day. It's been reported."

"Good." Faora flipped the switch to open the cupola hatch. She kneeled and looked inside the fighting compartment, then stood and turned her hard gaze on Rutger. "Why hasn't this mess been cleaned up?" she barked.

Rutger hadn't thought to warn her of the mess, nor did he want to think about it. "I was going to have maintenance take care of it."

She locked eyes with him. "We don't ask other people to clean up our messes. Get a bucket and a sponge and get this squared away."

Rutger didn't respond. His mind flashed to Duran's mutilated face and the blood-spattered compartment.

Faora's eyes narrowed, her voice taking a venomous edge. "You will clean up your commander's remains. That is an order. Trust me, I would do the same for you. Delegate it to your driver if you want, but it will be cleaned in the next twenty minutes. Do I make myself clear?"

"Yes, Staff Sergeant."

"Good. You and I will get along just fine if you can follow orders." She eyed the platoon's other tanks in the distance, then jumped to the ground. "While you take care of that, I'm going to inspect the other tanks."

Rutger said nothing. He returned to the house, found a bucket outside by the garden and filled it with water before returning to *Bounty Hunter*. There were rags and disinfectant in one of the tank's external storage compartments.

Rutger lowered himself through the gunner's hatch and turned on the interior fighting compartment lights to full brightness. There was a dark stain on the side of the fighting compartment above the commander's console where he had pushed Duran's body. In the light, he could make out faint specs of blood on the instrument panels and some clumps of brain matter that had fallen beside the main gun's autoloader. He thought he might vomit at the sight of it. After ordering AI to deactivate power to the commander's console, he used a toothbrush and rag to carefully clean up the mess the best he could. A faint bloodstain remained on the seat cushion after he'd finished, but the rest of the compartment looked clean. The solvents left a lingering chemical odor that couldn't quite trump the usual locker room stench.

Rutger sat in the gunner's seat and went through Duran's rucksack. He found a holo-card and swiped through it, found a picture of Duran in his younger years standing beside his wife and two young daughters. The girls aged as he swiped on, and he found more pics of Duran as well, images he must have taken himself and sent home. He paused on one of the last few pictures—Duran with a cigar in the side of his mouth, and Tyrone and Rutger standing before *Bounty Hunter*. Rutger remembered posing for the image, taken a few days after he'd been assigned as driver. Tears filled his eyes, surprising him. He'd only known Duran for a few months, but he'd been like a father to him. Now only images and memories remained.

An approaching vehicle intruded on his thoughts. He quickly flipped off the holo-card when he heard the thud of boots climbing *Bounty Hunter's* armored skirting. Wiping away tears, he pocketed the holo-card and gathered his things.

"Yeah, that Staff Sergeant's a real cunt," said a voice outside.

"No shit, but she set you straight," said another man, more distant.

The first guy chuckled. "Not like you said anything to her. Part of me wants to fuck her. The rest says run away."

Moments later, a bearded repair tech peered down into the open hatch. "Hey, buddy, didn't know you were in there. Sorry to bother you, but we have to make some repairs on this tank."

"No problem. I was just leaving." Rutger grabbed the pail of bloody water from the commander's seat and hoisted it upward. "You mind grabbing that?"

"Sure," the man said, grabbing the pail.

Rutger climbed through the hatch and stood on the turret. The burly tech had a large tool bag by his feet. Bathed in dim red light, another tech stood in the bed of a wheeled truck, unpacking a crate that probably contained the new actuator for the automatic defense weapon.

"I just finished cleaning inside. Mind letting the compartment air out a bit?"

"Yeah, no problem, man. We'll have to get inside anyway to conduct diagnostic tests on the weapons after completing repairs."

"Okay, thanks. You mind taking care of this?" Rutger gestured to the pail of bloody water.

"Sure," the tech said, shining a light into the bucket. He grunted in disgust. "What're these pink chunks floating in here?"

"What's left of my friend," Rutger said.

The two techs exchanged wide-eyed looks as Rutger jumped from the tank and departed.

In the predawn darkness, Bukar and the rest of third platoon sat squeezed under a hover bus awning with plexiglass sides outside a vacated school, taking shelter from the cold wind. No kids around now, and several roof sections of the elementary school had caved in, likely from artillery fire.

The men who sat in its cold shelter were in no hurry to go anywhere. Despite the cold, the platoon waited patiently for a briefing from their OIC, Lieutenant Palmer. Word had been received that the Repub forces had staged a breakout through Federation lines some 230 kilometers to the south. Rumor had it that 1st Battalion would be sent there to assist the Federation forces.

They waited forty more minutes, eating rations, talking, or catching up on sleep, before Lieutenant Palmer arrived from the battalion briefing. The men turned their attention towards him as he approached. Bukar stood in the back and stomped the mud from his boots, hoping to warm his feet as well. Temps had dropped below freezing last night accompanied by snow flurries, and more snow had been forecast.

"Good morning, gentlemen," Palmer said. "Everyone get a chance to eat and catch up on some rest?" The men grumbled affirmative responses, some wisecracking about the food or the weather. The platoon members liked or at least tolerated Palmer, a short, energetic, and personable man. They probably would have fragged him long ago had they disliked him. "Very good. As you've probably heard, we're moving south. Visors down, let's go over the plan."

Bukar lowered his visor and focused on the area map projected on HUD. "We're ordered to reach the town of Vlurg by 1800 hours local time," Palmer said. Vlurg appeared as a flashing blue star on the map. "Which gives us a little over twelve standard hours."

Bukar stared at the map and scowled. Vlurg was southwest of New Oslo, a hundred kilometers further from the Repub capital than their current position. The wrong direction from his sister. This didn't surprise Bukar. Conflicts rarely went as planned, and the Repub forces had caught the Fed yokels pants-down once again. Bukar wondered how many last-ditch offensives the Republic could launch in their vain attempt to reverse the war's course.

"We'll head west past Phase Line Gamma and meet with the dropships at Assembly Area Irene by 0830 hours for transport south to FOB Vulture. From there we'll travel east for approximately 90 kilometers to reach Objective Silver."

Only part of Bukar's mind listened as he thought of his sister. Three years older than Bukar, Adeze had practically raised him. Their father had been killed by police during a labor riot.

He'd been nine at the time. Arrested three years later for being a political dissident, their mother had died in prison, leaving only him and his sister. Bukar felt a sibling obligation to reach her. *I will get to you, one way or another. This is merely a temporary setback.*

"Any questions?" Palmer asked. There were none. "Okay, Platoon Sergeant, let's move 'em out."

The hardened face of Staff Sergeant Mardin appeared. "All right, you heard the man. I want a full checkout of the IFV's and skimmers before we move out at 0530." The men stood, some groaning or uttering minor complaints, though all had been expecting the news. "Ordnance checks, dropship prep, and equipment staged for embarkation by no later than 0800. Make it happen and quit your bitching. You can rest again on the flight."

Troopers filed past Bukar as he continued staring at the HUD map, almost transfixed by it, until only he remained beneath the shelter.

"Can I help you, Corporal?" Lieutenant Palmer asked, startling Bukar from his thoughts.

"No, sir," Bukar said, now focused on the shorter man. "I was just thinking about my sister in New Oslo." He immediately regretted saying it. *I shouldn't have mentioned it.*

Palmer seemed to take a moment to register the comment, as if he were concentrating on something else before he responded. "Are you from Scandova?" Palmer asked, surprised.

"No, sir, she moved here several years ago to pursue her art career."

"Oh...well, a lot of refugees have left the city. She probably got out with them." His positive thoughts seemed more like feigned interest.

"She wouldn't leave her work, sir," Bukar said with conviction. He'd asked her to leave when the political situation first hinted at civil war. She had refused his request.

"Look, this'll all be over soon. You know the business. Once the fighting is done put in for a leave chit, and I'll try to make it happen so you can look her up. You'd better get moving."

"Yes, sir," Bukar replied. He walked toward the platoon's staging area, where his fellow troopers were already performing final checks and loading equipment to deploy. As he strode toward the fighting vehicles, his thoughts remained on Adeze. *Lord, please protect her.*

SNOW BEGAN TO FALL IN HEAVY FLAKES. THE TANKS and IFVs of Bruiser Company glided through the streets of Vlurg as twilight fell, moving in blackout mode sans running lights. Seated in the gunner's seat, Rutger didn't need lights to see outside. Burnt, crumbling buildings and torched vehicles, civilian and military, shown on the holos. The streets were mostly empty, though Rutger occasionally spied civilians standing and staring with vacant eyes at the column of massive vehicles snaking toward the front.

After a 92-kilometer journey from their dropship drop-off point, Bruiser Company had arrived and linked up with elements of the 124th Federation Mechanized Infantry Division. Bruiser Company had been sent to where the Repub forces had penetrated furthest into Federation-held territory. Officially, they had come to reinforce the Feds, but their unstated mission, obvious to the veterans, was to stiffen the resolve of Fed troops in the sector.

They traveled down the same road Repub forces had used the previous night to attack Vlurg. After failing to take the town, the enemy had withdrawn to an unknown location. Bruiser Company's task was to find them.

Four-lane city streets soon gave way to a two-lane hardball road flanked by snow-covered fields. The tanks' active camouflage adapted to the change, further enhanced by blankets of snow accumulating atop the vehicles. Repulsors hummed and kicked up eddies of snow as they floated along like ghostly white apparitions creeping eastward. Second Platoon currently led the column. The rest of the company was half a kilometer back. Captain Hensley occasionally dispatched a tank or IFV to check out potential enemy hiding spots along the route.

Lieutenant Mosley's tank, *Hostile Intent*, led the way over the cracked and blistered road, with *Bounty Hunter* about sixty meters behind. The tanks behind them also maintained sixty-meter intervals. *Hostile Intent* kept its turret oriented forward, while the rest of the tanks in the formation pointed turrets outboard to cover the flanks and rear.

Rutger shivered in the biting cold. Duran had kept the fighting compartment closed and rather warm, which suited Rutger just fine, though staying awake on watch had sometimes been difficult. Staff Sergeant Faora, however, liked to keep the fighting compartment cold both in temperature and persona. She kept the commander's hatch in the protected open position, allowing freezing winds to howl into the cabin. *I'd kill to be a driver again.* He could have adjusted temperature in the forward driver's compartment to his own liking. Instead, he flexed his hands again to improve circulation as he monitored his screens.

They left the entrenched Federation positions around Vlurg behind, moving closer to the last known Repub positions around Lunwich, a small town along the highway. Fighting in the fields around Vlurg had been intense. They passed a burnt-out Federation tank, its melted barrel drooping limply toward the snow. Several destroyed APCs littered a field. Rutger assumed the smaller mounds of snow around them concealed corpses.

Intel revealed at the last briefing reported that Repub forces would soon attempt another offensive. If successful, they could possibly reverse the course of the war, or at least bring the Feds to the peace table. Rutger didn't care one way or another; he got paid either way. He only wanted to survive the war, then desert and return home to his wife and daughter. He'd debated his decision with a calmer head after Duran's death but hadn't changed his mind.

The convoy moved at a steady twenty-five kph, again watching for mines. The road had been clear so far. Directional mines along the road were still a concern, however, and Rutger hoped the active protection system would handle them.

The tank's bow rose as they headed uphill around a wooded bend. Rutger watched the terrain on the topography map slowly pivot as it scrolled downward. They were eight kilometers east of Vlurg. The road continued toward New Oslo as a blue line curving northeast across 180 kilometers of wooded terrain. A network of roads connecting smaller towns and villages cut across the route.

Snow-covered roofs on gray buildings in Lunwich appeared on the panoramic screens about two klicks away over the tree-tops, visibility still decent despite the falling snow. A recon drone had been dispatched to scout around Lunwich; it was quickly shot down on approach, leaving little doubt of enemy presence in town.

Lieutenant Mosley stopped *Hostile Intent* by a break in the trees to get a better view of the town on the rise above them. "Driver, halt here," Staff Sergeant Faora said over the intercom, sounding none too pleased about the column halting. *Bounty Hunter* slowed and stopped, the forward repulsors kicking up snow in front of the tank as they countered forward inertia. Occasionally buffeted by the wind, the tank floated a half meter above the road in dynamic stasis.

Rutger stole a glance at Faora. She had her visor locked down and he couldn't quite decipher her words, but the conversation was heated. *She's probably talking to Mosley.*

Duran had set the radios so the entire crew could monitor the various platoon, company, and battalion nets for situational awareness. He'd rarely switched to a private command channel or excluded the crew from a conversation. Faora had changed the radio settings so only the general platoon and company nets were audible. Rutger could still press a switch and listen in if he wanted to—Faora hadn't locked them out completely—but she would see a notification if he did, and he didn't want to feel her wrath.

Rutger grew bored as the column sat for what felt like an inordinate amount of time. Without access to the command net, he could only speculate regarding the delay. Perhaps Mosley was launching another recon drone or waiting for guidance from higher.

Rutger removed his gloves and fished a ration pack from the storage bin behind his seat. He hadn't eaten since before noon and wanted to grab a quick bite while they waited. He pressed the tab on the package that automatically warmed it up in thirty seconds. As his meal of tortellini cooked, he stared up at the town. When the tab turned from red to green, he peeled off the foil, grabbed his spoon from his armored vest, and shoveled a steaming spoonful into his mouth.

"What the fuck are you doing?" Staff Sergeant Faora hissed.

Rutger realized she was talking to him. "Just grabbing some quick chow while we—"

"Who said you could eat?"

"Well, Staff Sergeant Duran usually allowed us to—"

"What is your gun trained on?" Faora said cutting him off.

"What? There isn't a designated tar—"

"Where is the main gun pointed?"

"It's…it's just pointing straight ahead." Rutger stammered.

"And where do you think the enemy is at?" Faora asked. "Straight ahead? If you were them, where would you post your lookouts?"

On a view screen, Rutger spotted the tall blue spire on a multi-story structure over a kilometer away. "Probably in that building to the right."

"Brilliant deduction. Now train your gun on it."

"Yes, Staff Sergeant." Rutger slewed the targeting reticle onto the building.

"And toss that damn food out. I don't know what kind of tank Duran ran, but we will eat in rotation when I say."

"Yes, Staff Sergeant." Anger welled inside Rutger at her comment about Duran, but he complied, dumping the ration tin into the waste disposal slot behind him. He got what she was saying, but she didn't have to be an asshole about it.

Lieutenant Mosley's tank moved forward. He said over the platoon net, "Okay, people, resume advance toward the town in column. Stay frosty."

Faora shook her head and muttered something to herself before ordering Aubrey to advance.

Buildings in Lunwich loomed large on Rutger's holos at eight times magnification, most fairly modern in design and constructed from a mixture of wood, concrete, and plastic composites with blue solar roof tiles and large tinted windows. Rutger scanned the buildings, cycling through various spectrum displays for telltale signs of the enemy. The lead tank usually faced the greatest risk, but sometimes the enemy would engage trailing vehicles, either in an attempt to lure the other tanks into a trap or to block their axis of retreat. Rutger hoped the crews in the two tanks behind *Bounty Hunter* were alert and on their game.

Bounty Hunter was about 800 meters from the outskirts of town when the sharp hiss-crack of a Repub plasma cannon pierced the frigid air. A brilliant blue beam flashed from the town as bright and sudden as a lightning bolt and momentarily blacked out Rutger's center screen to shield his eyes. Lieutenant Mosley's tank flashed orange in a sun-bright flare and then ground to a halt on the road in a shower of sparks along the armored skirting. Black smoke billowed from a glowing scar on the front corner of its armored prow.

"Blue 1's been hit!" someone cried over the platoon net.

Rutger traversed the turret, scanning frantically for a target. He hadn't seen where the shot originated from. The AI extrapolated a likely yet vague area that covered a quarter of the buildings visible. Zooming in, Rutger couldn't identify a visible threat, just empty streets.

"Driver, shift us left twenty meters," Staff Sergeant Faora said over the intercom. "Now, damn it!"

Shit, I hope there aren't any mines! The tank dipped left as Aubrey shifted laterally, the repulsors kicking up a cloud of snow as they departed from the road.

"Gunner, report! Did you see the shot!" Faora demanded.

"Negative!" Rutger replied, panning over the buildings with the tank's advanced optics. The trailing tanks hadn't seen it either, since none had returned fire with their main guns.

In front of them, the crew of *Hostile Intent* started to bail out. Repub infantry in the buildings opened fire on the column. *Hostile Intent's* gunner and driver were already sprinting toward the wood line, blue bolts kicking up spires of snow around them. Lieutenant Mosley finally climbed from the commander's hatch. As he prepared to jump clear, a fiery blue bolt severed his leg at the hip in a flash of red mist. He tumbled off the tank, his screams flooding the platoon net for a second. They echoed in Rutger's mind and ate at his sanity as he stared in dumbstruck horror.

The threat detection warning wailed in Rutger's ear, snapping him out of inaction. Adrenaline suddenly surged through his veins. An unseen enemy was painting *Bounty Hunter's* hull with a laser rangefinder. The AI was already traversing the turret toward the highlighted source on Rutger's screen, a rooftop window over 1300 meters away.

"Gunner, suppress target, 30 mike mike," said Faora.

Rutger had the window lined up. "Identified. On the way," he said, mashing the trigger.

Bounty Hunter's rotary cannons sent streams of plasma bolts toward the window. The side of the building erupted in a gray cloud of orange flames. Pieces of the building exploded twenty meters in the air and cascaded down into the street. The lances of sun-hot plasma likely destroyed the laser rangefinder and everyone on the building's top floor.

The threat tone went silent. In the same instant, a flash of light and smoke to the left caught Rutger's eye. Three hypervelocity missiles leapt from a remote launcher staged in a lower floor window near his last target, leaving dense trails of smoke.

Rutger noted that the automatic defense weapon had been switched off from air defense mode. *Bounty Hunter's* automatic protection system would have to deal with them. Staff Sergeant Faora had taken control of the automatic defense weapon; she ripped streams of bolts toward flashes from heavy automatic weapons firing from dug-in hilltop positions.

Rutger rotated the turret with his right joystick and fired the autocannons again, walking the crimson stream of bolts across muzzle flashes in the buildings toward the source of the contrails. The other surviving tanks likewise pounded the buildings with autocannons and coaxial guns.

The shrieking missiles closed the gap in a heartbeat. *Bounty Hunter's* active protection system pods fired a sleet of self-forging projectiles. Two of the missiles exploded in thunderous booms; shrapnel pitted the tank's plasteel armor. The third missile streaked over the turret with only centimeters to spare and detonated behind them.

"Status report!" Captain Hensley said over the company net. "What the hell is going on up there?"

"Bruiser 6, this is Blue 4. We're being engaged from the town, force size unknown," Faora calmly replied. "Blue 1 is down. I'm in command."

After a second of dead air, Hensley replied, "Roger that, Blue 4. I'll break off a platoon and try to flank them to the south. Hold your position."

"Roger that, Bruiser 6." Faora turned to Rutger and said, "Keep your eye on the town. Slag anything that moves."

The enemy tank or whatever had taken out *Hostile Intent* was still out there, waiting or possibly moving to a new firing position, though sensors showed no Repub vehicles. Rutger stared at his screens, afraid to blink, waiting for the Repub tank to suddenly slide into view.

"Blue 4, movement to the left. Appears to be infantry," said Corporal Yurek, commander of *Dog Breath*, over the platoon net. "Looks like they're trying to flank us."

Rutger fought the temptation to look down at his tactical display and kept watching the town. He engaged another machine gun nest with the coaxial 15mm plasma machine gun. *Just do your job and trust everyone else to do theirs.*

"Roger that, Blue 3, pull back three hundred meters to your seven o'clock and stop them from getting a flank shot behind us. Break, Blue 2, displace two hundred meters to my nine o'clock and guard our flank."

"Roger that, moving now," the tank commanders replied in sequence.

Rutger felt his stomach twist at Faora's order. With a sinking feeling, he realized they were the only tank covering the town. No back up. It would be up to him to engage any threat up there. *Kill them before they kill me.*

Blood Shed and *Dog Breath* engaged the infantry on their flank a moment later. Rutger flinched slightly when their main guns fired, the cracking reports unnervingly loud through Faora's open hatch.

Right there! Rutger saw, or thought he saw, a Repub tank moving among some buildings. He zoomed in—nothing there. *Fuck!* This was no time for his mind to start playing tricks on him.

"Blue 4, Bruiser 6 actual. Pull back to Phase Line Epsilon," Captain Hensley said over the company net. "Feds have spotted a larger enemy force on our southern flank. We need to fall back and support."

"Fuck," Faora said, off the net. To Hensley she replied, "Copy that, Bruiser 6, falling back." Then over the platoon net: "Blue elements, pull back. We'll cover you."

"Copy," Blue 2 and Blue 3 responded.

"What about Lieutenant Mosley?" Rutger asked Faora.

"What about him? He's dead."

"But the body?"

"Isn't worth the risk."

Rutger stared out at Mosley's wrecked body and the spreading vermillion stain in the snow. Faora's attitude unsettled him. She was leaving the platoon commander behind, and he knew she would do the same to him if it ever came to that. *Fucking bitch!* He tried not to think about it, and slid the targeting reticle onto another machine gun position. Blue bolts zipped toward *Bounty Hunter*. He answered with a long burst of coaxial fire.

Behind, *Blood Shed* sprayed the tree line with its 30mm cannons as *Dog Breath* pulled back two hundred meters behind it and took an overwatch position, returning the favor as *Dog Breath* fell back. Trees splintered and fell, and soon the whole clearing was ablaze.

"Clear, Blue 4, we've got your back," said Sergeant Willard, ready to cover *Bounty Hunter* as they withdrew.

"Okay, our turn," Faora announced over the intercom. "Gunner, suppress area with main gun. Driver, back us up the way we came, nice and steady."

Rutger stared at the screen. *The main gun?* There were likely civilians hiding in the buildings. "I don't have a target, Staff Sergeant."

"Just level the fucking town! We need to get out of here before that tank in there gets any bright ideas. Maybe you can spot him while you're at it."

A cloud of snow blocked the gunsights as Aubrey reversed the repulsors and started backing up. The buildings soon returned to focus. Rutger swerved the main gun toward the nearest building and squeezed the trigger. The 150mm bolt gouged a 5-meter chunk from the building's front corner, the explosion raising a cloud of dust and fire. What remained of the multistory structure collapsed in on itself. The shockwave and heat from the blast rocked the settlement, shattering nearby windows and shaking snow from rooftops.

Rutger shifted his fire from building to building as they fell back, repeating the destruction and reducing the town to burning rubble. The tank jerked with recoil from every shot. The temperature inside the fighting compartment rose markedly, and Rutger kept a wary eye on the temperature gauge for the main gun tube.

No enemy tanks returned fire. Rutger ceased firing as they backed around the edge of the tree line. Steam rose from the main gun's glowing red muzzle. As Aubrey spun the tank around, Rutger caught a last look at Mosley's smoking tank and his crumpled form next to it. The image quickly and thankfully slid from view, but it wouldn't leave his mind. The handsome officer had been vibrant and alive hours before—now his body lay discarded in the snow as an afterthought.

Rutger thought of Serena and Callie. *What if that had been me?* He shook his head, and silently vowed that it wouldn't be.

CHAPTER

BUKAR LED PRIVATE TUCO THROUGH A DARK FOREST
of towering firs and powder-coated brush, their boots softly
crunching in the snow. They had been moving since dusk. The
time on Bukar's HUD currently read 2315. Four of Scandova's
dim blue moons hung indifferently overhead like distant billiard
balls. Twinkling fragments of the planet's rings shone on the
eastern horizon.

When Lieutenant Palmer had asked for volunteers for the
mission, Bukar had stepped up just to pass the time and occupy
himself. Anything had seemed better than lying in a cold fox hole
waiting for something to happen. He needed to keep moving, to
occupy his mind. When no one else volunteered, Tuco, one of the
platoon's junior men, had been volun-told to go. They'd traveled
on skimmers until they dared not go further—too great a risk of
sensor detection—and now they relied on their suits' active camo
as they moved on foot.

They moved silently, staying low and darting from cover to
cover through snow often a meter deep. Bukar couldn't wait to
ditch the heavy, unwieldy satchel charge slung over his shoulder.
He periodically stopped and listened as he checked their position

on his visor's map overlay. Night vision rendered the forest in stark monochrome, amplifying the already black-and-white environment. Despite his suit's environmental control system and the sub-freezing temperatures, Bukar sweated inside his power armor. *Another reason to keep moving.* He felt the cold seeping into his bones whenever he stopped.

Frosted exhalations blasted from his helmet's respirator. Bukar had never seen snow until joining the Berserkers, and the novelty of it soon devolved into hatred. The steamy jungles and urban sprawls on Beninia now seemed alluring, though he couldn't have left the planet fast enough all those years ago. *Just a kid with big dreams.* He let go of the thought. *Only the here and now matters*, he told himself, focusing on his breathing.

After stalking through the woods for half an hour, they finally reached the edge of the tree line. The grounded tank sat askew on the road almost half a klick away across a barren field of white. Bukar spotted no enemy in its proximity. It appeared unmolested in the moonlight. The company commander had debriefed the tank's two surviving crew members after their earlier engagement; they'd informed him the tank was only disabled. Bukar and Tuco had been tasked with destroying it to ensure the enemy couldn't hack the AI and access the crypto and force disposition information stored inside the tank's memory banks. *Typical. Let the grunts clean up the mess.*

The prospect of crossing the vast open field, not a stick of cover to be seen, unnerved Bukar. The settlement of Lunwich lurked on a hill in the distance. He could see the blown-out buildings and piles of rubble providing a myriad of hiding places. *Someone up there is watching the tank.* And they probably had crew-served weapons trained on it. He knew the mission would be dicey when he'd volunteered for it, but now it seemed like more than he'd bargained for.

Moonlight shined through Tuco's visor onto his face. The young man's eyes were wide with fear and apprehension. *Good, he is listening to his instincts.* Fear was justified, an intelligent reaction on a crazy-ass mission like this.

Now the hard part. "You ready?" Bukar asked over the proximity net.

Tuco nodded.

"Okay, good. We move slow and steady across the field until we reach the road, just a slow stroll. We don't want to attract attention with our movement. Let the active camouflage do its magic." Bukar said, studying the younger man's ruddy colored face. Tuco stared intently at Bukar, hanging on every word. "If there are any signs they have detected us, drop flat and freeze. Do not run. Got it?"

Tuco nodded mechanically.

"Tell me you understand," Bukar said.

"I understand."

"Good, let's move."

They set off slowly across the field. To cut down time of exposure in the open, Bukar elected to approach the road at a perpendicular angle before turning east and paralleling the road to the tank. Their objective seemed impossibly far away but also inviting, like the lures he'd once used for fishing. Bukar hoped the enemy hadn't been clever enough to post troops around the tank or in the tree line and use it as bait. *They probably have. I certainly would.*

They walked 600 meters across the field before reaching the relative safety of a ditch beside the elevated road. Though only about a meter deep, the ditch at least offered some cover as they peered down the icy highway toward the tank. It appeared practically undamaged but for the blackened hole in its prow. The hatches were still open, the main gun aligned with the hull and pointed up the slope toward Lunwich.

Bukar clutched his M-17 rifle and waited, watching and listening for a good ten minutes. He zoomed in with his visor and scanned around the tank, then checked the tree line on the field's other side. No movement save for trees waving in the wind. He watched the town for a few minutes. No lights or movement in the darkened buildings.

Satisfied as he could be, Bukar led Tuco to the tank. They crouched in its shadow, waiting for a hail of bolts to seek them out, but the night remained still and quiet save for the wind gusting and howling at times.

Then he noticed the corpse. The dead tanker's helmet and gloved fingers protruded from a snow drift that had accumulated along the armored skirting. Tuco noticed it as well, looking away. His eyes darting around fitfully, as he crouched beside the tank clutching his rifle.

"Stay here," Bukar said. He crawled from the ditch and mounted the tank. Staying low on the hull, he stuck his head over the side. "Hand me the other satchel charge."

Tuco raised it like an offering to a god, a burden he seemed happy to be relieved of.

Bukar shouldered the second bag and crept onto the turret, crawling forward on his belly. He peered over the commander's cupola, his rifle at the ready. Night vision revealed an empty cabin. He scanned the horizon again before dropping the charges and lowering himself in after them. The inside of the turret was cramped. He barely fit through the oversized commander's hatch in the bulk of his power armor, and he had to raise his arms above his head to slip through.

He looked around the cramped turret. A flashing red light on the top corner of his HUD indicated the helmet camera was recording. The smell of smoke infiltrated his respiration filters. Snow dusted the seats, consoles, and holo screens, but the electronics appeared undisturbed, no open panels or wires visible. The wind howled across the open commander's hatch overhead.

Bukar opened the green canvas satchel bags and set the timers on each large block of high explosives to twenty minutes, then he placed them under both consoles inside the turret as instructed. *More than enough time to reach the woods and wait.* They'd been ordered to visually confirm the tank's destruction.

The snow crunched beneath Bukar's feet as he dropped from the tank's hull. Tuco looked at him with frightened eyes, the trooper seeming to grow more apprehensive by the second. Eager to leave, Tuco started to rise. Bukar grabbed his shoulder and motioned for him to wait, then nodded toward the dead tanker. *We aren't going to leave you behind, buddy.*

Bukar tried to pick up the body but discovered it was frozen to the road. He turned his back toward the town to conceal the glow of his vibro-blade, the edge emitting a faint orange glow when he powered it up. He quickly cut the body free and noticed it was missing a leg. He sheathed his blade and hoisted the corpse, frozen solid and stiff as a board, over his shoulder.

Bukar and Tuco crept along the road's shallow embankment. They'd traveled about sixty meters when a mortar thumped in the distance toward town. A pop sounded overhead, followed by the hiss of a flare. Bukar and Tuco dropped to the deck and hugged the snowy ground. The flare illuminated the field like a premature dawn as it slowly dropped on a parachute, rocking in the wind and casting long, jumpy shadows. Bukar's pulse pounded in his head, and he prayed that their active camouflage would keep them invisible.

Looking down at the frozen corpse, he realized that the suit's active camo wasn't working. Perhaps the corpse had given them away. *No good deed goes unpunished. No…that isn't true. It was good karma to bring him.*

The flare began to flicker. Bukar's heart leapt at the hiss-crack of plasma bolts that pierced the night, blue streaks zipping overhead high to their left. Tuco started to rise and turn with his weapon. Bukar yanked him down. "Stay the fuck down!" Bukar growled. "They aren't shooting at us." Even with night vision, the enemy probably didn't have visual on them. *Recon by fire.* Bukar knew the trick—fire into the darkness and try to panic the enemy into returning fire and revealing their position.

The flare died out, leaving them in darkness again. Bukar waited, not daring to move. A second flare launched from the hilltop, this one further to their right, the glowing orb waxing and waning as it dropped. Between the sweat inside his suit and the frozen ground, Bukar began to feel invisible, icy fingers pierce his body.

The second flare died a few seconds later. No other flares launched as Bukar and Tuco lay motionless. A few minutes later, Bukar tapped Tuco on the shoulder. They rose and continued toward the woods. Bukar noticed the satchel charges' countdown on his visor—only 1:30 left, and they were nowhere near the tree line. *We aren't going to make it in time.* "Double time it, kid," Bukar grunted, starting to run.

Dual explosions from the satchel charges ripped through the night. Two pillars of flame erupted skyward from the disabled tank's open turret hatches, casting the field in brilliant light.

They chased their shadows down the hill toward the woods, Bukar balancing the unwieldy corpse on his shoulder. He heard Tuco's long, ragged breaths over his own as he sucked cold air in and out in huge windy gulps. Multiple flares launched with deep thumps from the town, igniting directly overhead and in front of them. The woods seemed impossibly far. Bukar knew that active camo couldn't conceal them now. The multiple flares cast their long shadows on the white field in stark relief.

Blue bolts blazed around them, kicking up plumes of snow as they sprinted madly toward the woods over 400 meters away. This time the mortars unleashed HE shells that shrieked down on them seconds later. Explosions blasted geysers of snow up around them, and hot shrapnel whizzed through the air as the Repub gunners tried to find their range.

Tuco dropped to the snow behind him, screaming and clutching his leg. Bukar turned and ran back to him. His foot remained attached by a few tendons, and gouts of dark red blood pulsed into the snow until his suit automatically applied a tourniquet to his leg. Tuco continued to thrash and scream in pain.

Bukar fought Tuco's flailing limbs for a moment before he could pull the painkiller tab on his power suit. The painers calmed him in seconds. Bukar grabbed the pull strap on the back of his armor and started dragging him, a herculean effort. Despite his suit's layer of artificial muscles, dragging the combined weight of the corpse and Tuco through the deep snow strained the suit's capabilities. Sweat began to flow freely down Bukar's sides as he awkwardly powered through the drifts.

Bolts continued to kick up snow around them, but the shots grew wilder as the range increased. Mortar shells still chased him, explosions and the hum of shrapnel shredding the frigid air. The tree line was so close. Bukar wheezed as he sucked in the cold air, his helmet struggling to warm it, his lungs and legs burning from exertion. The crack of bolts died off as he finally dragged Tuco and the corpse into the trees, where he collapsed behind the trunk of a thick fir. Bukar got a look at the corpse's gray face behind his visor, the man's countenance forever frozen in a contorted scream.

Mortar shells followed Bukar into the trees, felling branches and shattering trunks before suddenly ceasing. He stared back at the hilltop, his breaths still ragged. He zoomed in with his visor. No signs of enemy movement. Bukar awkwardly hoisted the corpse, grabbed Tuco's harness and started back toward their skimmers.

The snow in the forest was too deep to drag Tuco through, forcing Bukar to skirt the edge of the tree line. He thought of leaving the corpse, but he'd made it this far and stubborn pride wouldn't let him. He recalled Adeze helping him fight off gang members as a kid, after he'd refused to give up his backpack. His leg had been broken by a crowbar, and she'd carried him two kilometers to the local clinic. *We don't leave our brothers and sisters behind.*

Bukar paused about ten minutes later to rest and check on Tuco. He found the bottle of spray sealant in his med kit and liberally covered the grizzly wound in tan foam. Satisfied with his efforts, he got his bearings. The skimmers were half a kilometer away, and he could barely see the clearing where they'd hidden them.

Then he heard a soft whining sound on the wind. He tried to quiet his breathing as he strained to listen. The whining grew closer. *Drones!* One appeared in the distance over the trees on whirling turbofans. It paused for a second—loitering, turning, scanning, acquiring—before it rocketed directly toward them, the whine of its turbofans increasing in pitch.

No way to outrun it. Bukar dropped the corpse and Tuco and turned to face it, suddenly aware of how cold he was, his body numb. He shouldered his rifle as he grabbed Tuco and backed toward the cover of the tree line. Tuco saw it as well, mouthing gibberish over the proximity net as he frantically tried to reach the rifle slung behind his back.

The drone, short with a 1.5-meter wingspan, screamed toward them as it swooped low across the field like a giant gray bat. Bukar put his rifle's holographic sight on it and squeezed off two shots, both misses. A sharp cracking sound filled the dark expanse around him. Blue bolts leapt from the drone's nose and dug into the drifts at his feet, kicking up clouds of snow. One bolt passed so close that Bukar swore he'd felt the heat through his helmet.

He dropped to one knee and fired another burst while trying to control his ragged breathing. This time his bolts punched through the drone's fuselage and it broke apart in a shower of sparks. Flaming pieces plummeted softly into the snow.

Bukar didn't hesitate, since the enemy now knew his exact location. He sprinted back into the open, hefted the corpse and snatched Tuco's drag handle. Despite the cold, his pulse hammered in his hands as he scrambled desperately through the drifts toward the skimmers.

Faint whining sounds converged into an ominous hum that filled the night air. Still fifty meters from the skimmers, Bukar looked back. Two more drones swept in over the field on an intercept course, one 300 meters back and the other 100 meters behind. Their turbofans rose to a supercharged pitch, clawing the air as they swooped in for a strafing run.

He let go of Tuco, took a knee again and fired a frantic one-handed burst, the corpse still resting on his shoulder as incoming bolts kicked up the snow around him. The closest drone lost a turbofan and careened wildly into the trees, where it exploded in an orange flash.

The second drone raced in firing, its muzzle flashes turning the night into a crazy, strobe-filled nightmare. He unloaded his rifle at it, all bolts missing the mark. The drone streaked by and banked hard into a turn above the trees, circling around for another pass.

Reloading for the drone's next pass, Bukar heard a roaring noise grow louder in the distance. *Vehicle blower fans!* That meant dismounts. With the threat of enemy troops on their trail, they would have to flee from the drone and take their chances.

He grabbed Tuco and sprinted hard toward the skimmers. *Almost there!* They would have to all ride on one. The weight of Bukar, the corpse, and Tuco would test the craft's weight limit.

Sucking in great gulps of air, he watched the drone loom again over the trees. Everything slowed down and became surreal. The drone came in like a swooping grim reaper eager for a gruesome harvest.

Bukar had almost reached the skimmer when the drone opened fire, knocking him down. Yet Bukar felt no pain. He scrambled to his feet and noticed the smoking hole in the corpse's back armor plate. *Karma*, was all he could think.

He stumbled to the skimmer and draped Tuco over the handlebars, who grunted weakly in pain. The drone circled into another tight, banking turn. He fumbled with the rear cargo net and secured the corpse, then jumped on the seat and fired up the skimmer. Bukar leaned over Tuco and gunned the repulsors, wheeling the skimmer around in a tight ninety-degree turn. He rocketed forward just ahead of the drone's next salvo of bolts.

Blue bolts flashed around the skimmer as the drone gave chase. Bukar could have easily evaded the drone were he riding alone, but the overloaded skimmer moved and responded sluggishly to his inputs. *We're not fast enough!*

Bukar slalomed the skimmer left and right, almost dumping them off while trying to avoid the deadly blue beams. He waited for the moment when one would find its mark and punch through his armor to vaporize his insides. The skimmer bottomed out several times on the drifts kicking up clouds of powdered snow, losing speed and costing him precious distance.

Bukar steered drunkenly into a grove with low-hanging branches that barely cleared the skimmer as he rushed beneath them at over 150 kph. Shooting into the open again, the skimmer slammed into a drift-covered log and caught air, nearly bucking them off. It dropped like a rock before the repulsors arrested the descent and rocketed them forward.

Tuco groaned and thrashed a bit. "It hurts so bad. Am I dying? Am I gonna die?"

"You're going to be fine, kid," Bukar said. "Just quit moving and hold the fuck on."

The drone swept in behind them. Bolts carved up the snow beside them as Bukar swerved the craft violently. He felt fingers of concentrated ions punch into the vehicle's rear cowling, which exploded in a shower of sparks and metal fragments.

"Motherfucker!" Bukar screamed, trying to maneuver closer to the tree line. He whipped the skimmer left and right, slaloming through the trees with reckless abandon. He maneuvered through a tight gap between trunks and momentarily lost the drone, which had to slow and redirect course to resume pursuit. Bukar gunned the skimmer toward friendly lines, only a couple of klicks away now.

They shot into the open. *Shit!* Only open fields and death lay ahead of them. The drone hungrily gained on them, trying to get a lock on the skimmer. Bukar jinked again and again with stomach-lurching turns, almost losing control and flipping them.

The drone was almost on top of them. Bukar tried to ignore its proximity on HUD but knew it wouldn't be long now.

A pulsing streak of crimson lightning suddenly split the darkness overhead, blasting past the skimmer. The drone's icon disappeared on HUD. Bukar looked over his shoulder in time to see the drone dig a groove in the snow-covered field before it exploded. A nearby Berserker air defense weapon had detected the incoming drone and plucked it from sky.

"Praise God!" he cried, looking toward the stars overhead. Breathing a sigh of relief, he turned the skimmer toward their bivouac site and radioed that they were approaching.

CHAPTER 9

"STAFF SERGEANT," RUTGER SAID AS THEY SKIMMED over snow-patched farm fields north of Lunwich at over 75 kph, "are we gonna get any support from the locals today?" *Bounty Hunter* and second platoon were moving to cut off a sizable Repub force advancing into their AO twenty klicks to the northeast.

Staff Sergeant Faora rode with her commander's seat elevated, her head sticking above the turret. Rutger couldn't see her face, but it sounded like she was actually smiling, "I wouldn't bank on it. Probably a better chance of us winning the Galactic Lotto." She seemed to be in good spirits. The sun was out, and the brief spell of warmer weather had turned the snow into mud.

Rutger was beginning to get a better handle on his new platoon sergeant. Faora rarely spoke and was a harsh taskmaster but knew the business of war. Her quiet confidence was reassuring, but he missed Duran's relaxed manner and the stories he used to tell. Losing Duran seemed like an eternity ago, and he regretted dwelling on it. The image of him with half his face missing, and Lieutenant Mosley standing with his leg blown off often appeared when he closed his eyes.

He tried to push the memories from his mind as he kept a watchful eye on the threat sensor screen and the panoramic view ahead. He still worried about mines, but the enemy likely hadn't had time to plant any in advance, so speed was the order of the day. Faora probably would have moved faster if the chance of ambush or stumbling into the enemy in the fields, groves, and hedgerows wasn't so high.

The designated waypoint on the topo map finally slid into view. Faora ordered the tanks to fan out over the fields as they approached their destination, a broad, partially wooded hill with several buildings on it about 1.5 klicks away. Rutger zoomed to 20X magnification and scanned the buildings for potential threats. The small community of several prefab houses and sheet metal barns appeared to be a farming commune. Rutger saw no one, yet the place didn't appear deserted, and was untouched by the scars of war. *For now.*

"Keep an eye out for snipers, Staff Sergeant," Rutger said as they glided toward the hilltop.

Faora didn't answer, too busy searching the area with electrobinoculars.

They halted atop the hill next to the buildings. The position overlooked a long, sloping pasture that ended at a broad forest with several roads and cuts running through it.

"Driver," Faora said, "back us into that grove of trees seventy meters to our right."

Aubrey guided *Bounty Hunter* over and backed into the shadows of the tall firs beside some rusted, abandoned farming equipment that sat in tall yellow grass covered by rags of snow. Once satisfied with their position, Faora had him ground the tank and power down. *Bounty Hunter's* turret and main gun barely protruded above the slope of the hill, oriented toward the wood line over three kilometers away.

Dropping back into the fighting compartment, Faora looked at the terrain map and highlighted two positions. "Blue 2," she said over the platoon net, "position on the far-left flank behind the haystacks. Blue 3, move behind the northernmost farmhouse."

Sergeant Willard and Corporal Yurek acknowledged and moved their respective tanks into position. Their tanks' active camouflage chameleoning them into the background and buildings.

"Any threat of hostiles in this area?" Sergeant Willard asked. "I'm not so sure we should position so close to these buildings."

"This is a war zone, Blue 2. Consider this whole planet hostile. We need to cover this gap and stay dispersed. If it makes you feel any better, there haven't been any reports of partisan activity in this area."

"Copy that, Blue 1, Blue 2 out."

Blue 1. Rutger still wasn't used to the call sign which, at Captain Hensley's order, they'd assumed after Lieutenant Mosley's body was recovered. Rutger opened his hatch and stood to stretch his arms. Fatigue had become an issue among the troopers from the constant movements and standing watch at all hours. Machines were also breaking down; *Bounty Hunter* needed maintenance. Repulsor seven would soon fail if it wasn't recalibrated, and numbers two and three presently operated at 60% power. All of the platoon's tanks had a host of minor maintenance issues that eroded their combat effectiveness.

Faora let Rutger and Aubrey leave the tank one at time to relieve themselves and perform field hygiene, instructing them to stay well back from the clearing. As Rutger pissed behind a tree he noticed several male farm workers moving around one of the buildings. They stared at the tanks and talked amongst themselves. Rutger couldn't hear them, but their body language told him they weren't pleased to see the platoon.

A boy approached the men and pointed excitedly toward the woods. An older man quickly pulled his hand down and glanced around nervously. He said something to the boy, who then jogged toward the opposite tree line past several livestock pens, angling toward the bottom of the hill where the Repub force was expected to emerge.

Shit! Rutger zipped his fly and quickly climbed back into the tank. "Staff Sergeant, I think one of the farmers just sent a boy to warn the enemy."

"Where?" Faora demanded.

Rutger panned *Bounty Hunter's* periscope toward the woods and switched to thermal imaging. He and Faora spotted the boy's heat signature running along a game trail just inside the tree line. His body appeared stark white against the darker forest backdrop. By the kid's size, Rutger estimated his age at twelve or thirteen. He bounded downhill through the woods with surprising grace.

"He sure as fuck is," Faora said, taking control of the automatic defense weapon on the turret. The kid slowed a bit as he reached the bottom of the field. Faora tracked him with the targeting reticle as he moved. "Blue 2, Blue 3, be advised we have a runner at ten o'clock trying to give away our position. I'll take care of it." Despite the kilometer distance, the boy appeared large in her sights, his dark hair waving in the wind, the seams of his red hooded jacket visible. Faora's finger floated above the trigger on the joystick.

Rutger realized in horror that she intended to do more than just follow him. "You aren't going to shoot him, are you?"

Faora kept her eyes on her screen. "Would you rather have the Repub forces know where we are?"

"He's just a kid."

"I'm aware of that, Corporal. Do you think I get off on this shit?" She glared at him for a second before returning to her screen. "This is war. Things get messy. It's just the fucked-up nature of the business we're in."

Rutger knew she was right, but he almost wished he'd kept his mouth shut. His actions were about to get a child killed. *I might as well be pulling the trigger.*

Rutger fought the urge to close his eyes as Faora fingered the trigger. A single beam of crimson intersected the boy's body, bursting his torso. Its immense kinetic and thermal energy nearly blew the kid into two pieces. He spun around in a cloud of red mist, hands thrown toward the sky, a look of pain-stricken surprise on his face. He collapsed into a convulsing heap in the snow. Only his spine, shining pink and white in the sunlight, connected his torso to his lower half.

"Target neutralized," Faora announced.

Rutger sat stunned after witnessing the execution. He was hundreds of meters away, yet swore he could smell the ozone and burnt flesh. He realized it was likely the memory of what he smelled in the rear of the Repub vehicle's fighting compartment a week before. His anger turned toward the farmers who had sent the boy on a fool's errand. *They should have left things alone and stayed out of the way.* He panned over to the farmers to see their reaction, but the men had disappeared inside. He thought he heard a woman wailing through the tank's audible sensors.

No one spoke for the next couple of hours as they waited. Thoughts of his family, especially Callie, filled Rutger's mind. *It's a father's duty to protect his child.* The boy's father had either failed in his duties or simply hadn't cared. *Am I any better? I can't protect my family from lightyears away.* Though his family had moved to a better part of Port City before Rutger had joined the Berserkers, violent crime remained a concern. Images of his wife and daughter being mugged or worse flickered through his mind.

"Contact," Faora said, shaking him from his thoughts. He noticed the electronic signatures in the same instant moving southwest through the woods.

"Got it," Rutger said. "Multiple victors approaching on bearing 1-4-6-6." He zoomed in on the tactical display, which identified at least one platoon of enemy vehicles approaching the east end of the field.

"Blue elements, here they come," Faora said over the platoon net. "Hold your fire until I give the order or you're fired upon." She sounded relaxed and in control, a stark contrast to the growing anxiety within Rutger.

Minutes later, Rutger heard the distinct sound of powerful blower fans. A Repub hover jeep emerged from the woods a few moments later, acting as a forward scout. It paused and grounded at the tree line. Two Repub tanks emerged beside it and did the same. A Repub soldier standing in the jeep's passenger seat searched the hilltop with electrobinoculars. Large branches of foliage and sensor-scattering netting draped the vehicles' green and gray speckled hulls.

Sweat formed on Rutger's brow. Zooming in further, he glimpsed the outlines of several more tanks halted in the woods, apparently the vanguard of a sizable element given the electronic footprint they were now picking up. He glanced at Faora, who appeared unfazed by the sight of additional enemies.

The fusion-powered Repub HBT-6 tanks had thick frontal armor and a powerful 188mm plasma cannon that could pierce the frontal armor of the Berserker's Patton tanks at closer ranges. Their sensors and countermeasures weren't as advanced as those on the Pattons, but they could still hold their own against them.

Muddy slush sprayed from beneath the tanks when they engaged blower fans and began advancing up the slope, turrets nervously searching the hill and buildings above. Rutger watched them grow closer. Four more Repub tanks had stopped just inside the wood line, acting as overwatch for their advancing comrades.

"Gunner," Faora said, "target the trail vehicle, whichever one it is."

"Roger," Rutger responded, no stranger to the tactic. Destroying the trailing vehicle would create a logjam behind the leading tanks that would hamper their chances of retreat and keep them in the kill zone longer. He slid the main gun's pipper onto the turret ring on the second trailing tank. *Bounty Hunter's* AI shared the targeting information via micro-burst transmissions to ensure no duplication of effort.

A loud hiss-crack echoed across the valley as a crimson bolt from their left knifed into the lead tank. Its turret rose on a pillar of white flames and slid off the side of the tank's hull. The prow plowed into the ground and abruptly halted the burning machine.

"That son-of-a-bitch," Faora snarled. "Gunner, fire!"

Enemy tanks in the tree line were already firing on *Blood Shed*, which had unleashed the first bolt. The haystack it hid behind quickly transformed into a pyre, forcing the tank to fall back under a hail of bolts that clawed huge divots from the earth.

Rutger's pipper still lay on the trailing tank as it traversed its turret to fire on *Blood Shed*. He squeezed the trigger, and *Bounty Hunter* jolted as the main gun recoiled and sent megajoules of energy downrange. The red bolt punched a glowing, plate-sized hole in the prow just ahead of the turret. Black smoke curled upward like a braided rope from the grounded tank. Orange rockets on three ejection seats fired an instant later, blasting the crewmen fifteen meters into the air and an equal distance away from the burning tank.

The Repub tanks across the slope fired another volley before Rutger could find another target. A blue bolt exploded among the rusted farm machinery nearby. Pieces of scrap metal rang against *Bounty Hunter's* turret. Striking just short, a second bolt flung a fountain of mud over the bow as Aubrey engaged the repulsors. The shockwave from the near miss rattled Rutger's teeth. *Shit, that was close!*

The hover jeep went into a sharp turn, bent on retreating down the slope. It disappeared in an expanding orange sphere of super-heated metal halfway through its turn, blasted by a bolt from *Blood Shed* that reduced it to a glowing pile of slag in a ring of burning grass.

Repub tanks fired wildly from the tree line, dazzling blue bolts tearing apart the slope and nearby buildings. Dozens of brush fires smoldered on the slope, and the farmers who had tried to warn the enemy now ran from burning buildings, unwitting victims of their own cause.

Reflexes overrode fear as Rutger laid his orange pipper on another tank at the base of the slope. The glowing bolt he sent downrange struck the tank's turret beside the gun mantle. Sun-hot energy burned through tungsten-carbide armor and jetted into the fighting compartment, incinerating the crew in a heart-beat. Rutger doubted they'd had time to scream, let alone bail out.

Rutger almost had his pipper on a third Repub tank in the tree line when it suddenly began pulling back into the woods, the other tanks in the area following suit. Rutger wondered why. The enemy still had numerical advantage, and they now knew the Berserker tanks' locations.

The air defense warning chimed in his ear a moment later, answering his unspoken questions. *Incoming artillery.* The automatic defense weapon's doppler radar began tracking the storm of incoming shells as they arced inbound over the horizon. He hadn't realized that Staff Sergeant Faora had set it to air defense mode when the shooting started.

Faora noticed the threat as well. "Driver, get us the hell out of here!"

Bounty Hunter and the rest of Second Platoon's air search radars detected the rounds soon after they broke the horizon. The AI on each tank began to identify and prioritize the rounds for the automatic defense weapons. The self-guiding shells were a combination of cluster munitions and anti-tank seeker warheads traveling at over 3,000 meters per second. Three of the cluster munitions intentionally opened at high altitude to confuse the automatic defense weapons with thousands of bogeys.

Bounty Hunter rocketed forward, crunching through branches as Aubrey banked sideways and pivoted to turn into a different cut through the woods than they'd used before. The new route exposed less of the tank's stern to attack. Gaps in the trees ahead looked too narrow to Rutger as they approached, and he braced for impact. Aubrey threaded the needle with 120-tons of plasteel as they shot through. *We lost some paint going through here.* Halfway through the trees they began descending the hill's opposite slope.

The automatic defense weapon spun to life and started slinging bolts skyward as they exited the woods. Shells exploded far above the tank in a non-stop thunderstorm that rained bits of metal on *Bounty Hunter.*

"Blue elements, pull back—" Faora began to say before she noticed *Blood Shed* and *Dog Breath* already racing down the hill ahead of them. The air behind the retreating tanks flared with explosions as Repub artillery shells disgorged thousands of individual bomblets, too many for their air defense weapons to effectively counter. The houses and farm buildings disappeared in their wake, as a ripple of explosions began to overtake them and tear up the earth around them.

"Driver, gun it!" Faora yelled as they drove through the wall of flying steel, shrapnel rattling against the hull.

Faora tried to radio Captain Hensley as they flew back over the muddy fields they'd crossed only hours before. She eventually broke through all the comm jamming and requested counter-battery fire and a fire mission on the last known Repub position in the woods.

They'd escaped the arty barrage, yet tensions in the tank remained high, Faora plainly pissed at Sergeant Willard for firing on the enemy without orders.

"Blue 1, Bruiser 6, copy, over?" Captain Hensley called on the company net.

"This is Blue 1, go ahead," Faora responded.

"Requests for fire delayed by battalion due to priority targets in other areas. You're in queue, but it will be at least twenty mikes, over."

"Fuck off!" Faora growled, off the net. "Roger, Bruiser 6, cancel missions, Blue 1 out." She shook her head. "Fucking morons." Rutger didn't ask for clarification on whom the morons might be—battalion, Hensley, Sergeant Willard, her own crew. *Probably all of us.*

Half an hour later they moved into a defensive position in a wooded gap that overlooked the hill they'd just withdrawn from. Dark columns of smoke still rose from destroyed farm buildings and tanks burning in the pasture .

"Blue leaders, meet me by *Blood Shed,*" Faora said over the platoon net. Before they'd grounded or even acknowledged her, Faora opened her hatch and jumped to the muddy deck.

"Aubrey, stand watch," Rutger said. He opened the gunner's hatch and peered out at as Sergeant Willard and Corporal Yurek dropped down from their tanks. They approached Faora, both men standing a head taller than the staff sergeant. Rutger turned up his helmet's audio sensitivity and listened in.

"You've gotta be fucking kidding me! What kind of backwater bush-league bullshit was that back there?" Faora asked them.

Sergeant Willard threw up his hands and responded, "My target was about to fire, I had to do—"

"Bullshit! You spoiled that ambush intentionally."

"That was at least a company-sized element, maybe larger! We couldn't hold them and you know it. I'm not gonna die because you gave some foolhardy order that—"

Faora cut Willard off with a solid right to the jaw that dropped the sergeant to his knees. Willard raised a hand to his mouth; his gloved fingers came away bloody.

Yurek said, "Staff Sergeant, what are you—"

Faora silenced the corporal with only a glare. Willard stood and wiped blood from his lip. His eyes burned with hatred toward the platoon leader, and something else…surprise? Respect?

"Listen up you two and listen well," Faora said, punctuating her words with a pointed finger. "If one of you intentionally disobeys another order, I'll either shoot you myself or have you locked in the brig in solitary for a long, long time. Do I make myself clear?"

"Yes, Staff Sergeant," they muttered.

"I can't hear you!"

"Yes, Staff Sergeant!"

"Our job is to kill the enemy. If you hadn't tipped our hand, Willard, we could have easily taken out most of that unit and sent the rest running. We had the high ground, surprise, cover. Now we'll have to face them another day, and we might not have the advantage next time." She paused and glared at them. The men stood silent. "Okay, that is all. Mount up and wait for orders."

"Yes, Staff Sergeant!" The two tankers practically tripped over themselves to get away from her. Rutger quickly dropped back down into the turret as she turned back toward *Bounty Hunter*.

Faora climbed aboard and dropped back into the fighting compartment. Rutger glanced over at her, half a grin hiding behind his visor. He half admired her and half hated her, but she certainly had his respect. *She is one tough bitch.*

"Quit eyeballing me, Rutger, and mind your fucking screens."

"Yes, Staff Sergeant." His smile remained as he turned back to his displays. Maybe she respected him as well, perhaps just a little. *She's never called me by name before.*

CHAPTER 10

"JUST KNOW THAT DADDY LOVES YOU," RUTGER said, smiling while holding back a sob. "I'll try to be home real soon." He pressed the end message button on the holo-cube.

After taking a moment to compose himself, he started recording another message: "Serena, it's me again. I just got a message from my sister. I asked her to check on you and Callie since I haven't heard from you guys in over two months now. She says you're no longer at the apartment."

He tried to control his anger as he continued, "I know you've received my messages. Look, I know we both said some things we shouldn't have, but you knew what I signed on for when I took this contract. I don't like it any more than you do, but don't give up on me...on us. I'm coming home soon and I won't leave again. It'll cost us a lot of money, but I don't care. This just isn't worth it anymore. Everything's gonna be like before, I promise. Write me soon. I love you." He hit the end button and uploaded the messages into the tank's computer. They would be sent automatically when a strong enough signal was available and secondary traffic allowed.

He shivered. Cold, clear weather had returned, and he still hadn't fully warmed up after cutting branches from nearby trees and shoveling snow onto the deck of the tank to help camouflage it. *Bounty Hunter* and the other two tanks sat powered down in the darkness to reduce their electronic signatures, fusion bottles off, their auxiliary power units running the essential systems. To reduce their heat signature, Staff Sergeant Faora had turned the cabin heater to its lowest setting.

Rutger sat in the meat locker chill and watched the screens. The only bright spot on this night was Faora stepping out to check on the other tanks, allowing him enough privacy to take a shit in solitude and record some holo-vids.

The timer on the console finally beeped. "Okay, Aubrey your turn for watch," Rutger said over the intercom. "You awake in there?"

"Yeah, yeah, I'm awake," Aubrey responded groggily. *Probably sleeping like a baby up there.* The driver compartment was smaller and had its own heater, though Aubrey had to be careful not to crank it too high.

"Staff Sergeant stepped out," Rutger said. "She should be back in a bit."

"Roger that. Think we're gonna move again anytime soon?"

"No idea, you'll have to ask her." Aubrey seemed to look up to Rutger for some reason he hadn't figured out. *He didn't really know Duran, and Faora isn't the type to cozy up to.* Rutger found Aubrey's admiration sorely misplaced. *Don't listen to me, kid. I'm getting the fuck outta here soon.*

Aubrey didn't respond. He never initiated conversation with Faora and wasn't about to start now.

Rutger reclined his seat and curled up with his sleeping bag draped over him like a blanket. His toes felt numb inside his boots. He debated removing them to massage his toes but decided against it and closed his eyes. He slept fitfully, thinking of

Serena and Callie. Rutger's sister had heard rumors that Serena was involved with another man. He dreamed of a brawny guy with a giant cock having his way with his Serena. She had her legs wrapped around him as she moaned and egged him on to thrust harder. Rutger hadn't gotten any in so long that the image both tormented and aroused him.

Having grown erect, Rutger came to semi-consciousness. He considered opening his suit and jerking off for some release. He started to reach down when Faora dropped into the fighting compartment, her presence deflating his erection. She said nothing and began clicking keys on her console. The woman never seemed to sleep.

Closing his eyes again, Rutger slept fitfully. Dream images of Serena or Callie dissolved into the ghastly visages of Staff Sergeant Duran and Lieutenant Mosley.

Rutger had slept and awoken several times when he heard Aubrey say, "Staff Sergeant, I have multiple electronic contacts on bearing 2-3-1, four and half klicks and closing." Rutger snapped fully awake.

"I see them," Faora said. "Rutger, you awake?"

Rutger sat up and threw off his sleeping bag, feeling the bite of cold air in the compartment. "Yes, Staff Sergeant." He raised his seat and flipped on his displays.

"Blue elements, contact, see transmitted coordinates," Faora said over the platoon net.

Willard and Yurek acknowledged.

"Stay powered down and off the net. Don't do *anything* unless I do," Faora instructed.

Rutger's stomach flipped and knotted as he watched the threat display and external holos. The number of contacts increased to five as they grew closer. *Bounty Hunter's* AI identified them as Repub tanks.

Audio sensors amplified their blower fans, which grew louder and closer to their left. Second platoon faced northeast on the far end of Bruiser Company's left flank, anchoring their defensive position. Their vehicles sat isolated at the base of a large, wooded knoll, tucked in among trees with the forested slope to their backs. The rest of the company wrapped southwest around a long ridge. They had orders from Captain Hensley to engage any enemy entering their AO.

Rutger counted six signatures now. He stared out at the moonlit field in front of them, the tank's multi-spectrum optics brightening the night into a dull daytime of muted colors.

The first tank emerged from the forest, a dark silhouette traveling at an oblique angle from left to right across the field ahead. Rutger's trembling hands rested beside the firing control joysticks; he didn't dare to grip them until ordered. A second tank suddenly became visible, traveling almost in tandem with the first, only about two meters separating them. Tanks three and four appeared, likewise moving close together. The massive air-cushioned vehicles kicked up plumes of snow as they roared across the field, centimeters off the ground, their turrets sweeping back and forth.

"Rutger, track them," Faora said.

Are you fucking nuts?! The turret movement alone could give them away. Reluctantly, Rutger slowly traversed the turret, its motor's noise seeming to scream their position as he slid the pipper onto the lead tank.

"Get missile lock on them as well," Faora said calmly. "Be ready to fire on my command."

Rutger keyed a button to arm the missile launchers, and pushed the button on the side of the joystick that highlighted each tank with a red targeting box as they slid into view. He clearly saw their Repub markings from 900 meters away.

The last two Repub tanks powered out of the woods. *Three against six, but we have surprise and good flanking shots.* Rutger's finger hovered over the trigger as he tracked the lead tank. Adrenaline coursed through him, and time seemed to slow down. His fingers felt cold and tingly. He sensed Faora would give the order any second. He spied her from the corner of his eye, sitting hunched over and clutching the edge of her seat, as if she were about to pounce on the enemy tanks herself.

Two more tanks suddenly appeared on the tactical display. Their signals quickly split into two additional vehicles. *What the hell?* Rutger double checked the display and realized the tanks were traveling so close together that they appeared as one signal. Looking at his external holos, his eyes confirmed what the sensors showed—ten tanks, not six. *Oh fuck...*

"Staff Sergeant," Rutger whispered, as if he were afraid the enemy would hear. "Staff Sergeant," he said again.

"I see them. Wait for my command."

All of the tanks were now in the field. Rutger continued to track the lead vehicle, the turret basket slowly rotating under him. His pulse pounded in his ears as his mind raced. *Is this crazy bitch going to ambush a force three times our size?* Even if they each knocked out two tanks in the opening salvo—wishful thinking—Rutger doubted they could get the other four before they returned fire. They had a wall of trees around them—nowhere to maneuver but forward into the field. Rutger imagined a 188mm bore swinging to face them, followed by a searing blue bolt that blinded him before knifing into the tank and torching all three of them. *This is madness.*

He then thought of Staff Sergeant Duran, of getting revenge, but the feeling quickly fled. The anger and hate that had fueled his actions days before was now gone. Now he just felt empty and tired—tired of this planet, this war, sitting in this tank. He wanted to go home. He thought of Serena and Callie. *Fuck, I don't want to die here!*

His intestines writhed like a ball of snakes as the tanks continued across the field, rear flanks partially exposed now. He waited for the order to fire, which would set forth the motions to bring his own demise. Waiting for the surviving Repub tanks to turn and wheel and for the dazzling muzzle flashes that would reduce them to atoms.

But the order never came. The tanks moved on and disappeared behind a grove of trees, the roar of their blower fans steadily diminishing, until they were swallowed by the darkness.

Faora's voice over the radio startled him. "Bruiser 6, this is Blue 1, we had several electronic signatures to our front. Unable to get a visual. Do you want us to investigate?" Rutger couldn't believe his ears. She'd lied to the CO, though not completely. *More like she modified the truth.* She'd also transmitted on the command channel so he could hear.

"Negative, Blue 1. Transmit estimated coordinates of contact. I'll forward to intel. We still move out at 0500."

"Copy that, Bruiser 6, Blue 1 out."

Rutger hesitated to speak. He wanted to know why she'd did it, but feared her reaction. Nevertheless, he needed to know for his own sanity. "Why didn't we fire, Staff Sergeant?"

She studied him for a second in the glow of her displays.

"What about our order—"

"Our orders were to engage anything trying to pass into our AO. They were technically transiting out of it. Our job is to fight and get paid, not to die. If we were at full strength, or if they'd turned and headed toward the rest of the company, we would have been forced to engage. As it stood, we were outgunned and in a poor tactical position. All we had was surprise. It might not have been enough."

Rutger let her words sink in before he responded, "Yes, Staff Sergeant."

The reality of the encounter began to overwhelm Rutger as he lay back against the ejection seat. The compartment closed in around him in a wave of claustrophobia. He flipped open his visor and let the cool air hit his face. The adrenaline surge had worn off, leaving him feeling strung out and cold. He realized how scared he was at the brush with certain death. *And for what?* Bile rose in his throat; he fought back the urge to vomit. He took a long pull of water from his condenser canteen and tried to settle himself.

Helmet off, Faora sat in the command chair massaging her temples. Rutger now saw her in a different light. Her dark greasy hair hung over half her face as she took a long drag from a vape pen he had rarely seen her use. She stared at the map projection, looking just as tired as he was. Just someone trying to do a difficult job, just like him. *Was she just as afraid?*

The realization of her humanity should have put him at ease, but it did not. The tank that had once felt like a protective cocoon now seemed like a prison cell. He wanted to get out and run, but he had nowhere to go. *Not yet.* The futility of it all threatened to drive him mad. It didn't matter who won here, not even to the planet's citizens. The Repub forces were fascists, the Feds socialists. Shit, even on his allegedly democratic home planet of New Helena, the rich controlled everything. The political apparatus was nothing but a tool of control, window dressing for the people. *There's no winning in this life. The outcome is always the same. Only the people we love matter.*

He pondered that for a moment, feeling utterly tired again. Though not on watch, he knew he couldn't sleep, so he panned the optics up toward the constellations dotting the clear night sky. He thought about Serena and Callie light years away, and wished he could hold them in his arms.

CHAPTER
11

THE DEEP DRONE OF REPULSORS INCREASED AS THE tanks of Bruiser Company maneuvered up the side of a steep hill at just after 0630 hours. Columns of Federation armored vehicles, many moving in the wrong direction, choked the cracked and blistered hardball road. The morning fog had lifted somewhat to expose a dark forest pressing in around them.

Bounty Hunter and second platoon trailed the tanks of first platoon on the narrow road. IFVs from third and fourth Platoon brought up the rear. The road switched back several times as it climbed the hill, and the tank drivers had to move cautiously around clots of Fed vehicles to keep their machines from sliding off the road into the many ravines. Even with their powerful repulsors, the massive tanks relied on ground effect and needed the presence of ground or water to constrain the gravitational field, especially on a planet with 1.02 gravity like Scandova.

Rutger stared at the columns of men and equipment they passed as they snaked along the road. Covered in mud and snow, the vehicles all showed signs of battle. They had received word the previous evening that two Federation divisions had gained considerable ground forty kilometers to the north. Bruiser Company was moving to relieve a lead element and support a major assault in this sector. Battalion wanted to keep pressure on retreating Repub forces and force a breakout.

To Rutger, the entire war seemed like a disorganized, chaotic mess. He'd once believed that skill and superior equipment would rule the day. He'd always known that death was a possibility, but like all soldiers he'd believed it wouldn't happen to him. Now he knew war was random, death a statistical inevitability that increased the longer he fought. *Just hope it's over soon.*

After another half hour of starts and stops, they reached the Federation lines and halted. Aubrey shifted *Bounty Hunter* to the side of the road. Rutger looked down the column, hoping to see what lay ahead. Captain Hensley stood in the turret of the lead tank and spoke to a Federation soldier who pointed down the road and nodded several times.

Filthy Fed troops sat in fighting positions dug in along the road, their tripod-mounted heavy machine guns and portable missile launchers pointed east. They had various articles of non-issued clothing and blankets wrapped around them for warmth and were carrying an assortment of weapons. Many wore newer uniform items and carried M-17 rifles, but the haggard, unshaven men still looked like an armed mob to Rutger. Trash and discarded ammo cans littered the snow.

Rutger made eye contact with one of the soldiers, the man's eyes tired and vacant as he stared through him toward something beyond. *Man, what a wretch.* Rutger didn't know who to feel sorry for—the poor grunt, freezing and living in the mud; or himself, the man in the armored coffin about to be fed into a meat grinder.

Captain Hensley spoke over the company net. "All right, listen up. We're here to support an attack on the town of Rolette up ahead. Our Fed friends say there's a company of Repub tanks dug into the area, and at least three hundred enemy dismounts. First and second platoon will support the Fed assault until we reach the outskirts of town. Third and fourth platoon will follow in trail. At the edge of town, the troopers in third and fourth will sweep ahead with the Fed dismounts and clear out the town. The tanks will follow in support."

Rutger stared grimly at the blue and green arrows the CO had superimposed on the tactical map, showing the direction of attack. Green arrows symbolizing the Fed elements spearheaded the attack with Bruiser Company the blue arrows in trace. Icons of red resistance melted away as the arrows advanced over the holographic terrain and the computer estimated the Repub's path of withdrawal.

Looks great on tactical display. We'll see what happens when the metal meets the meat.

"Tanks from the 27th Federation Guards will lead the assault," Hensley continued. "Our job is to support them and stiffen their backbone. If they begin to falter, we need to be ready to continue the assault."

Yeah, if they could fight their own damn battles we wouldn't be here.

He looked over to gauge Faora's take on the plan. She was speaking softly on a private net, probably a last-minute discussion with Hensley. Rutger couldn't gauge her reaction when she finished. She ordered Rutger and Aubrey to perform their usual pre-checks as she studied the terrain map in further detail.

They received orders to move ahead, and soon reached the crest of a hill above a broad valley. Snow-covered farm fields stretched to the town of Rolette atop the opposite hill. Signs of the earlier failed attack were evident. Shell craters ringed with soot dotted the field among charred and twisted—mostly Fed—vehicle hulks. Dark pillars of smoke rose from Rolette.

This is probably a nice planet when it isn't ravaged by war. Rutger dreamed that perhaps one day he could move Serena and Callie to a planet like this. If Rutger found a good job back home and

Serena continued to work, they might be able to save enough money to buy a plot of farmland. Rutger was city bred, but the idea of working the land and being outdoors appealed to him.

They sat there as elements of the Federation unit moved into position. As he waited for the signal to advance, Rutger continued to dwell on Serena and Callie. He wondered what they were doing back home. He pictured Serena, with her big brown eyes that always seemed to see right through him. Her short brown hair framed a slender throat, and he recalled coming up behind her and kissing it, feeling its softness, his hands roaming over her breasts. She was delicate yet strong. His heart ached for her, and he realized that he was the weak one, unable to provide for them and forced to whore himself out as a merc. A melancholy queasiness washed over Rutger, further dampening his mood.

Rutger's life back home, his memories of Serena and Callie, no longer seemed real. Had he even appreciated his life back then? In hindsight it seemed that he'd just been floating along, letting life happen around him, never an active participant and never taking control.

But here in the mud and snow on Scandova, life was painfully real. The prospect of imminent death tended to order his thoughts into razor focus, making him feel more alive than ever, even as he realized all he had taken for granted back home. *And now I'll probably die here.*

Faora's voice snapped him back reality. "Okay, people, we're positioning on the right flank. Watch your spacing and keep your visual scans up."

Led by Captain Hensley's tank, *Bad Medicine*, Bruiser's eight other tanks fanned out over the field, the first unit behind the Federation Guard tanks. The Berserker tanks all showed scars of battle. There were numerous spots on the tanks were the exterior nano paint that facilitated their active camouflage had been chipped away and where sections of armor had been gashed or pitted. The tanks appeared as a dirty patchwork of active camo and brown base paint spattered with mud and snow.

The two tank platoons formed up in a skirmisher line. Aubrey guided *Bounty Hunter* to the far-right flank. Lieutenant Kelly and first platoon had the left flank. The IFVs of the two infantry platoons trailed the tanks. Captain Hensley in *Bad Medicine* would lead the assault from the center of the formation beside Lieutenant Inkari, the company XO, in *Draggin Lady*.

Bounty Hunter sat in a hover as the other vehicles jockeyed into position, loose snow blasting from beneath them, about forty meters separating each vehicle. *I hope the snow in the field is more compacted than this.* Rutger worried that blowing snow might impede visibility, especially since the wind was blowing in their direction on the far-right side of the formation. He considered the flip side as well. *It might keep us hidden from the enemy.*

Rutger scanned the horizon and Rolette in the far distance. No movement visible, but he felt a keen sense of foreboding nonetheless. They would be advancing over five kilometers of relatively open terrain. His stomach constricted into a cold knot just thinking about it. Stout armor and exceptional speed could not guarantee that they would reach their objective.

The Federation tanks up ahead began to advance in an armored wedge of over three dozen vehicles. The Feds used the same HBT-6 tanks as the Republic. Their blowers cut trenches in the snow as they accelerated forward in a curtain of blowing whiteness.

"Time to earn your paychecks, people," Captain Hensley radioed. "Move out."

Hensley's order tripped an avalanched of steel as the tanks of first and second platoon steadily accelerated and maintained their spacing. The IFVs of third and fourth platoon trailed 200 meters behind them.

Friendly artillery rounds screamed overhead as the Federation's planned bombardment commenced. Repub batteries responded by firing on the advancing tanks. *Bounty Hunter's* AI tracked the rounds, and the automatic defense weapon, set to air-defense mode, spun to life and pumped computer-precision bursts that detonated the incoming munitions. The heavens rumbled angrily, and the sky was soon painted with orange flashes and the brilliant tracks of plasma bolts as they detonated the incoming munitions. Occasionally, rounds the AI determined to be non-threatening would fly through the plasma curtain and explode out of effective range.

"Red 1, Blue 1," said Captain Hensley, "maintain spacing and stay sharp. Remaining elements, follow in trace."

Snow clouds stirred up by the Fed tanks ahead reduced visibility. Aubrey drove on using sensors as much as sight, keeping the armored skirting only a few centimeters above the snow to maximize micro-terrain and present a low target profile as they skimmed over the snow at 75 kph.

Rutger scanned the horizon on his holo-screens, catching glimpses of gray buildings and snow-covered trees on the opposite slope through the snow squalls. Orange flashes and puffs of black smoke from the Fed's arty prep began to appear on the hill. Ahead, clusters of derelict vehicles and shell craters pointed the way toward the town. No response from Repub infantry or tanks yet, but he knew they awaited among the buildings. Despite the tank's rolling motion over the terrain, the horizon appeared fixed. The main gun and external weapons mounts were gyrostabilized and remained level with whatever point they were fixed on, enabling them to shoot accurately on the move.

Grossly contorted and blackened, dead Federation soldiers lay in the snow amid the derelict vehicles they passed. Snow filled one woman's open mouth, and one of her hands, dark and withered from frostbite, reached toward the tank with gnarled fingers that beckoned Rutger to join her. He quickly looked away. *Stay focused!*

Rutger's center console screen, set to the tactical display, showed dispositions of friendly forces as they progressed toward Rolette. The Guards' vehicles, green square icons, had reached the halfway point. Still no sign of Repub grunts or tanks. *Maybe they pulled back?*

As if to satisfy his curiosity, strobing bursts of plasma fire ripped from over a dozen Repub machineguns in the town and surrounding fields. Blue bolts snapped above the tanks, the enemy gunners trying to find their range.

Yeah, didn't think so. Rutger searched for targets as Aubrey banked the tank side to side in evasive maneuvers.

To their left, *Blood Shed* fired its main gun. A yellow flash appeared atop the hill, followed by a massive secondary explosion. Rutger couldn't identify what they'd hit, unable to see much of anything through the snow the Federation tanks churned up ahead.

"Steady, boys," Captain Hensley broadcast over the net.

Ahead of *Bounty Hunter*, the prow of a Federation tank suddenly lifted into the air on a column of fire before dropping back to the deck and sliding to a halt. The powerful explosion reverberated through the fighting compartment. Rutger instinctively flinched. When he looked again, black smoke billowed from beneath the tank. The driver scrambled from the forward hatch. The top hatches opened a second later, and the commander and gunner hopped clear as *Bounty Hunter* flew past.

"Mines!" Faora shouted over the intercom.

Aubrey and the other drivers immediately hauled back on their controls and decelerated to less than 25 kph, the forward repulsors kicking up a curtain of snow ahead of them. Rutger's restraint harness dug into his shoulders. He quickly recovered and activated the ground-penetrating radar.

"Stay in the tracks of the vehicles ahead of you. Keep pushing forward," Captain Hensley said, his voice calm and steady.

Two dozen red enemy icons suddenly lit Rutger's tactical display like a Christmas tree. The Repub tanks on the outskirts of town had been powered down; *Bounty Hunter's* sensors detected their electronic signatures when they fired up their fusion powerplants.

Flashes of fire erupted when the Repub tanks emerged from hiding on the left side of town, rising up to fire from their dug-in positions before quickly dropping back down. Blue beams tore through the air at the advancing tanks and kicked up plumes of snow as gunners searched for targets. Fed and Berserker tanks turned their turrets in unison and returned fire on the elusive threats.

The Fed tanks began to break formation, some stopping while others continued to advance or took evasive action. Fed gunners sprayed the hilltop with main gun bolts and 15mm cupola-mounted plasma machine guns, raising smoke and snow around the Repub positions. Clouds of steam condensed around the searing tracks of the energy bolts; a thin haze soon blanketed the battlefield. On tactical display, none of the enemy armor icons flashed or disappeared to indicate damage or destruction. *Great pyrotechnics show, but it won't get the job done.*

"Infantry on the rooftops, two o'clock!" Faora said.

Rutger rotated the turret toward the target, able to see individual Repub troopers shouldering bulky multi-tubed missile launchers at eight times magnification. "Identified." He fired the main gun. The top of the holo-screen flashed over, but the image returned to crystal clarity in time for Rutger to see the top half of the building disappear in an expanding orange shockwave that vaporized the enemy infantry.

The offensive had gone to shit the instant the Feds began taking fire. Berserker forces now led the charge. Aubrey banked *Bounty Hunter* around several destroyed or halted Federation tanks. Firing on the move, the Berserker armored vehicles blasted targets on the hilltop and in town. First Platoon and the remaining Fed tanks on the left flank fought on toward the hill, making steady progress and taking out targets on the outskirts of Rolette. The positions in town weren't so easy to target, however.

Repub troops continued to pound the advance with a plethora or antitank weapons from a score of rooftop positions. Their tanks used the buildings as cover, the streets and retaining walls acting as cutouts to fire from. Rutger recognized a dire situation. They needed to kill as many enemies as possible to soften up the town, otherwise the Fed and Berserker grunts would have a hell of a time clearing the place out.

Repub fire increased in intensity. Plasma machine gun bolts and guided missiles flew wildly at the advancing vehicles, most missing. The moving tanks were difficult to hit. Pods on *Bounty Hunter's* automatic protection system *whoomped* as they destroyed the incoming missiles.

Bounty Hunter's AI identified and locked on to several infantry positions in the buildings to their right. Rutger thought-fired a salvo of the tank's self-guiding Javelin missiles. A swarm of self-guiding missiles shrieked out from the tank's rear turret launchers and rocketed towards their targets. He watched with grim satisfaction as the buildings erupted in a wave of explosions that silenced many of the weapons.

A Repub tank's main gun ripped the Federation tank directly ahead of them with a 188mm plasma bolt. The blue bolt stabbed through the turret with a white flash that produced a shower of sparks and flames. The smoking Fed tank grounded in the snow. No one bailed out or ejected.

"Tank one o'clock, 1900 meters," Staff Sergeant Faora said.

Rutger was already traversing the main gun toward it. His gunnery screen marked the target between two buildings with an inverted red triangle. Rutger couldn't get a good visual on it; the sensor-scattering netting draped over it provided excellent camouflage from optical sensors. He placed the orange circle of the targeting reticle on what he thought was the turret and fingered the trigger. The tank exploded in an orange hemispherical blast. Flaming pieces of sensor-scattering netting fluttered through the air like burning confetti.

A blue main gun bolt sliced diagonally across the top of *Bounty Hunter's* turret, carving a glowing, meter-long gash in the armor. It traveled on and destroyed the left-rear missile pod. *Bounty Hunter* rocked and shook from secondary explosions that threw Rutger against his restraints. The lights dimmed inside the fighting compartment for a split second. Rutger's screens flickered for an instant before returning to sharp clarity. He searched frantically for the tank that had hit them.

The AI identified the threat and traversed the turret eleven degrees starboard. The red threat box hovered over a set of buildings on the right outskirts of town about two klicks away. *Bounty Hunter's* electromagnetic sensors couldn't provide exact targeting information due to the range and interfering buildings. A second shaft of blue light shot from the structures and missed them by only a few meters.

"Shit, no target!" Rutger said. *There!* At twelve times magnification he barely saw the tank glide into an alley between two buildings, its main gun pointed straight at them. It had the usual Repub camo paint scheme, except for an odd-looking splotch on its prow, white and orange, that Rutger couldn't quite make out at long range. "Wait, I see it. Identified." He set the glowing pipper on the tank's prow.

"Fire already!" Faora said.

Rutger squeezed the trigger an instant too late, just as the tank slid hard left and disappeared behind a long rectangular building. The crimson bolt struck another building further on, which collapsed into a giant cloud of dust and debris.

Shit! "Miss," he reported.

"Stay on him," Faora ordered.

He didn't know which side of the building the tank would pop out from, so he traversed the turret left and fired the main gun twice in quick succession, hoping to get a lucky shot or flush his quarry out. The building disintegrated from the thunderous flashes of crimson. A wave of heat from the barrel filled the fighting compartment.

The tank did not appear from behind the rubble. *Which side? Or is he falling back?* He doubted it was the latter. The tank's commander seemed to be a crafty tactician. He believed the tank would keep moving left, so he slew the turret on the adjacent alley and waited.

Then it appeared, backing out and emerging to the right of the rubble. *Fuck!* He'd gambled and lost, now realizing he should have kept the gun centered so he could have responded equally fast in either direction.

"Right side! Right side!" Staff Sergeant Faora said. She seized the override controls and attempted to swing the turret particle cannons over in time.

Too late—the blue bolt struck *Bounty Hunter* forward on the right side, just below the turret ring. The starboard front repulsors winked off. "Hit!" Aubrey shouted as he lost control. The starboard side of the prow plowed into the snow and spun them violently around, the tank's enormous inertia almost rolling them over.

Though his restraint harness held, Rutger's helmet slammed against the turret wall. *Bounty Hunter's* systems crashed momentarily at the massive overload of energy, then began to rapidly reboot. The holo screens and displays flickered back to life. Temperature in the fighting compartment, already high, began to spike as a thin haze of gray smoke smelling of ozone and fried circuits started filling the cabin.

"Report!" Faora shouted in a hoarse voice.

"Front repulsors offline," Aubrey said after a brief pause. "Shit, we can't move!"

Rutger tried to traverse the turret onto the enemy tank, but the bolt or the crash had damaged the turret ring, which failed to respond. The turret motors whined in protest to his joystick movements.

"Turret is down," Rutger choked out.

Another main gun bolt cracked by, just missing *Bounty Hunter*. The dazzling brightness blacked out the view screens for a moment.

"We gotta get out of here!" Faora shouted. "Punching out!" She reached for the black and yellow stripped handle between her legs.

"No! Wait—"

An orange flash and a blast of intense heat filled the cabin, then there was darkness.

Rutger's head spun, throbbed, ached. His blurry vision refocused to clarity. He lay sideways in a shallow snow drift, still strapped into his ejection seat. The sounds of explosions and cracking plasma bolts came from every direction. Everything hurt, but pain meant he still lived, and he wasn't missing any appendages when he checked. His muscles trembled as he manipulated the harness release. He unbuckled and collapsed on his side. Pain radiated through his body.

With great effort, he raised his head and tried to gain his bearings. Ahead of him, *Bounty Hunter* was a fountain of flames. Struck by a second blue bolt just as Rutger and the rest of the crew's ejection seats lifted them clear of the massive secondary explosion. Even forty meters distant he could feel the intense heat radiating from the burning hull.

He'd been briefed about ejections after joining the tankers. *It's worse than they told me.* No parachutes—the chairs just shot from the tank about 30 meters into the air before plummeting back to earth around 30 meters from the tank. Ejection was a last resort for escape, usually used only in the most dire circumstances. Bailing out of the hatches was the sane and standard option if time permitted.

Rutger tried to stand, only to collapse, his head still spinning. He tried again, his equilibrium returning somewhat, and staggered to his feet. Looking across the white battlefield, he watched the Berserker tanks whisk past smoldering wreckage of destroyed vehicles to disappear in the distance.

He looked around, searching for Aubrey and Faora. Still a bit loopy, he watched in rapt fascination as a Federation tank emerged from the haze behind him. It bore down on him like a charging green and white elephant from only 40 meters away. His pain disappeared as another jolt of adrenaline shot through his veins. He struggled to get out of the way, staggering, his boots slipping in the snow. *Don't you fucking see me?* He looked at the prow only meters away and waited for the end.

Someone yanked the back strap on his body armor and pulled him out of the way. They collapsed in the snow as the hover tank roared by less than half a meter away. The tank's blower fans buffeted them with snow.

"You okay?" Faora shouted from beside him, even louder than usual. The blast and ejection appeared to have deafened her.

"Yeah," Rutger croaked as she helped him back to his feet.

They found Aubrey a few moments later, shaken but unhurt. Rutger had feared that he'd been killed in the blast and felt joy at seeing him. The three of them crouched as they ran back toward friendly lines.

A Berserker IFV approached. The driver saw them and swung over to pick them up. Kicking up snow, it remained at a hover as infantry troopers in power armor hauled them up the rear ramp.

The vehicle surged forward before the ramp had even closed. Fortunately, it carried an undermanned squad and the three of them were able to find a seat in the cramped compartment. Rutger squeezed in across from a tall trooper with coal black skin and a handsome face, his visor raised. BUKAR was stenciled on his chest plate above a small, black Christian cross. He flashed a brilliant white smile at Rutger, who didn't understand what the man was so damned happy about.

"God shines his blessings upon you today, my friend," Bukar said.

Rutger studied him for a moment. The man's pleasant smile and demeanor was almost as jarring as the ejection from the tank.

"Yeah, I guess so," he muttered. He sure as shit didn't feel lucky, even though he'd survived.

Fighting continued to rage outside. Nearby blasts occasionally jolted the vehicle. The rear of the fighting vehicle felt hot and claustrophobic. Rutger's headache worsened. He began to feel nauseous and wondered if he had a concussion.

Rutger replayed the last moments of his duel with the enemy tank and cursed himself for making the wrong choice. He saw the massive bore right before it fired, and the subsequent events then played in slow motion. He looked at Faora and Aubrey crammed in on the opposite side. Aubrey had his eyes closed. Faora stared sullenly forward. An immense feeling of guilt washed over him. His mistake had almost cost them their lives, as well as his own.

Overwhelmed, Rutger closed his eyes and pushed the brush with death from his mind. His thoughts returned to Serena and Callie. The IFV traveled on, ever closer to its objective, while Rutger felt his wife and daughter slipping further away.

CHAPTER 12

BUKAR STOOD BAREFOOTED IN WARM, WET SAND
on a Beninian beach. The sun baked his back as he stood with
his long, powered surfboard tucked under his arm, waiting for
the next set of towering waves to come in. Then he saw it—a
rising swell approaching the beach. He dashed for the water,
mounted his board, engaged the jet propeller drive, and started
riding toward it. The wave kept climbing—it was going to be
a big one.

The wave lifted him and almost threw him backward before
he did a bottom turn and mounted the surging wall of water.
Steering the board with his feet, he positioned it at a 45-degree
angle, riding the wave as it crested toward shore.

Then he was in the barrel, a tunnel of water curling around
him. He was about to shoot through the opening when the wave
suddenly crashed down on him, its titanic force pushing him to
the bottom and raking him over the coral. He kicked hard toward
the surface, never quite reaching it.

He gagged, no longer at the bottom of the ocean but strapped
to a chair and tilted back as thugs poured a giant can of water
into his mouth. He fought the restraints, gagging and drowning.

An armored boot jarred him from his dream. He woke up swinging.

"Easy, Preacher," a familiar voice said. Bukar awoke in a dark, bombed-out cellar. Staff Sergeant Mardin's stubble-covered face hovered over him.

"It's me. Didn't mean to startle you," Mardin said in a low voice. "You awake?"

"I am now." Bukar wiped the sleep from his eyes and focused on the platoon sergeant. He shivered in the cold as he checked his watch: 2205. "Sorry about that. What's up? Are we moving out already?"

"Nah, we still got business here. The old man wants a recon patrol. You up for it?"

He cleared the last vestiges of sleep from his mind. "Yeah, sounds good. Beats freezing my ass off here."

Mardin took out a holo-disk and illuminated a local terrain image. As his eyes adjusted to the light, Bukar could see a couple of small hills that overlooked fields dotted with groves of trees. Several irrigation canals crossed the area, and the main east-west highway ran along the right edge. Blue, green, and red dots represented positions of friendly and known hostile forces. Repub forces had withdrawn from Rolette after the earlier assault, and the Berserkers were holding in place with their Fed allies to prevent a potential counterattack.

Mardin highlighted an area close to the highway. "Faint signals have been detected in this area, and command thinks the Repubs might be bringing up reinforcements for a counterattack. Captain Hensley wants us to get over there and get eyes on. Watch for seismic sensors. Last patrol the Feds sent out didn't come back."

"Who am I taking?"

"Niles and Reyes volunteered. You can pick the other two."

"Sims and Dominguez available?"

"Yeah, they are. I'll have them report to you. You need to leave in twenty. The old man wants you back before 0400 hours."

"Okay."

"Watch yourself out there, Preacher. Especially coming back. The Feds are awfully trigger-happy. Good luck."

Bukar stood in the crisp night air and waited for the men. A sliver of one of Scandova's moons hung just above the horizon. Blue bolts flashed upward from the Repub lines at incoming artillery, followed by distance reports of intercepted rounds. Bukar prayed: *Almighty God, please protect us. Guide my hands and actions tonight, and deliver us from the eternal darkness of man's sins.*

The four troopers arrived. Bukar led them inside the blacked-out house. The men looked haggard but alert. Mud and frost covered their armor. Other troopers in the room lay asleep on the floor or in contorted positions on whatever furniture they could find, their weapons close at hand. Cases of ammo and grenades were piled in one corner.

"Geez, I thought our house was cold," said Niles, his visor up, breath frosting in the chill. Beside him, Reyes slurped a spoonful of steaming soup.

"What's the word, Preacher?" Sims asked. He didn't appear happy to be there.

"Recon patrol," Bukar said. "Old man wants us to snoop and poop behind the Repub lines. They've picked up some electronic intel, but they want an eyes-on report."

"Damn, maybe I should unvolunteer," Niles said.

"Shit, at least you did volunteer," Sims said. "This ain't my idea of a good night's rest."

"You'll be able to sleep soon enough," Dominguez said. "Permanently."

Bukar briefed them on the patrol route, keeping it short and succinct. He'd worked with all of these men before, professionals all around, but even pros needed guidance sometimes. "Ensure you turn off all active sensors and comms. Passive only, not even proximity comms. We communicate by hand signals as soon as we depart." He eyed the men for a moment. "And don't fire unless fired upon. The Repubs know what we're up to. The last Fed patrol didn't come back." He let that sink in. "Take only essential gear. Weapons and grenades."

Bukar led them to the forward outpost located in the open-air ruins of a bombed-out house, where a pair of Berserker troopers stood watch behind a heavy plasma machine gun.

"Halt," an electronically amplified voice called in challenge.

"Bukar. Recon patrol. Thunder."

"Flash," the voice responded. "Come on in."

Bukar's HUD identified the troopers' names as Kendrick and Thomas. Kendrick pointed to the field in front of them. "We got remote mines and trip flares along this front. Go right about fifty meters down this street and you'll find a path through the lines by the last house."

Bukar carefully scanned outside the walls before stepping into the darkness. Four shadows followed behind him. The wind howled through blasted windows and stubborn building walls that refused to topple. They made their way to the shattered remains of the house the trooper had identified.

Bukar advanced into the snow-covered field and headed for the nearest patch of woods. They ran at a crouch, the soft snow absorbing the sound of their footfalls. The snow kicked up around them in eddies as they finally made it to the wood line, which swallowed them up like a great dark beast.

Bukar followed a path preset in his HUD, periodically stopping to listen and scan the area ahead for decent cover, avoiding obvious areas where the enemy might have set up an observation post.

They walked for two klicks, darting between patches of woods or crouching while following shallow ditches. Bukar had turned up the thermostat on his power armor, but it did little to stave off the bitter cold since sweating while on the move was inevitable. He likened the thermostat control to those in cheap hotels: there for psychological effect, to give one the illusion of having some control over the surroundings.

They followed a curving path along a lengthy tree line and reached the edge of a broad, barren field. Looking at the horizon, Bukar thought he felt eyes upon him, yet he noticed no enemy movement. The open field stretched for 200 meters without a stick of cover, so they high-crawled on hands and knees, weapons resting in the crooks of their arms. Bukar kept a close eye on HUD for any signs of the enemy, hoping passive sensors would pick up something.

His helmet's audio sensors registered the soft buzz of fan motors. Bukar dropped to the deck and froze, the other men following suit. He raised his eyes slowly and saw the drone about forty meters away, flying low and slow to avoid detection. He felt naked and exposed in the field, and wished his body could melt into the ground.

The drone continued along its flight path, the fans growing softer in the distance. Quiet reigned again. The clouds and sliver of the moon stood silent vigil above. *A close call.* Bukar began to wonder if he'd pressed his luck volunteering for this mission. His time would come, he knew. *But only when the Lord wills it.*

After fifteen more minutes of slow crawling, they cautiously approached a shallow irrigation canal crusted with a thin layer of ice. He motioned for the men to wait and crawled the last few feet to the edge. He took out his vibro-blade, cut a large, jagged hole in the ice and then carefully slid the sheet out of the way.

He motioned toward the water before slipping quietly into the hole, where he activated his helmet's environmental seal and turned on the oxygen. Each helmet had a small crystal that emitted oxygen through laser photosynthesis, providing about a one-hour air supply. Missions on worlds with unbreathable atmospheres or vacuums required more extensive backpack kits.

Slipping below the ice, Bukar felt the water's frigid embrace as though his skin were wet, though the armor was watertight. The canal was about a meter deep. He barely fit beneath the ice and had to crawl along the muddy bottom toward the waypoint on his HUD over two meters away. His patrol followed. It seemed to take forever in the dark, cramped confines. He began to lose track of time and distance in the murky water, his HUD the only navigational aid. A couple of times he thought he heard noises and paused, hoping his bubbles wouldn't give him away if someone was watching the canal.

Reaching his waypoint, he halted and carefully cut a hole through the ice. He came up slowly, the water dripping from his armor. He crawled out and hoisted himself upward into snow-dusted grass. His men likewise emerged slowly until all were out.

A hand grasped his shoulder as he went to stand—Reyes, who nodded toward the canal's other side. Not twenty meters away, the vague shape of an armored man squatted in the snow, his back turned to them as he took a shit.

Bukar waited, pulse hammering in his ears. The man finally finished up and headed toward his fighting position in the distance. Bukar waited until he disappeared inside a foxhole, then began to slip away, crawling along the tall grass to avoid disturbing it.

They reached another tree line after crawling 100 meters. Bukar's stomach and back muscles had begun to ache from exertion. Using night vision, he spotted two soldiers in a fighting hole about fifty meters down the tree line. Bukar slowly slithered forward, his armor pressed against the snow, and led the patrol past the position into the tree line. Safely concealed in the woods, they picked their way carefully through branches and bushes.

Sounds of voices and machinery drifted into Bukar's ears. He led them a short distance out of the woods to the top of a low knoll. Pressed into the snow, he peered over the edge.

About a company of Repub infantry were digging fighting positions, well spread across the field and along a distant tree line. Turbine-powered heavy equipment whined and churned, scooping out positions for several air-cushioned tanks and APCs. Some of the armor had already moved into the positions under sensor-scattering nets. Several trucks sat parked by the trees, Repub soldiers unloading them in a hurry and stacking the crates next to a bunker.

Bukar recorded the scene with his helmet camera. Niles and Reyes, spread out beside him, did the same, noting grid coordinates of positions, while Sim and Dominquez watched their six. He noted the time: 0214.

Time to get the hell out of here.

Bukar led the team back the way they'd come, making excellent time along the familiar route. Returning along the same path presented a risk, but they had a limited time hack and not much choice. False dawn lit the sky by the time they paused in a tree line atop a low ridge overlooking the final field before their lines.

Bukar spotted figures in the far distance stealing toward them. He signaled the men to get down. "Enemy patrol," he said, figuring proximity comms were now safe to use. His mind spun with a plan. "We are going to bag them."

"I thought this was a recon patrol?" Niles said.

"It is. We got our intel, but a prisoner would be even better."

"You're nuts. We're just as likely to get shot by our people."

"Just shut up and wait for me to open fire."

Six armored figures in white camouflage continued toward them. Bukar could make out their weapons and their darting heads as they approached the recon team's position. His pulse quickened. His fingertips tingled from adrenaline. The Repub soldiers warily approached the wooded hill. Bukar began to take up slack on the trigger as their point man halted the patrol at the tree line and inched forward, scanning ahead. He paused, his gaze passing over Bukar and the team lying prone on the hill under protection of active camouflage.

Satisfied, the point man motioned the patrol forward. Bukar let them approach to twenty meters before opening fire with a twenty-round burst, his patrol joining in. Repub soldiers fell to the deck, injured or dead, but a couple found cover behind tree trunks.

"Flank them!" Bukar shouted, "I'll keep you covered." Over holographic rifle sights, Bukar watched his patrol swoop down.

"Still two moving down here," Reyes said, though the enemy hadn't returned fire. Two soldiers emerged from the trees with their hands up.

Bukar stood and headed toward them. The severely wounded gasped for breath, their entrails and goblets of blood splattered across the snow. Dominguez had two soldiers, an older man and a young woman, at gunpoint as Sims searched them for weapons. A trail of blood dripped from a long gash on the man's arm. His eyes burned with hate.

Reyes jerked the woman, apparently unhurt, to her feet. She trembled at the sight of them.

"What about the wounded?" Sims asked as Dominguez and Reyes bound the prisoners' wrists behind them with flex cuffs. Bukar perused the torn bodies before him, several still conscious and moaning in agony as their adrenaline wore off. Seared holes dotted their torsos. Almost all were missing appendages.

"We have to leave them. They are in God's hands now," Bukar said.

"You mercenary pigs!" the female prisoner said scornfully, spitting toward him.

"Let's go. We have to move," Bukar said.

They headed down toward the field, Bukar and Reyes in the lead. Niles and Sims followed, prodding the prisoners with their rifle barrels, with Dominguez in the rear. A couple of minutes later, shouts and thrashing came from the trees behind them.

"Shit, we got company!" Dominguez said.

"They must have had some other friends out here," Bukar said as they picked up their pace across the field. "Get the prisoners moving!" He knew they would try to drag their feet.

Several plasma rifles opened fire, blue bolts sizzling overhead. Bukar and his men dropped and began spraying muzzle flashes in the woods with crimson bolts. Bolts from the Repub patrol pulsed the night wildly, the enemy either unaware or unconcerned for their companions.

"Incoming!" Bukar shouted as mortar rounds exploded in the distance. Another volley quickly followed, the explosions waltzing toward them as the enemy adjusted fire. The ground shuddering from each incoming blast. Since the shells posed no threat to their positions, Berserker and Federal air-defense weapons allowed the rounds to fall unimpeded.

The female prisoner began screaming hysterically beneath Niles, who kept her pinned to the ground while returning fire. The male prisoner somehow escaped from Sims and bolted toward the tree line. Bukar and Sims blasted him simultaneously, their bolts chewing across his back and nearly cutting him in two. Shrapnel whizzed over and around them as mortar explosions crept closer.

"C'mon, move it!" Bukar shouted over the cacophony of battle. Sims and Niles scooped up the female and half-dragged, half-carried her across the field while Dominguez used his light machine gun to lay down a stream of covering fire.

Bukar and Reyes dropped and provided covering fire as Dominquez displaced. They bounded across the field in that fashion toward the darkened buildings only 400 meters away. The explosions grew distant behind them and finally ceased.

"Recon patrol coming in, thunder!" Bukar transmitted over the net between ragged breaths.

"Flash, come on in," a trooper responded.

A flare popped overhead and cast them in an eerie glow as they ran hunched over toward their lines.

"Get down!" Bukar bellowed as a plasma machine gun ripped from a position on the Fed side of the lines, sending bolts zipping past. The patrol hugged the frozen earth and crawled toward a nearby ditch as blue death flashed overhead.

"Fucking Fed idiots!" Reyes yelled. "Nice welcome. I'm tempted to fire back!"

"Good thing those yokels can't aim for shit," Sims said.

"Bruiser 7," Bukar called over the net. "Tell those Fed dipshits to cease fire!"

The fire lifted a moment later. Bukar's team sprinted the remaining distance to the safe path through their lines.

"Is that you, Preacher?" called a tense voice over the net as they reached the shelled-out house marking the path through the mines and trip flares.

"Yes, recon coming back. Hold your fire."

Staff Sergeant Mardin awaited them. "What the hell happened out there?"

"We took out a Repub patrol on the way back," Bukar said. "Took a prisoner as well."

"No shit?" Mardin said, eyeing the female prisoner in the moonlight. "What are our friends up to?"

"They are digging in. Looks like reinforcements are moving up as well."

"Shit, that means we attack."

Bukar nodded. "Yeah, probably."

"The intel boys will want to question her right away. Report to the captain, then get some rest. You look like hammered shit."

Bukar led the woman down the empty street, holding her bound hands with his free arm, as he steered her around piles of rubble to the company outpost, a shelled-out two-story office building a couple of blocks from the line. Captain Hensley's tank sat grounded outside. Bukar pushed through a black-out tarp covering the door.

"Where's the Captain?" Bukar asked the trooper on watch, a lance corporal.

Eying the prisoner, he pointed toward a pair of muddy composite boots hanging over the edge of a cot in the corner.

"Sit over here," Bukar said to the prisoner, motioning to a stack of ration boxes. "Are you thirsty?"

She nodded without making eye contact. Bukar gave her a plastic water bottle from a nearby case. She fumbled with the cap and drank greedily. "Keep an eye on her," Bukar said to the trooper, who nodded and laid his pistol on the desk. The woman eyed it warily.

"Corporal Bukar reporting in, sir."

Captain Hensley sat up with a snort and massaged his eyes, looking like a zombie from fatigue. "So what did you see?"

Bukar turned on his holo-disk. "Repub forces are digging defensive positions about half a klick north of this road," he said, highlighting the area. "They are bringing in armor, at least four tanks and several APCs, as well as supplies."

"Yeah, I didn't figure they had the numbers to counterattack. They're just buying time while they strengthen their defenses around New Oslo," Hensley muttered, more to himself than Bukar. "How was it out there?"

"Not bad, nothing harrier than usual. We brought you a present." He motioned toward the prisoner.

Hensley appraised her for a second before saying, "Outstanding, Preacher. You'd better get some rest. We'll likely be on the move again soon."

"Yes, sir." Bukar turned to leave, then stopped and looked back. "Sir, what will happen to her?"

"Battalion will likely send their intel boys up here. They probably won't bother with questions, better to just do a brain dive and then hand her to the Feds for processing. Why?"

"No reason, sir. I was just wondering. Have a good night... what's left of it."

He couldn't help but wonder what would be left of her by the time the Feds finished their "processing."

BUKAR FINISHED SPLASHING COLD WATER ACROSS his face, trying to wash away some of the sweat and grime from the previous night. Midmorning sunlight shone through a broken window. Shells were falling again in the area, the distant blasts rumbling the house. He'd gotten five hours of uninterrupted sleep—a reward from Staff Sergeant Mardin, he assumed—a rare luxury in a combat zone, not that he'd slept well.

Grabbing his weapon, he left the house and checked the squad's supplies of rations and ammo, finding both satisfactory. Dominguez needed a new earpiece for his helmet's radio, and Sims's visor was on the fritz. Needing a break from the line, Bukar had offered to walk to the rear for replacement parts.

He headed toward the command post, happy to stretch his legs. He wanted to check in with the head shed before reaching the rear area 1.5 klicks away.

The female prisoner wasn't in the CP. "Where is the prisoner that was here?" Bukar asked Terrano, the trooper on watch.

"The intel guys showed up a couple hours after you dropped her off. They did their thing, and when she came to they handed her over to Fed soldiers."

"How long ago?"

"About a half hour or so."

Bukar nodded. "I'm going to the rear for some helmet parts. Need anything?"

"Yeah, a pass out of here."

"Can't help you with that. When Staff Sergeant Mardin gets back, let him know I went to the rear."

Headed for the rear, Bukar spotted the golden domes of a church in the distance. *If I have time, I should stop and pray.*

He soon entered the Federal area of the encampment, where soldiers busied themselves with vehicle maintenance and weapons cleaning while others huddled beneath tarps stretched from tanks or APCs, warming food or vaping tobacco.

Bukar walked toward the supply area. Countless civilian air-cars and wheeled vehicles had been destroyed in the fighting. Drivers and passengers sat frozen in death, slumped over controls or spilling out from open doors. Dead civilians lay scattered about, some crushed into unrecognizable smears by grav tanks or air-cushioned vehicles. A heavy-set older man frozen waxy and gray sprawled on a park bench with one hand clutching his abdomen, his intestines piled on the sidewalk beneath him. Smoke still rose from some of the gutted buildings, and glass crunched beneath his boots. Outbound artillery fire occasionally thundered overhead.

Rounding a corner, Bukar heard a woman's anguished cries on the wind. He flipped down his visor, shouldered his rifle and cautiously moved down the street, stopping at a large house that seemed to be the source of the noise.

The door stood ajar. He stepped inside and listened. Moans, grunts, and coarse cheers came through a heavy wooden door atop a short stairway. He mounted the stairs, avoiding the broken glass, and hesitated.

It ain't none of your business.

Yes, it is. We are all God's children. His conscience remained skeptical, however. *You keep sticking your nose where it doesn't belong. You should know better by now.*

Two years before, getting involved had gotten him busted from sergeant back to corporal when he'd beaten his platoon sergeant bloody for torturing a civilian. Bukar grudgingly accepted torturing enemy soldiers for intel, but the staff sergeant's victim had been a young girl who'd obviously known nothing of the enemy's whereabouts. Though the command had terminated the staff sergeant's contract for misconduct, rules were rules. Despite his justifiable reason, Bukar was demoted for striking a superior.

He knew himself too well. He couldn't walk away from this incident, either. *Okay, let's do this.*

He kicked in the door and surprised a group of Fed soldiers busy gang raping the female prisoner he'd captured. They'd stripped off her uniform pants and torn open her field jacket, exposing her breasts. A burly sergeant took her from behind while another waved his skinny cock in her face. Primal terror filled her eyes. Blood dripped from her busted lower lip.

The Feds turned in surprise, one reaching for his plasma rifle. Bukar put a blinding bolt through the floor next to the man's feet. The sergeant behind her withdrew, and the rest slowly backed away from the woman while buttoning their trousers.

White-hot rage filled Bukar. "You animals! Get away from her! Is this how you treat your fellow man?" Silent, the men stared at him blankly. "Get her clothes. Now!"

They stood frozen for a second, eyeing his steaming rifle barrel, before one of them turned and produced a pair of motley green fatigue pants. He offered them to the woman like a gift. She glared at him as she snatched the pants and began pulling them on.

"And her boots."

The soldiers sized up Bukar as she dressed. The burly sergeant sneered and said, "You have no authority here. What gives you the right? She's the enemy…we were just having a little fun."

Bukar's face hardened. "God is my authority."

The sergeant chuckled. "Whatever you say. Who knew fucking mercs had a conscience?" He grinned, exposing a mouthful of gleaming metal dentures. "Look, you made your point. We'll bring her back to HQ no worse for wear."

"She is coming with me."

"Sure about that? Your command signed her over to us. You take her and I'll report you."

Bukar watched as the soldiers having regained their composure edged closer to their weapons. He was playing a dangerous game now. If he killed these men, he wouldn't be justified and would be locked away for a long time, or perhaps worse, and be made an example of. He didn't want it to come to that, but he wasn't leaving without the woman. "Then report me. Corporal Bukar: B-U-K-A-R."

The sergeant snorted. "You wouldn't act so tough if you weren't holding a rifle on us."

Bukar opened his visor, lowered his weapon and stepped toward the man. "God is my strength. The rifle is just a tool," he said, nose to nose with the sergeant.

The sergeant stared into Bukar's fiery eyes, yet quickly looked away, not liking what he saw. "Fine, take her."

"That is what I thought."

Bukar turned to the woman. She was holding her torn pants up by the fly. He motioned her toward the door and then backed out, not taking his eyes off the soldiers. Outside, she backed nervously away as though expecting him to attack her next. She shivered in the cold as her fearful eyes studied her towering ebony savior.

"Come with me," Bukar said, steering her quickly around the corner. His heart hammered as he considered the righteousness and stupidity of his actions. As they continued down the street past troops and destroyed vehicles, Bukar studied her in the daylight. Slender and a head shorter than himself, her baggy uniform concealed a lithe frame. *An attractive woman.* In a different time or place he might have desired her, but not now. *Not anymore.* He'd been celibate for quite some time. He still desired women and occasionally masturbated, reliving intimate escapades of his youth, but the idea of a relationship no longer appealed to him. He'd seen too much and lost too many people who'd been close to him. His relationship with God was enough.

Moving down the road, Bukar's eyes roamed over the vehicles and troops they encountered. None of the troops they passed questioned him, but he could take no further chances protecting the prisoner. He spotted an older woman's corpse lying in the street and quickly removed her blue insulated jacket, handing it to the woman. She shrugged it on, ignoring the bloodstains. Bukar retrieved a belt from a male corpse nearby to hold up her ripped uniform trousers. She stared at him questioningly after cinching her pants.

"Go," Bukar said. "There is a refugee camp on the far side of town. Hide there until the troops clear out of here."

She didn't move.

"Go! Those soldiers will be looking for you." He could do nothing else for her.

The woman turned and started walking away, then stopped to look back. "Thank you," she said softly. "I'm Taraia, by the way."

"Bukar. I'm sorry about what happened to you."

"It's war. It's not your fault."

Bukar nodded before adding, "Go with God's blessings."

He watched her go. She was so young. *Just a girl playing soldier.* She turned down an alley, and he suddenly felt alone, though he smiled briefly at having helped someone for a change.

Bukar saw the church spire again in the distance. It made him think of all the human suffering God seemed to ignore. *Why does He allow it?* He continued to ponder his faith and humanity's inherent flaws as he made his way toward the rear.

CHAPTER 14

"RUTGER, GET YOUR ASS UP!" ROARED STAFF Sergeant Faora, who stood in the open door to his room in the hab trailer.

Rutger sat up and rubbed sleep from his eyes, trying not to look pissed at the interruption. "I'm up, Staff Sergeant." His head throbbed from a hangover. A half-empty bottle of snythos stood on the nightstand.

"Well, get your ass dressed. Find Aubrey and meet me over by the airfield. Our tank arrived this morning. We need to get it checked out and resupplied. It's now 1005 hours. Meet you there in thirty."

"Yes, Staff Sergeant."

Rutger shrugged on his jumpsuit and went to Aubrey's room a couple doors down. They'd been lucky getting single rooms in the transitory barracks. Most of the combat troops arriving at FOB Vulture were shipped directly to the front, but they'd been languishing with the rear element for three days while awaiting a replacement tank.

Rutger shielded his eyes from the sunlight as he stepped outside with Aubrey. Forward Operating Base Vulture bustled with activity as they walked through the camp toward the airfield. The roar of dropships and aircraft grew louder as they approached. His stomach growled; he'd slept in and missed breakfast. Three hot meals a day of real food had brought his appetite back. During a physical exam the previous day, he'd learned that he'd lost over fifteen pounds in the last two months.

Staff Sergeant Faora had all but disappeared upon their arrival, leaving Rutger and Aubrey to their own devices with their only orders being to remain on base. While exploring the massive base, Rutger had found the morale area and checked for electronic messages. Still nothing from Serena—only a message from his sister asking how he was holding up.

The first night he went to bed early and slept nearly fourteen hours, enjoying the luxury of an actual bed. He still felt mentally exhausted the next day, but his body felt more energized. Pissed at not hearing from Serena, Rutger decided to check out the pleasure bot trailer the following night. The line was over four hours long, so he bought a bottle of synthos instead and got drunk in his room while watching a reality game show on holovid.

Since then he'd left his room only to visit the chow hall and medical. The base felt like a different world; the war didn't seem real here. He'd quickly come to resent the rear-echelon troops with their clean uniforms and relaxed, cavalier attitudes, though perhaps it was just jealousy. He'd been one of them not long ago. Unable to take their own, many of the rear troops purchased war souvenirs from several vendor trailers by the front gate: flags and patches of Federation and Republic forces, scarves worn by Repub troops, knives, inert grenades, and even traditional post cards. Rutger was happy to stay in his room, far from the clueless remfs.

Rutger and Aubrey signed in with flight-line security at the airfield. They waited inside a hangar while Staff Sergeant Faora stood in the distance talking to ground personnel and signing paperwork on a data pad.

"Sam, is that you?" a feminine voice called from behind Rutger.

He turned and stared into the violet eyes of Lance Corporal Nicole Giaconi. She gave Rutger a hug, surprising him. He stood there awkwardly for a moment before hugging her back. Her breasts felt nice pressed against him.

"What are you doing here?" she asked.

"Waiting for a new tank."

Nicole hadn't changed much since the Berserker Logistics Course: shiny dark hair in tight braids on her scalp, a gorgeous white smile that dimpled her freckled cheeks whenever she flashed it. She wore a tanker uniform, the only noticeable change.

"My TC is over there signing for it," Rutger said. "When did you become a tanker?"

"They were short drivers, so I got transferred over from the motor pool about a month ago. I didn't even know you were in our battalion. I see you got promoted to corporal, congrats. Are you still a driver?"

"No, I'm a gunner. I'm with Bruiser Company, second platoon. Who are you with?"

"Anvil Company, first platoon. Wow, a gunner already. Impressive."

"Yeah, well, the units are shorthanded all around." *Dropping like flies during a cold snap.* "So what are you doing here?"

"Checking to see if a shipment of parts came in for our tank. We got hit by a drone swarm attack a few days ago. How long have you been in tanks?"

"Glad you're okay. I got moved over shortly after we got planet side."

"Have you seen much action?"

"Yeah...enough to have a tank shot out from under me."

"I hear you. I've gotten my fill as well. It's not what I expected it to be..." She looked away, voice trailing off.

"Yeah, I know."

"Rutger! Move your ass," Faora barked. "You can chase tail later. We're catching a ride to our mount!"

Embarrassed, Rutger said, "Well, it was good seeing you, Nicole. I gotta run, but maybe I'll see you around later. I'm in the transitory barracks, H block."

"Okay, take care of yourself, Corporal."

Rutger jogged to where Faora and Aubrey waited beside an anti-grav truck. Faora shot him an annoyed look as they boarded the worn vehicle. She sat in the cab, with Rutger and Aubrey relegated to threadbare, collapsible canvas seats in the bed. The driver engaged the repulsors, and the vehicle lurched away from the hangar. The truck's motion rocked Rutger to drowsiness. He closed his eyes.

"You know her?" Aubrey asked.

No, Sherlock, we just met a second ago. "Yeah, we were class-mates at the logistics course."

"Damn, she's a looker for sure. I had to wait over four hours for a pleasure bot, but I'm telling you it was worth it. She did things—"

A dropship firing up its ion jets drowned out Aubrey, the high wine growing louder as the pilot spooled up the engines. A larger dropship rippled the air with intense heat as it flew in with two giant shipping containers strapped beneath. Aubrey kept mouthing words, oblivious to the noise. Rutger didn't give a fuck about whatever he was saying. He felt confused at seeing Nicole. Nothing had happened between them at the schoolhouse, but now he couldn't stop thinking about her.

Several rows of Berserker vehicles and shipping containers were staged along the airfield fence. Rutger and Aubrey jumped from the truck and followed Staff Sergeant Faora, who weaved between several IFVs and lesser vehicles until they reached their replacement tank.

It was brand new, its squat and angular body covered in field-brown nano paint. It had no name, just a hull number: 372. Aubrey and Rutger climbed aboard while Faora dealt with the yard superintendent. Rutger peered down into the gunner's hatch. Sheets of protective plastic film still covered the ejection seats.

"It's brand new!" Aubrey said like a kid on Christmas morning.

"I know," Rutger said, waiting for Faora to finish her business before getting into systems checks and inspections. He knew this was one of those times you couldn't win as a junior enlisted person. If he took the initiative and began without her, she would chew his ass for not waiting on her order; and if he waited, she would chew his ass for not taking more initiative. Just another situation where he was a powerless junior enlisted man.

She didn't appear pleased at all when she finally finished up and walked toward them.

"The tank is brand new, Staff Sergeant," Aubrey said. "Isn't that great?"

"No, not at all," Faora said. "It means that it isn't broken in, and we have a lot more prep work to do before we head back to the front."

Rutger's stomach knotted and his blood went cold at that word *front*. That they would return to the fighting was a given, but the tank's arrival made the fact ominously imminent. *Shit, we might be on the move by dusk.*

"Let's get this over with," Faora said. "I'll do the external inspection. You two do your full preflight checks, everything they taught you at the schoolhouse, no stripped-down field shit. We want to ensure everything is functioning properly before we roll into combat."

Used to the usual locker room stench in the fighting compartment, Rutger developed a minor headache from the fresh, overwhelming smells of new plastics, wiring, and unsoiled upholstery. He sat in the gunner's seat and perused the controls. Though the same model as their previous tank, this Patton was an updated factory variant. The dash cluster looked slightly different, but the multifunction displays and main viewing screens were the same.

Rutger flipped the main power switch; the gauges and displays flashed to life. He scanned the readouts for irregularities as he tested the requisite switches and control buttons. Lowering his visor, he synched his commo helmet with the AI, and information on the various systems scrolled across his HUD. Fresh air blew from the vents when he checked the life support systems.

Staff Sergeant Faora slid in next to him. Rutger tested the hatch controls, which swung down and sealed with a heavy thud, electronically locking.

A rapid, mounting whirring arose when Aubrey powered up the fusion reactor. He engaged the repulsors moments later, and the tank began to rise on its inverse gravitational field.

Rutger continued his checks of the turret and fire control systems. The main gun gyros were functioning properly. A red warning light flashed on the console; he'd forgotten about the breach cooling pump. The light disappeared when he switched it on. After checking external cameras to ensure the surrounding area was clear, he traversed the tank's turret through all its stops.

"Everything checks out, Staff Sergeant," Rutger said. "We just need ammo and countermeasures."

"Good," Faora said, eyes glued to her readouts. "We'll take care of that in a bit. George, has the tank been named?"

The AI's synthesized voice answered, "No, the tank has not been named."

Faora turned to Rutger. "I'm terrible at that kind of shit. You can name her."

Rutger thought it over. Callie flashed to mind, but it was bad luck to name a tank after a loved one or even a girlfriend. He then thought of Duran—the man warranted a tribute. *Bounty Hunter II*."

"Works for me," Faora said. "George, name her *Bounty Hunter II*. Display in standard font."

AI manipulated the layer of nano-paint, and *Bounty Hunter II* appeared in white block font on the main gun barrel.

"Let's take her for a spin, Aubrey," Faora said. "Just take it slow while we're breaking in."

They topped off with ordnance at the ammo dump before putting the tank through its paces, checking the control surfaces and test firing all weapons outside the base perimeter. They replenished ammo again upon returning, and got topped off with fuel as well before grounding the tank in a staging area near the front gate. The tests had taken a while; it was now mid-afternoon.

"You guys have the rest of the day off," Faora said. "We return to the front tomorrow, so get whatever you need to get out of your system. We leave at 0530 sharp, so I expect to see both of your ugly mugs here by 0500, not a minute later. Do *not* make me go hunting for you, or you'll wish you were never born. Do you copy?"

"Yes, Staff Sergeant!" Aubrey and Rutger replied.

"Rutger, you need to report to the S-1 office before you knock off. There are some administrative matters you need to take care of."

"Roger that, Staff Sergeant."

Rutger headed to battalion HQ, located in a two-story warehouse across from the landing field. Several command vehicles sat outside, their large communications arrays pointed toward the heavens. Rutger followed data and power cords from the vehicles into the building, then a series of signs that pointed him to the S-1 office.

Clerks dutifully pushed data in the admin shop at a long table with several holographic consoles, while others updated status boards with current unit locations and strengths. Some of the personnel wore Berserker uniforms, while others were contracted help from the local population.

"Can I help you, trooper?" an admin sergeant named Cruchner asked Rutger.

"I'm Corporal Rutger with B Company. I was told to report here by my—"

"Right, follow me." Cruchner motioned toward a side hallway and led Rutger inside a small office with a holo console on a makeshift wooden desk. He glanced at Rutger's name tape and started typing and scrolling through various windows. "Okay, here it is."

Rutger couldn't read the screen from his side due to the privacy filter, the holographic projection appearing as a green refraction. "What's it say?"

"Your wife is divorcing you," he said, matter of factly. He reversed the image so Rutger could read it. A printer behind Cruchner spat out a paper copy several pages long, which he handed to Rutger.

"What the hell?" Rutger said. "There's got to be some kind of mistake. You sure you got the right Rutger?"

"Yeah, I'm sure, Corporal. Unfortunately, I see it all the time." He shook his world-weary head.

Rutger read the hard copy from the local magistrate's office in Port City. It took a while, his nonplussed gaze lingering on legalese passages he couldn't quite understand, though the entire document mystified him. *This can't be happening. Why the fuck is she doing this?* "This is almost two months old. Why am I getting it now?"

"We only received it the other day. It wasn't considered priority traffic."

"My wife leaving me wasn't considered important?"

"I don't prioritize the traffic, Corporal. I'm sorry."

Rutger sat dumbfounded, still in disbelief.

"I need you to fill out this form." The sergeant slid a data pad to him. "You need to decide if you want to keep your elected benefits and beneficiary the same, and whether you want your funds routed to a different account."

Rutger stared helplessly at the data pad, then back to the legalese gibberish on paper. "I don't understand any of this. What is it telling me?"

"It says that you've abandoned your duties as a husband, and that she is seeking sole custody of your daughter. You are no longer obligated to provide healthcare coverage to the family, but you're still required to pay the stipulated credits in child support."

Rutger continued staring at the form. "Can I somehow contest this?"

"Not here you can't. You'll have to go there or hire a lawyer to file a motion. I'm neither qualified nor permitted to provide legal counsel, but off the record, I would advise you to terminate benefits since she isn't requesting any. It eats up a lot of your pay. Check these boxes if that's what you want to do."

"But…my daughter needs medical insurance."

"Your wife isn't requesting continuation. She must have gotten her own benefits."

And how the fuck did she manage that? Even if she were working again, the cost of benefits for both her and their daughter would eat up most of her pay. That was why he had left in the first place. Rutger somehow checked his temper as he began to realize the obvious. He checked the appropriate boxes to terminate benefits and funds.

After signing the paperwork, he started walking in shock to the transitory barracks. His stomach erupted in rumbling, mild pains, but his appetite had disappeared, even though he knew he should eat. Once they shipped out, he wouldn't see a fresh-cooked meal for a while, perhaps never again. *I don't care.*

He purchased a bottle of synthos at the post exchange on his way to the barracks. He didn't feel much like socializing, so he simply drank and watched the other troopers as he walked. Many seemed to be taking their drinking seriously, so he assumed he wasn't the only one going back forward.

He stopped by the morale tent and saw the line for the pleasure bots. With both male and female versions, the androids were quite adept at what they did, able to change their hair and eye color and body contours to match a person's preference. They even could match the looks and techniques of the current adult vid stars. They were known to suck a man dry of both his urges and his money. Rumor was the Berserker's got a cut of the services provided by the vendors, allowing the organization to recoup some of the salary they paid to soldiers. He was tempted to wait, but when he saw the line continued around the corner and all the way up the street he frustratedly move on.

He'd downed his fourth shot back in his room when Aubrey came knocking, wanting to know if he'd like to go grab a bite to eat. "No, I feel like shit," Rutger called through the door. "Go without me. I'll see you tomorrow."

Silence from outside, then, "You want me to fetch a doc, Corporal?"

"Just go!" *I just want to be by myself.*

After another long pause Aubrey said, "Okay, suit yourself. Come find me if you change your mind. I'll try to hold a place in line for you."

Don't fucking bother. He said nothing and poured another shot.

The liquor put him in an oddly juxtaposed state of boredom and animation. "Fucking cunt!" he shouted at the walls. "I'll fucking show you!" He grabbed his holo-pad and sent several nasty, profanity-laden rants to Serena. He then polished off the bottle, followed by the half bottle still on the nightstand.

As darkness fell outside, Rutger's head lolled forward and his eyelids drooped. He removed his trousers and uniform jacket, yet hadn't the energy or desire to completely undress. He collapsed onto his bunk, head spinning with thoughts of Serena. He regretted sending the messages, but they couldn't be deleted and it didn't matter anyway. His rantings wouldn't get her back, nor, from the look of things, make her dislike him more. His drunken thoughts eventually slipped from Serena to Callie, and then to the past. He then thought of the future—and feared.

He was back in *Bounty Hunter.* "How bout a drink, Rutger?" Staff Sergeant Duran asked from the command chair. He turned and offered Rutger a bottle of synthos. As Rutger reached for the bottle, half of Duran's face slid away and splattered on his lap, exposing the slick white sheen of his skull. Bloody teeth grinned at Rutger. "Come join me…it isn't so bad. There's no pain, only darkness."

Knowing it was a dream didn't make it seem any less real to Rutger. The plasma cannons started firing, their rhythm slow and offbeat. They needed maintenance.

Rutger awakened and realized the cannon fire was something else. He lay there trying to sober up. Somebody was knocking on his door.

He got up and stumbled into a wall, found the door, and opened it. Nicole stood in the hallway's harsh light, smiling tipsily.

"Do you mind if I stay with you?" she whispered. "I don't want to be alone."

"Okay," Rutger slurred, stepping back. He suddenly became aware of his boner showing through his boxer briefs.

Nicole stepped past him and unzipped her jumpsuit, revealing a black sports bra and panties. "No funny business, okay?" she said, eyes shining with seriousness. She brushed a lock of hair from her eyes and slipped into bed.

"Okay." Rutger slid under the sheets from the other side. She grabbed his arm and pulled it around her.

"Good night," Rutger said.

"Good night," Nicole said.

Within seconds, she who wanted no funny business turned over and began kissing him, quickly, urgently, reaching for his boxer briefs. He found himself on top of her, inside her, feeling her every move as she gasped and moaned beneath him. For a few moments he forgot about Serena, concentrating only on Nicole and how she made his body feel. He reached his release and rolled aside.

She curled up next to him and put her head on his chest. He suddenly felt guilty for not being faithful to his wife, or ex-wife, and for perhaps taking advantage of his drunk friend.

His guilt didn't last long; they made love again minutes later. He held her afterwards, and before drifting off he stared at the shadows in his room. For the first time in a long while he didn't feel lonely. He fell into a dreamless sleep.

CHAPTER 15

HEAVY SNOWFLAKES DRIFTED DOWN IN THE PRE-
dawn darkness as the tanks of Bruiser Company sat hovering
over a highway that ran toward the city of Cavour.

A bitter chill ran through Rutger despite the tempest of emotions raging inside of him. *Can't she ever close that fucking hatch?*
He knew better than to look over at Staff Sergeant Faora. He kept
his eyes glued to his screens.

They'd returned to the front three days before. Still untested,
Bounty Hunter II vibrated around Rutger. He knew the tank
would be tested today, because they were about to spearhead the
assault on Cavour.

But Rutger's thoughts were elsewhere. *I can't believe she's divorcing me and trying to keep me from seeing Callie.* He still hadn't come
to terms with that reality, though it really didn't change anything.
What? I'm not good enough for her, but that bitch still wants my money.
He knew he shouldn't look at it that way though. Technically the
money would be child support for Callie. Either way, he was stuck
here and they were light years away, same as before.

It could be worse. You could be out there. He shuddered at the
thought while watching the grunts of third and fourth platoons

trudging over snowy fields toward the tree line on their left. Their white and green active camouflage blended perfectly with the dark forest, the spire-like trees swallowing them like the jagged teeth of a great beast.

Task Force Marauder, consisting of the 5th Berserker Battalion and the 2nd Federation Army, had secured over sixty kilometers of territory during his absence in the rear, which already seemed an eternity ago to Rutger. The stress of returning to the front had already fatigued him, grinding him down mentally and physically. He missed a warm bed. *And I miss Nicole.* The thought of her made him smile for a second before vanishing in the storm of emotions whirling inside him.

Repub troops reportedly packed Cavour. Now confined to a smaller AO, enemy forces had concentrated into larger units, their defenses ever more elaborate as the task force drove east toward New Oslo. Though on the ropes with no real chance of victory at this point, the enemy fought on desperately, making the Federation and Berserkers pay with blood for every centimeter of ground.

Thankfully, civilian traffic on the highway had decreased. *No wonder.* Burnt-out vehicles and dead bodies lay strewn beside the road, pushed from the hardball by bladed engineer vehicles. Republic forces had lost civilian support in this area, and rumors abounded of them shooting civilians who attempted to flee toward Federation troops.

So stupid. They'd be better off sending them to us. Refugees slowed the Berserkers almost as much as the Fed yokels dragging their feet. For an army fighting to preserve their nation, the Feds never seemed eager for battle. Rutger somewhat understood, but their delays gave the Repub forces more time to prepare their defenses.

Faora's voice in his earpiece snapped him back to the moment. "Listen up, boys. We'll be leading the assault on Cavour. Anvil Company will be on our right flank. The Twenty-Seventh

Federation Guards will be moving up on the highway to our south. Cyclone Company will be in reserve in an overwatch position with the remaining Fed support elements. We've got grunts and drones scouting ahead, and early recon has confirmed dug-in enemy positions ringing the outskirts of the town." Blue arrows showing the Battalion's attack plan appeared on the tactical display. "After we cross the LD, there are several belts of trees that cross our AO. They provide natural bottlenecks of enemy fire, so watch for them. They could also contain enemy sappers."

In a saddle between hills, Cavour overlooked acres of pastural fields. Their objective was a wooded hilltop north of town. Anvil would secure orchard-covered hills to the south while Federation forces secured the road into town.

The broad valley plain narrowed as it neared Cavour. The tree belts Faora had spoken of had been planted as snow breaks across the valley. They would cover most of the 6.2-kilometer distance to the objective over open ground. The trees would offer some cover from enemy line-of-sight weapons but would limit Berserker and Fed tank fire as well. Zooming in on a sat map, Rutger noticed several spots in the trees where bottlenecks could occur.

"We have air support today as well," Faora said. "Our gunships will provide CAS during our final approach to the objective."

The mention of air support didn't relieve Rutger's anxiety. In short supply, air assets didn't have a long life expectancy against the enemy's plethora of air-defense weapons. They moved at greater speeds than grav tanks but weren't generally much higher off the deck, and they didn't carry as much armor. *This must be a tough objective.* The command wouldn't have committed air assets to the assault otherwise.

They sat tight for over two hours while the grunts moved up through the woods. Time crawled, and the waiting started to eat at Rutger. He thought self-preservation would make him reluctant to attack, but it only multiplied his misgivings. Life sucked—why try to enjoy what might be the final moments? *Attack already and be done with it. Whatever that means for me...*

Fifteen minutes later they received orders to stand by as tracked drones started moving forward. Rutger zoomed in and watched the boxy drones with morbid fascination as they moved into the field. The autonomous vehicles quickly picked up speed, their rubber tracks throwing up rooster tails of snow as they accelerated across the white void. They fanned out, turrets scanning back and forth. Each had a rack of guided multi-purpose missiles, a 15mm plasma rotary cannon, a 40mm automatic grenade launcher, and an advanced sensor suite. They were thinly armored, alas, and in short supply.

The tracked drones had shipped to the front in the same convoy as *Bounty Hunter II*. Rutger switched to one of their feeds and saw the first tree belt growing closer. The buildings of Cavour loomed above in the distance like dark, brooding monoliths under an ash gray sky. Then the feed suddenly terminated in a blue flash. *So much for that.*

The other drones continued, firing as they zig-zagged erratically to evade bolts. Red target icons appeared and multiplied atop the topographic map as the drones drew enemy fire and identified targets. All were destroyed in the next couple of minutes.

The machines did their job. Time to do ours.

"Bruisers, move out," Captain Hensley ordered over the company net.

A phalanx of steel spread across the field as Bruiser and Anvil companies turned off the road and crossed the line of departure. First platoon took the lead, followed by second and trailed by the IFVs of third and fourth platoons. To their right, Anvil Company assumed attack formation. The staggered rows of the two formations stretched across the field like a swinging gate. Rutger pulled up the tank call signs on tactical display and saw Nicole's tank, *Apocalypse*, in the lead row. Drones and grunts hadn't detected any mines. The tanks accelerated to a moderate 55 kph, which would give the infantry on the left flank more time to finish clearing the woods. After that, the grunts would continue to their respective assault objectives.

"Bruiser elements, Bruiser 6, artillery preparation commencing. Begin target suppression," Captain Hensley ordered.

The lead tanks opened fire, main guns recoiling, reports cracking sharply through the frigid air. Orange spherical flashes lit up hilltops in the distance.

Repub soldiers on the heights answered with strings of blue bolts from heavy machine guns that kicked up fountains of snow and steam around the tanks. Blue flashes from their air-defense guns lanced skyward, finding and destroying many of the rocket-boosted shells in the Fed's artillery preparation. Berserker gunships followed the artillery with gun runs on the Repub positions.

Bounty Hunter II raced past the burning wreckage of the first tracked drone. Snow had melted around the still-glowing hulk, and scorched pieces of it lay scattered in the snow for meters around. *That could be us next.*

The two tank companies kept firing as they advanced, obliterating buildings and sending up plumes of dirt from dug-in positions around the town. Enemy fire intensified as they drew closer.

Rutger searched out targets from their position in the second row of tanks, zooming in on buildings in his assigned sector of fire. Every time he was about to pull the trigger, another gunner beat him to the punch. The AI normally prevented duplication of effort on targets, but there were too many packed close together for AI in every tank to keep up. *Fuck!* he thought, watching a tripod missile launcher crew disappear in a megajoule fury of ionized cobalt that literally vaporized them. Great that they'd died, but he wanted to be the trigger man.

A blue bolt from far to the left barely missed *Bounty Hunter II*. The AI identified the source as a 210mm self-propelled artillery piece. Normally used for lobbing shells long distances during indirect fire missions, the big gun now direct-fired anti-tank plasma rounds line-of-sight.

He zoomed in looking for a shot. The Repub vehicles fired through cuts in the woods and from positions dug well into the hills. Rutger saw no actual targets, just random muzzle flashes as they fired. He centered his pipper over the source of one of the flashes. The main gun bucked as he squeezed the trigger. The crimson bolt splintered a clump of trees and set them ablaze, but another muzzle flash came immediately from the shadows, the enemy gun still in business.

Adding to the torrent of blue bolts were guided missiles that launched with telltale plumes of smoke. Automatic-defense weapons took out most of the salvo; the few remaining missiles streaked far above the wildly maneuvering tanks. The enemy weaved a thick web of crossfire from scores of entrenched positions on both sides of town, and the Berserker vehicles were about to be ensnared.

Targets called out and orders relayed jammed the nets with chaotic, staticky gibberish. The tank formations had grown ragged by the time they started moving in a loose echelon around the first tree belt.

Rutger tried to push the chaotic noise from his mind and focus on acquiring targets, but at present the tree belt obscured his view of the hilltops. *Bounty Hunter II* banked slightly as they followed first platoon around the wall of trees, straight into a hail of enemy fire. One of first platoon's tanks erupted in a blue flash followed by a fountain of sparks. Rutger watched helplessly as *Black Label* ground hard in the snow, dark smoke starting to rise from the hull. The crew flung open the hatches and abandoned the tank. Sizzling blue bolts just missed the other tanks as they flew through the gap.

"Bruiser 6, we lost Red 2," said the tired voice of Lieutenant Kelly, first platoon's commander.

"Copy, Red 1. Watch that gap, people!"

The next row of trees came up quickly. One of Anvil Company's tanks to their right exploded, twin columns of flame jetting skyward from the turret hatches as the tank plowed nose-first into the snow. No survivors. *At least it was quick.* Rutger checked the tactical display, thankful to see the kill wasn't *Apocalypse.* The enemy's strategy of zeroing heavy weapons on breaks in the tree belts was working a little too well for Rutger's tastes, and they had several more to pass through.

"Crossing Phase Line Kendra, pop smoke," Captain Hensley ordered as they approached the next gap.

Rutger pressed a button and fired *Bounty Hunter II's* smoke grenades. The cylindrical grenades launched one hundred meters ahead of the tank in a diverging arc before exploding into a shroud of thick gray smoke laced with nanos and chemical agents to disrupt sensors. Blue bolts sliced through the smoke as the advance continued toward the next break. The tank rocked, buffeted by an explosion meters behind as they raced for the gap. The eerie flashes of manmade lightning ahead looked like the gateway to some hellish netherworld.

This is suicide.

CHAPTER

BUKAR MOVED RAPIDLY AND STEALTHILY THROUGH the woods with his metal companion, a sensor bot named Turk, a few paces ahead to his right. He felt cold again despite the brutal pace he was setting. He and Turk were at the point position, advancing one hundred meters ahead of third and fourth platoons as they pushed northeast through the tree line.

Running out of time. Seconds and minutes ticked by on HUD, but Bukar already moved as quickly as he dared; any faster and they would be jogging through the woods. *Don't rush to your death.* He recalled a lesson from his infantry instructors. *Slow is smooth, and smooth is fast.*

His eyes darted over every tree, bush, and fallen log, collecting just as much data as the bot's optical sensors and processing it almost as fast. He had two distinct advantages over the bot: his gut intuition and the ability to feel fear. Self-preservation was a powerful operating code hard wired into human DNA over eons. *The enemy positions must be close now.*

Now and then Bukar checked the spacing between himself and Turk. The bot didn't move with human stealth, but his armored carapace featured active camouflage that blended well into the white and green surroundings. The many optical sensors on his squarish head provided 360-degree and overhead vision.

Bolts cracked through the air like lightning ahead and to the right, blue flashes barely visible through thick forest cover. Artillery thundered in the distance. He was too far into the trees to see what was happening, but he could sense the heavy weapons close by as they crept ahead.

MG POS 110 METERS, Turk texted, having identified the source of firing ahead.

ROGER, Bukar thought-texted back. His helmet sensors had also located the position, but they couldn't reveal the enemy lying in wait under sensor-scattering cover. They might stumble upon such a position at any moment. Bukar studied the terrain map on HUD, looking for likely ambush points by considering where *he* would set up an ambush. His pulse pounded in his head from physical exertion and the mental exhaustion of monitoring HUD while keeping close watch on their surroundings.

Ironically, he knew his anxiety would ease once the enemy opened fire, for instincts would take over and silence his racing thoughts. He'd been all over the galaxy as a merc and knew that war came naturally to the human species, as if it were God's perverse gift. *Perhaps it is. The Lord works in mysterious ways.*

Bukar certainly had the gift, which he'd honed to a razor's edge while working with the Berserkers and other outfits. His sister had her art—he knew how to kill. Though she ironically had been the first to teach him that, to kill and to survive. There had been others of course that had trained him in the arts of war. But he had learned his formative lessons from his sister in the slums of Emeraldville, and they would forever share that bond.

He remembered how young and naïve he'd been, his ambitions greater than his limited skills and common sense. It had been his final job, the hustle of a local crime lord that would set he and Adeze up for life, enough credits for them to leave the planet and start anew.

But crime, alas, was an even more fickle business than war, and a supposed friend double-crossed him for a few lousy credits. He didn't even resist when the gang came for him, knowing he was good as dead. They took him to an abandoned warehouse and chained him to a chair before a camera, planning to make an example of him by broadcasting his torture and murder live on the local holo-cast.

They didn't factor in Adeze coming to his rescue. She surprised them, shooting two of the gangsters before they had a chance to react. In the ensuing battle she moved with a deadly dancer's grace—shooting, kicking, stabbing. She untied him and they fled, but good deeds never went unpunished. A parting bolt sliced past her face as they ran from the warehouse, blowing off her goggles and blinding her.

Afterward, on a chartered ship off world, he held her and cried for them both. She never once blamed him or even complained. Bukar bore the true scar from the incident. He had to live with the guilt, a burden that weighed on him heavily still. Even so, his burden had transformed him from a brash boy to a contemplative man and had also helped him find religion. Adeze even thanked him years later, for blindness had brought her closer to her art. She eventually received bionic replacements, but she turned off her bionic eyes while painting to further enhance her psychic gifts.

Bukar heard a metallic click ahead and instinctively dropped. Turk froze at the sound, programmed to do so, then gestured toward his right. A machine gun opened fire. Bolts blasted through the bot's torso and tore off his pointing arm in a shower of sparks and metal fragments. SENSOR BOT "TURK" DESTROYED, scrolled a red message atop Bukar's HUD.

Bukar pressed his body against a giant tangle of roots as a second burst cut overhead. Fear crept into his gut and seized his stomach like an icy, clutching hand. Lieutenant Palmer's voice scratched in his ear: "White 1 Bravo, this is White 6. What's your status?" Bukar ignored the call. Silence returned. He waited a moment longer before peeking out of cover to see several gray helmets barely protruding above the parapet of a well-concealed trench twenty meters to the right. Steam rose from the barrel of their machine gun.

Bukar took a grenade from his harness, pulled the pin and thumbed the selector switch to *contact*. The enemy had opened fire before all targets had entered the kill zone, a crucial error on their part. Turk and he had stumbled into what appeared to be the far-right flank of a network of enemy positions.

Bukar heard the squads coming up behind him, their boots crunching through the snow. "White 1 Bravo, White 6. Do you copy?" Lieutenant Palmer persisted.

Bukar stepped from behind the tree, threw the plasma grenade, and quickly ducked back into cover. The Repub soldiers spotted him too late, just beginning to raise their rifles when the grenade exploded in their midst. Screams followed.

Bukar moved like a wraith from tree to tree toward the trench, his rifle at the ready. Three men lay dead in the trench. A survivor sat with his head tucked between his knees, sobbing, while another, a female, grasped his shoulders from behind.

"C'mon we need to get out of—" Sensing Bukar's presence, the female soldier turned and froze, unable to speak.

Bukar squeezed off a burst that spread her upper body across the trench. The sobbing soldier didn't look up as Bukar pulled the trigger. A smoking hole bored through his helmet, blowing his brains out the back to decorate the rear wall of the trench.

Additional fighting positions lay ahead, each equipped with a crew-served weapon trained on a gap in the tree belt to attack

Berserker and Fed vehicles. Bukar estimated roughly a platoon occupying the area. The gunner in the closest position spun a heavy machine gun toward Bukar and fired early, most of his bolts flying far overhead, but one hissed by Bukar's right ear.

Bukar dropped into a kneeling position, put his holographic sight on the man's head, and squeezed the trigger. Helmet pieces and brains flew before the man slumped over the weapon. Other soldiers frantically yanked the man off the gun and returned fire. Snow and dirt flew around Bukar as he dived into the trench a nanosecond ahead of the bolts.

Blue flashes tore over his head. On his visor, pink flecks of goop mingled with brown mud: pieces of the female soldier's lungs. The dead crew's plasma machine gun sat on the parapet above him.

He lobbed a grenade without exposing himself, using the distraction to grab the machine gun by the tripod and pull it from the parapet. He checked the weapon to ensure it was ready before pulling a plasma grenade from the dead woman's vest. He thumbed the switch and tossed the grenade. When it exploded, he rose with the machine gun and fired from the waist, working streams of bolts up and down the positions as hot matrix cases piled up around his feet. Several Repub soldiers dashed from their positions only to be cut down by a fire hose of blue death.

A grenade sailed toward him, and he hit the deck. It landed outside the trench, but the concussion reverberating through the trench wall dumped loose snow and dirt atop him.

Bukar keyed his mic. "White 6, this is White 1 Bravo."

"What the hell's going on up there?" Lieutenant Palmer answered.

"Enemy positions in front of our objective. I need fire support on the following positions." Bukar designated the positions on his HUD map. Artillery support would likely take too long or be intercepted, so he opted for direct fire support from the ground vehicles. As he radioed in the fire mission, he threw another plasma grenade blindly toward the enemy positions.

"Say again, White 1 Bravo. I can't hear you."

"Fire support, 30 Mike Mike and Javelin missiles set for air burst."

"Come in, White 1 Bravo. Can't make out your last."

The enemy had the nets jammed. "Fire support, coordinates: 354, 367, 372."

"Copy, White 1 Bravo," a different voice responded.

A moment later, Bukar heard the ripping crackle of 30mm plasma bolts. He peeked over the parapet as a deadly sleet of crimson sawed through the trees, splintering trunks and kicking up clouds of snow. The fire raked the enemy positions from left to right, then back again.

Bukar ducked at the first air-burst explosion of a hypersonic javelin missile above the treetops, followed by several more. Hot shrapnel and smoldering wood shards whizzed through the air, cutting down Repub soldiers in their trenches.

He peered from the trench a few seconds after the final explosion. A gray haze hung in the air and several small fires dotted the hellish landscape. Through his respirator filters, Bukar smelled explosive residue mixed with human filth. Shrieks of pain and agony drifted over from the Repub positions.

Bukar jumped from the trench and bounded between the few remaining trees toward the enemy positions. In the first trench he found one man still alive, his lower jaw missing. Blood covered the chest plate on his armor. Bukar dropped him with a mercy shot.

"White 1 Bravo, White 6. Are you still there?"

"Yeah, you can move up. Clearing positions now."

"Copy, 1 Bravo. Moving up."

Bukar advanced to the next trench, mopping up hole by hole. He was about to climb from a trench full of bodies when he heard an echoing cry followed by a panicked voice in standard yelling, "Help me! Help me!"

He peered over his sights, wary of a trick. A young Repub soldier staggered through the haze toward him. His helmet was missing, exposing dark skin and black curly hair. He wore a service pistol on his belt. Bukar's finger tensed on the trigger, then he noticed both of the soldier's arms were missing below the elbow.

The kid couldn't have been older than 18. Blood ran from his nose and ears. Bukar figured he was in shock, and the missile blasts had likely deafened him. The animal fear in his eyes and his dark skin reminded Bukar of himself years before—young, scared, and in over his head. A boy playing a game that even most men would never master.

Bukar rose slowly from the trench. The boy saw him and walked toward him, but he froze a few seconds later, recognizing the enemy.

Looking around, Bukar saw no further threats. Even so, he waited in the trench and motioned the soldier to approach. He could help this young man, whose combat days were over. *He will be free of this war and still live a good life, Lord willing.*

Crimson bolts snapped past Bukar and knifed into the boy's chest, dropping him to the snow in a cloud of red mist. Bukar stared in disbelief for a moment, then angrily turned around as the first squad of Berserker troopers moved in. *Will this madness ever end?*

"Getting a little slow in your old age, Preacher?" one of the troopers asked. He lifted his visor and spat. "No worries, we greased his ass for you."

Bukar slowly climbed from the trench. "You didn't need to shoot him. He was unarmed."

The man examined his handiwork. "No shit, I guess he was. Were you gonna give him a hand?" He laughed at his own joke.

Bukar stared at the trooper, then back down at the boy. He laughed as well at the cruel absurdity of it all. *Unarmed.*

Lieutenant Palmer approached out of the haze. "What's so funny?"

Bukar looked at him, trying to stifle his mad laughter. "Nothing, sir."

"Okay..." Palmer said, still confused regarding the amusement. His bearing returned. "Good work, Preacher. I'll have Rivers take point the rest of the way."

Bukar stopped laughing, deadly serious again. "I would prefer to do it, sir."

Palmer studied him for a moment, then nodded. "Okay, it's yours."

Bukar glanced down at what remained of the armless boy, and tried to forget him as he set off up the slope.

17

CHAPTER

"BRUISER 6, WHERE'S OUR DAMN AIR SUPPORT?"
Staff Sergeant Faora asked.

"Blue 1, I'm working on it," Captain Hensley said. "Kelly lost
another tank. Prepare to become lead element of the assault."

"Copy, Six."

Rutger winced at the news of another tank down. *Now we'll
be first through the gap.*

The attack had faltered due to the murderous fire zeroed on
the breaks in the shelter belts. First platoon had stopped behind
the next tree line. Second platoon moved up behind as blue bolts
ripped overhead.

The rising roar of ion engines came from *Bounty Hunter II's*
rear. A formation of three Dragon gunships raced overhead, flying nap of the earth and barely clearing the tanks.

They halted and hovered just below the treetops. Then they
rose above trees and unloaded their racks of missiles toward the
hilltop positions. White contrails hung like streamers over the
battlefield as they ducked to a low hover and slid further down
the tree line before rising again to unleash streams of crimson

darts from their fuselage-mounted rotary cannons. Rutger hoped they had eliminated most of the hilltop artillery.

As the gunships banked and accelerated away, jettisoning scores of decoy flares, blue bolts from an air-defense weapon struck the trailing bird. The left engine mount disintegrated in a cloud of black smoke, sending the gunship spinning out of control and pirouetting down to explode in a massive fireball.

The enemy arty fire slackened momentarily beneath the Dragons' onslaught, then resumed in intensity in defiance of the plumes of soil that were kicked up by the incoming rounds. They'd taken out one gun according to the tactical display. So *much for that thought.*

"Driver, move us to the front," Faora said.

Bounty Hunter II accelerated forward. Rutger scanned for targets with sonic imaging through the dissipating smoke screen. *Bounty Hunter II* approached the next cut in the trees where a steady stream of massive blue bolts already tore through the area. *We'll never make it through there!* Then he noticed several trees downed by arty fire during the enemy's pre-assault registration, when they'd put the guns on target.

And the idea hit him: *The trees!* Planted by man, the tree belt was only four or five rows thick. He pivoted the turret toward the tree line.

"We need to hold here," Rutger said.

"What are you fucking talking about?" Faora said. "You heard our orders, we—"

"We need to stop, dammit. There's a better way to do this!"

"Driver, halt!" Faora snarled. "You're holding up the entire company, Rutger. This better be worth it."

Aubrey touched *Bounty Hunter II's* skirting to the ground, friction acting as a brake against the tank's massive inertia. Once stopped, he brought the tank back to hover. The column halted behind them.

No time to explain. Rutger swerved the main gun onto the tree line and fired. A crimson flash hit the woods and expanded into a hemisphere of orange that shattered the first rows of trees for several meters in each direction. Trees around the blast burst into flames at the immense heat discharge.

"We don't have time to play fucking lumberjack!" Faora roared.

He ignored her, lowered the pipper slightly, and fired twice in quick succession. Temperature in the fighting compartment rose considerably. Each bolt knifed deeper into the tree line, felling additional trees and sending flaming wood fragments flying.

"Blue 1, this is Bruiser 6. What is the fucking hold up?" Captain Hensley demanded. "We need to move now!"

Rutger ignored the CO's angry voice and fired again. The explosive flash died seconds later, completing a ragged gap through the woods and exposing the field beyond. *Not quite a clear shot, but we might slip through.* Stumps and partially felled trees still burned in the new gap, however, some of them pretty high. *Maybe we can knock them down driving through.*

"Rutger, switch to clearing charge," Faora ordered, apparently seeing his plan.

"Copy, on the way!"

Rutger thumbed the trigger. The tri-barreled 80mm mortar unit in the bow of *Bounty Hunter II* fired a net laced with explosives into the gap. A ripping report shook the hull a moment later. The clearing charge had felled the remaining trees or blasted them to smithereens, clearing a path almost ten meters wide through the tree belt.

"Driver!" Faora ordered. "Take us through the gap!"

Aubrey turned the tank and glided between infernos of trees to either side. The remaining branches and smoldering scrub scraped at the armored skirting as they shot through the conflagration. Despite the tank's environmental controls, the air in the fighting compartment reeked of burning wood. They emerged on the other side like a phoenix arising from the fires of hell.

Faora radioed the results to the CO, then ordered second platoon to follow through the gap.

"Bruiser 6 to all Bruiser and Anvil vehicles," said Captain Hensley over the battalion net. "Hold positions and use main guns and breaching charges to clear through the tree lines."

Bounty Hunter II accelerated up the sloping field, well ahead of second platoon. The smoke cleared, and the wooded top of Hill 581 became visible. Rutger traversed the main gun thirty degrees to port to target enemy guns partially visible through the trees.

Thinly armored, the self-propelled guns weren't designed to go toe-to-toe with tanks. They had been dug into defilade and positioned with limited fields of direct fire, all trained on the tree line breaks. This worked against them now as Bruiser and Anvil Company tanks poured through the newly cut gaps and spread out over the slope.

Rutger fired the main gun twice in quick succession at the boxy turret profile of a self-propelled gun. The bolts shot through a precut firing line in the trees and knifed into the turret with deadly accuracy. Thin titanium armor blazed white for an instant before the ammunition inside exploded. A massive secondary explosion flattened trees for meters around and blasted pieces of the vehicle skyward.

Surprised to see the Berserker tank waves coming through the trees, several Repub infantrymen in fighting positions at the edge of the tree line jumped and ran from their holes. Their panic spread, and others followed in a retreating stampede up the hill.

The other self-propelled guns continued to fire. A blue bolt blew a giant hole in the ground only five meters in front of *Bounty Hunter II*, buffeting the tank and showering it with snow and grit.

Rutger sought the next artillery vehicle as Faora aimed the 15mm automatic defense weapon at the fleeing infantry, her long bursts cutting down soldiers with surgical precision. Many began to crawl through the snow in terror as bolts blew apart their comrades in grizzly red flashes.

Rutger slid the orange pipper over the next artillery piece and gave it a double tap from the main gun. The first bolt hit the sandbagged embankment surrounding the position, transforming the sand into a cloud of molten glass, while the second struck the vehicle and reduced it to a glowing orange fireball that engulfed fleeing troops.

Engrossed in finding and destroying the remaining self-propelled guns, Rutger barely noticed the automatic defense pods belching fire and destroying an incoming missile. Like all of the Berserker tankers, he was obsessed with exacting revenge. He found the next firing position empty. The vehicle had already fled. He was about to engage another position when a tank from the right flank of Anvil Company beat him to the punch by perhaps a second. The vehicle wasn't even in that tank's sector of fire, but the battle had become a free-for-all, the gunners bent on destroying anything they came across.

Anvil company encountered stiff resistance initially from infantry backed by Mantis air defense platforms atop their objective, Hill 641. The enemy's resolve began to erode at the loss of the self-propelled guns and at the sight of the armored vehicles pouring through the gaps in the trees. Meanwhile Rutger, unable to locate more artillery targets, fired on fleeing infantry with the automatic defense weapon, taking over so Faora could concentrate on her duties.

The dual 30mm cannons on the trailing IFVs began to lace the hilltop with a near constant stream of crimson bolts. The tracks of plasma like glowing beads on a rosary of death. Repub soldiers ran up the slope from the murderous onslaught. The crackling bolts fell trees and kicked up plumes of snow as they cut through the soldiers, scattering their appendages and filth over the orchard like human fertilizer. Wounded soldiers gnashed their teeth and moaned as they drug themselves across the snow like seals.

Rutger stole a glance at the tactical display. Fed forces on the south side of the road had started to advance now that the bulk of the resistance had been eliminated. *Fucking typical.* But not unexpected. *If the yokels were worth a shit, then we wouldn't be here.* Behind the Feds, combat engineers were starting to clear the road of mines so reinforcements and support units could move up.

Aubrey slowed *Bounty Hunter II* slightly as they reached their initial objective. In the woods near the top of Hill 581, Repub troops continued their retreat, dragging and carrying wounded personnel. Those foolish enough to fire were quickly cut down. Their blood trails in the snow pointed the way for Berserker tanks.

"Driver, don't slow. Punch it and follow the road," bellowed Faora over the intercom as Bruiser Company tanks advanced past the tree line positions. The *road* was more like a path cut through the woods on the edge of town. Aubrey goosed *Bounty Hunter II's* repulsors. The momentum felt like shove in the back as they headed up the curving track in a cloud of snow.

Around the first bend they encountered fleeing Repub artillery troops who scattered before them, their eyes wide with terror. Rutger swept the narrow path and surrounding trees with a steady stream of crimson bolts from the coaxial machine gun. A few soldiers dropped to the snow and covered their heads with their hands, their screams barely audible in the fighting compartment. Rutger didn't even feel a bump when *Bounty Hunter II* plowed over them, its gravitational field reducing them to red smears, as they left a hell-lit trail of death behind them.

Bounty Hunter II emerged from the forest. The other side of Hill 581 descended in a gentle slope into a narrow valley about 1.5 klicks across. Repub vehicles parked in utter disarray packed the snowy field: troop transports, ammo haulers, support vans, and two retreating self-propelled guns. Frantic to escape, Repub soldiers pushed and jostled to board trucks and jeeps before the Berserker juggernaut arrived.

Caught them with their pants down.

"Kill the bastards," Faora said.

Rutger was already on it. "George, prioritize targets."

The AI automatically assessed and prioritized the Repub vehicles. George swiveled the turret to engage a communications van, not only to cut the enemy comms but to destroy its jamming equipment. Repub troops began to frantically pop smoke grenades, but the AI had already identified the vehicles' locations.

Rutger fired the main gun before the pipper had slid all the way on target. The comm vehicle disappeared in a glowing cataclysm.

Before the weapon had finished recoiling, the computer traversed the turret two degrees to engage another victim. Rutger fired, and a self-propelled gun exploded in a shower of orange slurry. The sheer force of the blast sent the turret tumbling over the front of the vehicle. What remained of the air-cushioned chassis plowed into the snow.

Time for you fuckers to pay!

George picked out a couple of plum targets, an air-cushioned ammo hauler beside a multi-axle troop transport, which were both starting to pull away. Repub troops clambered up the transport's sides, desperate to get in the bed and get the hell away. One of them glanced back as Rutger fired the main gun. The ammo hauler erupted in an apocalyptic fireball that obliterated everything within a 100-meter radius, leaving only a smoking crater. The remains of troops and transport fluttered down like burning tickertape.

Additional Bruiser tanks poured over the hill and joined the fray. Columns of black smoke from the burning vehicles littering the valley began to form a dark haze. The corpse-strewn field looked like a scene from Dante's Inferno.

Rutger kept firing, pulsing the field with the main gun and particle cannons, pouring fire into the writhing mass of metal and men. A sick smile crept over his face as he unleashed pent-up fear, anger, and adrenaline in a mad frenzy. The weapons' residual heat turned the fighting compartment into a sweltering oven.

"Gunner, cease fire," Faora ordered.

She had to repeat the command twice more before Rutger stopped.

CHAPTER 16

"WHAT'S THE HOLD UP?" ASKED CORPORAL BUKAR from the number two seat in the troop compartment of *Crazy Train*.

"Drones are showing a massive roadblock ahead," said Staff Sergeant Mardin, eyes glued to the screens at the IFV's command station. "Damn Repubs blew away half the side of a mountain. We're being routed around on a logging trail that circles north."

"Roger that," Bukar said, feeling the IFV reverse and pivot off the main road. He pulled up a map overlay on his HUD. The tanks and IFVs appeared as blue boxes crawling over the narrow dirt road carved into granite bluffs overlooking New Oslo, the Free Norden Republic's capital.

We are so close.

The detour didn't surprise Bukar. They'd rapidly advanced another twenty klicks toward New Oslo the day after sweeping through Cavour. The enemy had grown more desperate, their resistance less organized but concentrated in particular areas. They were running out of places to flee. Some of the Repub troops were determined to fight to the last man, while others provided only token resistance before surrendering, often as entire units. Each encounter was a unique obstacle, and all took too much time to sort out for Bukar's liking.

Thirty minutes dragged on as they rocked over the forest trail. Bukar synched his HUD to the vehicle's external cameras to watch the tanks and IFVs ahead in the column, their turrets scanning the dark trees lining both sides of the road. They occasionally passed small houses in clearings while climbing the slope. Several times Bukar noticed civilians in tattered clothes watching them pass. Some waved and others scowled, all depending on their political persuasion.

Night vision automatically kicked in as the sun began to drop behind the wooded slopes. The road curved sharply left to avoid a rocky outcropping, and Bukar momentarily lost site of the convoy ahead.

The sharp report of a 188mm tank main gun echoed from the head of the column.

"Contact front!" shouted a tank crewman over the net.

The IFV jolted to a halt, throwing Bukar against his restraints. An orange and black cloud mushroomed over the front of the column. Bukar scanned the trees anxiously through the camera feeds, feeling like a caged animal in the IFV's cramped hold.

Four Mantis air-defense vehicles suddenly appeared on HUD, perched atop a rocky rise to their front. Their crews tore off sensor-scattering netting and opened fire on the convoy. The ripping sound of 40mm cannons echoed through the valley. Automatic protection systems on Berserker armor began blasting guided missiles streaking down from above.

Inside *Crazy Train*, Bukar tensed in his seat as a hailstorm of bolts struck the vehicle, the impacts sounding like jackhammer blows in the troop compartment. Sparks erupted from several bundles of overhead wiring in the hold. The gunner panned the vehicle's dual rotary cannons upward toward the threat. A thunderous report sounded from above a few moments later after he commenced firing.

"Dismount!" Staff Sergeant Mardin bellowed. "Get in the trees!"

The rear ramp crashed down, and troopers at the rear of the hold started ducking through the rectangular hatch. The roar of battle filled his audio sensors. The first two troopers got out unscathed and dashed to the right, but the third fell to the ramp in a blue flash and a spray of vermillion blood. He thrashed about, his screams drowned out by the whip-like crack of bolts streaking by. The next two troopers hurdled over him. Bukar reached the ramp. Lance Corporal Niles lay on his back, missing his groin and most of his intestines. There was no helping him. *Lord, save his soul.*

Bukar stepped over him and ran from the vehicle. Sizzling bolts flew by his head so close his polarized visor dimmed to protect his eyes as he wheeled behind the IFV and dove into the trees. Explosive streaks of red and blue energy crisscrossed above, making it sound as if the sky were being torn open. A gray haze and the sharp tang of ozone hung in the air.

Mardin stepped onto the rear ramp as the IFV exploded in an orange fireball. He disappeared within the expanding shockwave of flames.

No! Bukar had known the platoon sergeant for almost five years, yet he hadn't time to mourn. He ducked behind a tree as pieces of *Crazy Train* rained down like fiery comets. Dual cannons on IFVs ahead and behind sprayed the ridge above with crimson bolts, trying to suppress targets and gain fire superiority. Other squads of Berserker grunts hastily poured from their vehicles to the relative safety of the tree line.

Chaotic orders, counter-orders and status reports jammed the nets as commanders tried to make sense of the ambush. The collective agreement seemed to be that they needed to fall back and regroup.

The Mantis' autocannons continued to belch glowing strings of blue bolts from above. Troopers dashed from the IFV ahead as bolts punched through the thin roof armor. Flames billowed from the crew compartment and sprouted from the hull hatches. Twin pairs of rockets flashed, the crew opting to eject. They flew off to parts unknown, one arcing uphill into the woods and the other down the slope somewhere. A couple more troopers stumbled out and fell, rolling on the deck and slapping at the flames engulfing them. Their cries filled the proximity net until their radios cut out from the heat.

A bolt ripped past Bukar's head as he crouched on the slope and watched the column. Drivers of the lead tanks and IFVs began to reverse and pivot erratically, trying to escape the kill zone. An IFV from fourth platoon backed off the edge of the road and slid down the embankment. Several troopers jumped out of the way, but one didn't make it, his scream cut short when the IFV ground over him, leaving behind a red, pulverized carcass in the snow. The driver gunned the repulsors and tried to scuttle sideways across the grade, but the IFV just wallowed further down the slope, finally lodging between two trees. The crew bailed out and ran for the rear.

Trying to make sense of the situation, Bukar pulled up a tactical overlay on his visor, the topographic map awash with blue dots moving toward the rear and red enemy dots ahead and on the ridge above.

Bukar closed the map. Reyes, Sims, and Castro from first squad lay next to him. "We need to move up this road and see what the fuck is going on."

The men nodded without replying, following Bukar around the bend toward the front of the convoy while staying as low as possible. Bolts snapped over their heads into the trees, felling branches and sending smoldering splinters flying. They encountered several troopers running in the other direction, their eyes crazed with fear and shock. "Fall back!" a corporal yelled. "We have orders!" Bukar ignored all of the fleeing troopers.

Thunderous reports sounded as withdrawing Berserker tanks unleashed their main guns on the vehicles atop the ridge. A Repub Mantis burst into flames, lighting up the hillside.

Circling around a thick clump of bushes, Bukar found Lieutenant Palmer and about a dozen troopers from second squad sheltering behind a fallen tree along the embankment, engaging roughly a company of advancing Repub infantry supported by two tanks.

"What's the plan, sir?" Bukar asked, dropping in behind him.

"We're providing cover fire for the remnants of fourth platoon." Palmer nodded toward troopers from fourth platoon running down the road to the rear, several assisting wounded comrades. "They left several wounded up ahead along the road, but we can't reach them. We can't hold this position much longer. Our armor is pulling out. We need to fall back."

A Repub tank's main gun bolt hit the tree line twenty meters to their left, as if to punctuate Palmer's assessment. The blue flash raised a cloud of steam and shattered several trees, peppering the men with splinters.

"I'll go get them, sir," Bukar said.

"I can't let you do that, Preacher. We lost a man who tried already."

"We can't leave them behind. Let me try, sir."

Palmer stared at him. "Very well, we'll cover you the best we can. But we can't save you if you're hit. Higher wants us out of here ASAP."

"Understood, sir."

Bukar low-crawled toward the wounded men as plasma bolts dug divots in the muddy road to his right. He paused in the cover of a ditch after about twenty meters to get a better look ahead. His HUD showed numerous Repub infantry approaching through the woods, the massive tanks advancing up the road forty meters behind them.

About twenty men in green and gray digital camouflage uniforms cautiously approached, trying to flank Bukar from the left. He put the holographic sight for the 40mm grenade launcher mounted beneath his M-17 dead-center on the formation and squeezed the trigger.

An orange explosion erupted in the middle of the group, filleting men with shrapnel and dropping troopers for several meters around. He pumped two more quick grenades into their flanks as troops behind them opened fire. In a storm of flying bolts, he launched his last two grenades, cutting down several more troopers. The survivors bellowed orders and curses as they retreated through a cloud of smoke and snow, pulling wounded comrades with them.

Bukar crawled to the end of the ditch and spotted the wounded troopers on the road. He leapt to his feet, raced past a burning IFV and reached the first man down, his left leg missing below the knee. He howled in pain as Bukar scooped him up and threw him over his shoulder. He stepped to the next wounded trooper, a female with her hand pressed against her side, some entrails slithering through her fingers. She stared at him with glassy eyes as he grabbed the drag handle on the back of her armored plate carrier and dragged her toward Lieutenant Palmer's position.

A Repub tank's main gun cracked. The ground to Bukar's right heaved from the massive blast, the shockwave causing him to stagger drunkenly over the shaking earth. He stayed on his feet and kept moving. Seconds later he dumped the wounded troopers at Lieutenant Palmer's position.

"We gotta fall back," Palmer said as Bukar turned to fetch the third trooper. "Captain Hensley requested a priority artillery barrage. Rounds are gonna start falling any moment. We gotta scoot. Now!"

"What about the other trooper?"

"There's no time!"

Bukar turned to go. Palmer grabbed his shoulder. "Don't you hear that?" Palmer said, shaking him. "That tank moving up is gonna blow us all to hell in a minute."

"I'll take care of it."

"It's your ass!"

"I know."

A trooper preparing to retreat crouched a few meters away with a multi-barreled missile launcher strapped across his back. Bukar wordlessly took the weapon from the trooper and slung it across his back, then began crawling down the ditch toward the burning IFV next to the last wounded trooper.

Almost there, he peered from the ditch and spotted a Repub tank less than a hundred meters away, moving toward the burning hulk of the lead Berserker grav tank. Dozens of Repub infantry advanced behind the metal behemoth in a skirmisher formation. The tank began traversing its tube toward him.

With a tremendous flash and explosion of flaming debris, the cab of the derelict IFV blew apart, the shockwave knocking Bukar off his feet. He unslung the missile launcher and crawled past the burning IFV, the heat intense despite his suit's thermal insulation.

The tank's main gun cracked again, the blue flash hitting the slope above him. He could feel the force of the superheated air like an invisible hand slapping him as the bolt discharged its wrath. Dirt, rocks, and flaming branches rained down around and atop him as he readied the launcher. Bolts snapped toward him from infantry in the trees, the tank having revealed his position.

Bukar put the holographic targeting reticle on the tank and got a lock. He ducked behind cover just as a hail of bolts tore up the ground where he had stood. With a solid lock, he keyed the switch to fire the three missiles simultaneously, hoping the flames leaping from the IFV would mask the missiles' signatures from the tank's countermeasures, because he only had one shot at this. Stepping back, he launched the missiles over the IFV's burning hull. The flash of igniting rocket motors blinded him momentarily.

Three quick reports sounded. Bukar dropped the launcher and shouldered his rifle. The tank's massive smoothbore cannon still pointed at him, but the vehicle sat grounded and lifeless on the road with two glowing holes punched through the turret. Black smoke billowed out when a crewman pushed open turret hatch, slid out and rolled off the hull. He was missing an arm.

Bukar looked over at the last wounded trooper, identified on HUD as PRIVATE LAWSON. He darted toward Lawson and scooped her up in his arms. He then saw a second hover tank come around the bend and halt beside the destroyed tank. Though frightened and knowing he needed to haul ass, Bukar paused when he noticed a symbol on the tank's prow—a grinning skull wearing a crown of dancing flames.

Move! He dived off the road with her just as the tank fired its main gun.

His visor went black. The explosion hurled them over ten meters down the slope. They rolled and skidded together before finally coming to rest.

Bukar lay on his back, lungs spasming to replace the air knocked from him by the shockwave. He felt like he'd been mercilessly beaten by one of the street gangs back home. He struggled to his hands and knees, breathing again, smells of smoke and ozone filling his nostrils.

*Oh no…*he thought, hearing a keening whistling that gradually rose toward a continuous shriek. He struggled to his feet and found his rifle in the snow.

INCOMING ARTILLERY! flashed across the top of his HUD, and a fresh surge of adrenaline shot into his veins. He scooped up Lawson with a grunt and threw her over his shoulder, then half-crawled, half-sprinted up the slope to the road, lungs burning when he finally reached it. He looked to where the skull tank had been—gone. He turned and ran for the rear as the first arty rounds arrived.

The force of the blasts from behind knocked him forward. He crashed onto the muddy road on his side, spilling Lawson, who grunted in pain. Bukar stood, hoisted the trooper once again, and rushed past the second burning IFV.

Even though I walk through the valley of the shadow of death…

The next salvo struck, closer, a giant hammer blow that flattened him face-down in the mud. He staggered to his feet again with the injured trooper, who moaned something unintelligible.

I will fear no evil, for you are with—

More rounds screamed in and erupted behind him, growing ever closer. The ground heaved and the overpressure of shockwaves slapped and careened him about. He felt shrapnel embedding in his armor but heard very little, his helmet's audio system cutting off the tremendous noise.

Your rod and your staff, they comfort me.

His legs pumped like pistons, the muscles heavy with lactic acid. Despite the neuromuscular layer of synthetic myofibrils in his suit assisting him, he labored to carry his extra burden.

You prepare a table before me in the presence of my enemies.

The artillery barrage began to grow distant behind him. He spotted the retreating convoy 200 meters ahead, troopers spread out in the trees along the road. He reached them and almost collapsed. A medbot helped him lower the body, then Bukar dropped to his knees in utter exhaustion.

Chip marks and embedded shrapnel shards covered Bukar and Lawson's armor. The medbot had raised her visor. She looked like shit, but she was alive. Her eyes anxious, pain etched across her pale face. But she was alive. The bot examined her and administered a dose of painers and nanos in an IV pack to help stop internal bleeding.

Surely goodness and mercy shall follow me all the days of my life: and I will dwell in the house of the Lord forever.

"She should be okay," the medbot said in a distant, tinny voice.

"Praise be to God," Bukar said, louder than he'd meant to.

Lieutenant Palmer approached Bukar. "You okay, Preacher?"

"Yes, sir." He wanted to collapse right there, but pride kept him upright. He had saved three troopers, after all.

"Great work," Palmer said, slapping him on the shoulder. "Head back to the rear and get with the first sergeant. He's working on personnel assignments as we reorganize. We'll be moving again shortly. It looks like the barrage bugged out the enemy."

"Yes, sir." Bukar walked toward the back of the convoy, his mind replaying what had just happened. Despite momentary feelings of elation and satisfaction from saving the wounded troopers, a sense of foreboding washed over Bukar as his adrenaline wore off. *I'm running out of time.*

He needed to reach New Oslo.

CHAPTER 19

"BRUISER 6, BLUE 1 IS AT CHECKPOINT TROPHY," Staff Sergeant Faora reported to Captain Hensley.

"Roger, Blue 1, continue the mission."

Task Force Marauder had advanced over twenty kilometers during the night and had met only slight resistance entering the broad valley New Oslo occupied. Bruiser Company had been tasked with clearing the section of highway leading to the southwestern part of the city. To their north, Anvil and Cyclone were clearing the network of roads forming the main westerly approach. The armored vehicles of Bruiser Company now approached the outskirts of the city on a four-lane divided highway, *Bounty Hunter II* in the lead. Surveillance feeds and radio reports from forward elements had not prepared Rutger for what he saw as they came over a ridge.

On the horizon, columns of black smoke from preparatory arty and air strikes rose from the city to mix with dark gray clouds looming overhead. Civilian vehicles and pedestrians fleeing the city packed all four lanes as well as the embankments of the raised highway. People rode on car hoods and in open trunks.

There was a sea of civilians on foot carrying children, bags, suitcases, and whatever worldly possessions they could tote.

A long column of Repub logistics vehicles smoldered in the distance, victims of artillery or Federation air power. Wrecked and abandoned civilian vehicles further choked the flow of traffic. Rutger noted that many of the vehicles were air cars, but after seeing several burnt wrecks along the way, he surmised that the drivers quickly realized any vehicles detected above the horizon were quickly targeted with air defense weapons.

Faora reported the situation without emotion to Captain Hensley, who ordered them to deploy into the sloping fields alongside the highway to bypass what they could. They moved at a slow but steady pace this way for a couple of kilometers until trees began to press in on the highway, forcing them back to the hardball. The refugees scattered at their approach and screamed when the massive tanks plowed and knocked aside dead vehicles in their way. Their tank-like ships cut through a sea of humanity as they advanced toward the city.

They reached the outskirts of New Oslo. Captain Hensley ordered first and second platoons, along with a scouting infantry fire team from fourth platoon on skimmers, to continue for two more kilometers while the grunts of third and fourth platoons swept some building chokepoints along the road, which had to be cleared to prevent surprise attacks from the rear.

Bounty Hunter II had led the advance for almost a kilometer when the first obstacle appeared.

"Bruiser 6, this is Black 2-1. Be advised that the road ahead is blocked," reported Sergeant Gromile, in charge of fourth platoon's recon element. "We'll continue to scout ahead, but you'll have to find an alternate route or call the engineers to clear, over."

"Copy, Black 2-1," Hensley said.

"Looks like a roadblock," Faora said over the intercom, watching the remote holo feed from the infantry. "Could be an ambush. Stay sharp."

Rutger zoomed in on the problem area as they advanced. Four hundred meters away, an assortment of burnt and abandoned vehicles stacked three or four high jammed an underpass, likely pushed into place with bulldozers by enemy engineers. On and offramps to either side had been destroyed with shearing charges, leaving nearly vertical escarpments of dirt and concrete. The grav tanks could likely surmount them in a high hover, but that would expose their thin belly armor and vulnerable repulsors. The Fed follow-on and support forces behind them, equipped with wheeled and air-cushioned vehicles, would be stranded behind them.

"Driver, hold here," Faora said.

The convoy of armored vehicles halted behind *Bounty Hunter II* as Faora requested the combat engineers to move up.

"Roger that, Blue 1," Captain Hensley replied. "We need to keep pace with the other task force elements, so make sure this doesn't take all morning."

"Copy, Bruiser 6."

Rutger tensed at the thought of being ambushed and scanned the surrounding area. Permacrete buildings two and three-stories tall lined the highway, set back twenty meters or so from the road. Past the overpass stood rows of squat gray apartment buildings overlooking the freeway.

The river of humanity continued to flow on both sides of the highway, the pedestrians able to squeeze around the roadblock. The fleeing kids made Rutger think of Callie. They looked tired and scared as they warily passed *Bounty Hunter II*. *I hope Callie never has to experience something like this.* New Helena had a fairly stable government despite scattered incidents of civil unrest. *Then again, so did Scandova.*

"Keep your eyes on those civies," Faora ordered. "There could be insurgents mixed in with them."

"Yes, Staff Sergeant." The civilians in close proximity had forced them to switch the automatic protection system from active to passive mode. It would still react to incoming missile threats but would not engage proximity targets that came within five meters of the tank, which made Rutger warier of the possible civilian threat.

Faora popped her hatch, and this time Rutger followed her lead despite the cold. From the north came the thunder of heavy weapons and the sharp lightning crack of plasma bolts. Anvil and Cyclone companies had apparently encountered some resistance. Close by, the occasional report of a plasma rifle to their rear confirmed enemy in the area. As Faora stood in the hatch and glassed the area with electrobinoculars, Rutger kept a wary eye on the civilians, zooming in with thermal imagery to detect weapons. He watched the tactical display too, where blue dots from the grunts of fourth platoon spread out on skimmers into an industrial complex overlooking the road.

The combat engineers' IFV drove by and approached the obstacle.

"The cavalry is here," said Sergeant Tran from the combat engineer squad over the proximity net.

"Fucking took you long enough," Faora replied.

"Ouch! Somebody woke up on the wrong side of the bed. Don't worry, Blue 1, we'll have you rolling again in no time."

Rutger watched the engineers and a large support bot dismount to examine the wall of vehicles. Civilians continued to skid down the destroyed ramp embankments or stream through the narrow gaps along both sides of the underpass.

Time dragged on, unnerving Rutger as he watched the engineers strategically place explosive charges. His thoughts drifted to the ambush that had occurred two days before. Positioned at the rear of the convoy that night, *Bounty Hunter II* hadn't seen any action. But he remembered driving past a tank from first platoon, *Gang Bang,* after the road had been cleared. A 188mm plasma bolt had punched through the front mantle to incinerate the crew, turning the gunner and commander into charred, shrunken statues. The driver had gotten out and dropped to the ground before the tank but was killed by a follow-up strike. The spray of molten metal and glowing ions had burned skin and muscles right off his blackened bones. Staring at the barbecued corpses, Rutger had thought, *Better them than me. Stay alive...and get home.*

"Contact front," reported Sergeant Tran, snapping plasma bolts accompanying the call.

Faora dropped into the turret as Rutger checked his displays. "Sniper, building right, 550 meters," Rutger said, already traversing the turret onto a fifth-story window. On thermal imaging, the sniper's body appeared white against a dark backdrop.

"Fire!" Faora commanded. "Search and assess."

Recoil from the main gun jerked the tank. The crimson bolt blasted the building's upper corner to dust and vaporized the sniper. Civilians outside screamed and ran, some stumbling and falling, dazed or blinded by the main gun's blast. More targets extrapolated by the AI populated Rutger's threat display, at least a half dozen personnel, likely snipers. Unfortunately, the targets were in buildings beyond the roadblock, and he didn't have a shot.

Ten minutes passed as the engineers and snipers exchanged fire on the far side of the roadblock.

"Green 2, this is Bruiser 6. What's the status on the roadblock?" Captain Hensley asked the engineers' commander over the company net. Receiving no answer, he queried several more times. Nothing.

"Bruiser 6, Blue 1," Faora called. "The engineers are still working on it, but they're taking sniper fire and we aren't in a position to support."

"Find out what the holdup is, Blue 1. We're behind schedule. Bruiser 6 out."

"Green 2, Blue 1, do you copy? Any Green 5 element?" Faora couldn't raise the engineers. She tried to pull up their helmet feeds, then looked over at Rutger. "Must be intense local jamming. I need a visual. Get out there and see what the hell's going on."

Rutger hesitated for a moment. "Yes, Staff Sergeant." He grabbed his submachine gun and stuck his head through the hatch. The crack of bolts seemed closer with his head above the turret. Muzzles flashed in the distance past the overpass, but he had no targets at this range. *Safe as it's likely to get...* He dropped to the hull deck and then slid off the tank.

Civilians continued to pour through the narrow gaps between the roadblock and the sides of the overpass, giving Rutger a wide berth as he ran into harm's way. He squeezed past the wall of wrecked vehicles and spotted two engineers hunched behind a concrete road divider about twenty meters to the right. Crouched behind a wrecked vehicle a few meters ahead of them, a third engineer sprayed bolts wildly down the road. Blue bolts pocked the pavement, showering the area with grit. Several dead civilians lay in contorted positions beside the road.

Rutger tried to reach the engineers on proximity net but got no response. *Fuck!* His testicles constricted and his stomach clenched as he prepared to sprint toward them. He took off, running hunched over toward the barrier through a storm of glowing bolts. He dived the last few meters and came up in a crouch behind the barrier.

"What the fuck is the hold up?" Rutger asked the closest engineer.

"We can't blow the obstacle!" the man blurted, eyes wide with fear.

"Why the hell not? What have you guys been doing?"

"We placed the charges, but we can't get to the detonator. Sergeant Tran has it." He nodded toward a trooper lying about twenty meters to the right behind a wrecked car beside the wall of vehicles. Tran sprawled in a vast pool of blood, smoke wafting from a hole in his armor. He clutched a green detonator box in his left hand.

"Don't you guys have a support bot?" Rutger asked.

The man nodded toward smoldering electronic wreckage on the ground nearby.

"Shit."

Rutger peered over the barrier and spotted several Repub soldiers firing from behind a burned-out truck about 100 meters away. His helmet's AI recorded their coordinates. A bolt snapped past his face as he ducked down, his visor polarizing to prevent him being blinded.

"Blue 1, use missiles to engage targets designated, how copy?" There was no response. Rutger turned back to the engineer, "What the fuck is up with all the comms?"

"We have a jamming field up to prevent anyone from detonating the explosives prematurely."

Rutger's mind raced, looking at how close the charges were. *Fuck it.* "Deactivate the jamming field. I need to talk to my commander."

"We can't do—"

"Just fucking do it already."

The engineer stared at him dumbly for a second but keyed his wrist computer, happy to have someone else take charge. Rutger tried comms again.

"We read you, Blue 1 Golf. Stand by."

A pair of missiles streaked over the overpass and exploded on target, evoking a few enemy screams. The fire slackened. Peering over the barrier, Rutger saw no enemy moving around the truck hulk, now burning again. Beyond the truck, several more Repub soldiers ran from a building into a group of fleeing civilians, using them for cover, while another half dozen approached from the opposite flank. *Damn it, it's like fucking whack-a-mole out here!.*

Rutger turned to the engineers. "We gotta get that detonator and pull back."

"I'm not fucking going out there," the nearest engineer said. The other said nothing and stared at him.

"It's your fucking job, asshole!"

"I don't give a fuck what you say. I'm not going out there."

Rutger turned to other one, who continued to stare at him wildly, unmoving.

"Fine, I'll go, you fuckin' pussies. Can you cover me at least?"

The two men nodded, then turned and began firing, each taking a separate flank. Rutger sprinted toward the detonator. Bolts whizzed by all around him as he slid behind the car. He carefully pried the detonator from the dead sergeant's grip, lest he detonate the charges in the roadblock right next to him.

Rutger took a couple of deep breaths to ready himself before sprinting back to the engineers. He dived in between them and the barrier and came to his knees, then peered over the barrier toward the enemy, sucking huge breaths of air after his harried run.

"Okay, we gotta run for it," Rutger said. He turned and saw nobody. To his left he spied them bolting for the gap in the overpass. *You fuckers!*

Rutger jumped up and sprinted toward the gap through bolts and flying pavement chunks, the short trip seeming to take an eternity. He made it through and sprinted for *Bounty Hunter II*, weaving through the throng of panicked civilians. Already in their IFV, the engineers took off for the rear. *Thanks for nothing, assholes!*

Chest heaving, he clambered aboard the tank and dropped into the turret. He flipped the power switch on the detonator and looked at the overpass on exterior view. Civilians still streamed around the barricade or slid down the steep embankments.

"Go ahead and press the button!" Faora said.

"But there are civilians!"

"So what? It's gonna be our asses if we don't get moving!" Blue bolts began streaking toward them from troops atop the overpass, kicking up sparks and pieces of slag as they pelted the tank's armor. "Blow it now. That's an order!"

A woman clutching a child in her arms had just emerged from the gap around the roadblock. *God forgive me.* He pressed the button, annihilating the mother and child and many more civilians in a tremendous explosion that rocked the tank and blasted metal and concrete a hundred meters into the air. Debris rained down on the tank and civilian mob, scattering them into a panicked stampede. A cloud of dust and smoked washed over the tank in a gritty tidal wave.

As the drape of smoke cleared, dead civilians could be seen scattered about the roadway, some of them crushed by falling debris. A bloody and haggard woman emerged from the haze and walked slowly past *Bounty Hunter II*, her face an unblinking mask of terror and shock.

Rutger felt like he was going to throw up.

CHAPTER 20

"BUILDING CLEARED," CORPORAL BUKAR AN-nounced on the platoon net, marking the multistory office building clear on HUD as well. His fire team—Sims, Dominguez, and Reyes—followed him back down the stairs, being careful to avoid the windows, not an easy task since entire sections of the building had glass walls, most of them blown out.

As they approached the lobby exit, bursts of plasma fire punctuated by booming grenades echoed down the street. Numerous corpses littered the streets, both civilian and combatants, and the putrefaction of death hung in the air despite the bitter cold.

"Sounds like second squad has their hands full," Reyes commented.

"Yeah," Bukar said. "We need to keep pace. We're a couple buildings behind."

Bruiser Company had been tasked with clearing New Oslo's financial district and one of the main roads leading to the Klarven River, which split the city, before nightfall. They'd been clearing buildings all day. First squad had the right side of the street, second squad the left, with third squad working on the next street over, where they linked with second platoon. To speed the process, each squad had been broken into fire teams by Lieutenant Palmer. The teams leapfrogged from building to building, clearing the way for the tanks and IFVs following in support. If Repub armor was detected, the tanks would be called in to take care of it.

Fortunately, most of the buildings were empty, and the tide of civilians they had encountered on the approach to the city had diminished to a faint trickle. Resistance hadn't been as stiff as expected. The work was fatiguing and repetitive, but Bukar didn't mind. *Every building is one step closer to Adeze.*

"Okay, move to the next building," Bukar said over the proximity net as he took point. They moved out, staying low and warily scanning the windows next to them and across the street.

Five Repub soldiers burst from a building ahead and sprinted toward the next intersection.

Bukar raised his rifle. "Halt or we'll shoot!" he shouted, voice booming through his helmet's electronic speaker. They had gotten several groups to surrender, a tactic that would hopefully encourage others to follow suit. It was a preferable outcome to slaughtering them all. Higher command and the grunts alike didn't want the enemy fighting to the last man like cornered rats.

They didn't stop. Bukar and Sims got a bead on them and fired as the lead man began to turn the corner. Bukar's first bolt took the leader in the neck, decapitating him in a spray of vaporized blood. The flurry of bolts sliced through their targets, concentrated beams of plasma burning through uniforms and armor, causing the bodily fluids inside to flash boil and explode. "Cease fire!" Bukar ordered. Several bodies still convulsed on the deck. What had been living and breathing people, men and women with hopes and futures, were reduced to quivering piles of meat by the squeeze of a trigger.

Bukar and his team approached the next building. The smell of shit from the troops they'd cut down wafted toward them.

Men usually voided their bowels in death, and Bukar still found the smell repulsive.

Second fire team entered the next building with Bukar in the lead and began a cautious sweep. If they found a locked door, they fired bolts through it and the adjacent walls before entering. Tossing a grenade into the room first was the best practice, but they hadn't nearly enough to do so at every room, so they saved them for when they might be most effective.

They quickly and methodically cleared the first three floors. Heading to the fourth floor, Bukar rounded the corner to the stairwell and froze upon spotting a grenade trip wire suspended across the stairway, a sure sign the enemy waited above. Bukar was relieved that he'd detected the telltale wire, which were hard to spot even with advanced helmet optics. They'd lost several troopers to the nasty booby traps.

Bukar motioned Reyes ahead while Sims and Dominguez covered the stairwell. Reyes clipped the trip wire, ensuring that he didn't let the taught wire snap. Bukar took the lead again and carefully ascended the concrete stairs. He found the fire escape door atop the flight propped open by a brick. He grabbed a grenade from his webbing, thumbed it on, and tossed it through the opening.

Boom! He sprinted into a spacious room full of cubicles. Glass-walled offices lined the left wall. Crouching low, he approached the first office. The smoked-glass window shattered above him, blasted by a hail of blue bolts that flew over his head. He dropped to his knee as Sims took the soldier out from the cover of the hallway.

A Repub soldier's helmet and rifle appeared at the next office door. Bukar stitched him with a short burst from his plasma rifle. Red mist hung in the air as the body slumped to the floor.

Bukar stayed hunched over as he and Sims advanced to check every office. Reyes and Dominguez searched the center cubicles.

Bukar paused at a rustling sound coming from behind an office door. He thumbed another grenade, kicked in the door, and tossed it into a large conference room before diving aside. The plasma grenade exploded with a tremendous boom and flash, shattering the glass wall and several glass partitions nearby. A half second after the blast, Bukar and Sims stood and strode forward with weapons shouldered to sweep the room.

Two Repub soldiers had died immediately, one writhing in agony on the floor. Two live soldiers kneeled behind an over-turned conference table raised rifles to fire.

Bukar and Sims sprayed the men with crimson fire. The sizzling bolts tore into wood, uniforms, body armor, and flesh. The heavy wooden table began to burn around fist-sized holes punched through it. Despite their helmets' filters, the smells of burnt flesh, wood, and plastics singed their nostrils.

He and Sims moved and stacked up by the next door, which stood ajar. Running low on grenades, Bukar held his rifle around the corner and sprayed the room. He knew it wasn't the most thorough way to ensure a room was cleared, but it had its uses. His empty magazine clattered on the tile floor, followed by the click of a fresh one slammed home. He crouched and peered around the corner to the second conference room and found it empty.

His visor HUD showed the locations of Dominquez and Reyes, blocked from view as they crouched behind the cubicles. They had almost cleared to the opposite corner of the room. Bukar crept toward the final office on his side.

A long burst of blue flashes ripped out in front of him, shattering glass and tearing out chunks of the opposite wall.

Bukar jumped back. "Watch yourselves, tango in the corner!" He knew he'd escaped death by a mere step and an itchy trigger finger.

"Copy that," Dominquez replied. "We'll draw their fire."

From his right, crimson bolts tore through the glass wall and wood-composite door. Bursts of blue bolts cracked from the room in response. Bukar peered around the wall through the broken glass and scanned the room over his sights. A Repub soldier crouched behind an overturned desk, reloading her weapon while another soldier raised his rifle to fire back blindly toward Dominquez and Reyes.

Her eyes went big as saucers when she saw Bukar. She fumbled with the magazine in a frantic attempt to reload her rifle. Bukar's rifle chattered, sweeping bolts over both soldiers. Their uniforms smoldered as they crumpled to the floor in two bloody heaps. The man moaned, his intestines spilling out beside him. Bukar strode forward and put a final burst across his back.

"Room cleared," Sims announced as he finished sweeping the remaining rows of cubicles. Reyes and Dominguez plopped on top of a pair of desks to rest their legs. Sims sat down in a rolling office chair, his armored bulk barely fitting between the armrests.

Bukar resisted the temptation to sit and took a pull of cold water from his condenser canteen. He marked the building clear on HUD, then checked his team over. They looked as tired and dirty as he felt, but he knew they couldn't rest for long without becoming lethargic. *Bodies at rest stay at rest.* "All right, let's move out."

"C'mon Preacher," Reyes said. "Can't we take five after that?"

"I'm tired as well, but we have to keep moving. Only six more blocks to the river. We can rest then."

The men didn't respond, but they understood he was just doing his job as an NCO, that it wasn't personal. Even so, they took their time getting up. The whole operation had been a skull drag to this point.

They filed from the building behind him and continued up the street. Second squad advanced along the opposite sidewalk. Two IFVs had come forward to support, now forty meters behind as they glided along, turrets scanning the area. *We'll clear one more, then go back for more ammo and—*

A slug cracked through the air. A second squad trooper fell clutching his shoulder, moaning in pain over the proximity net before it cut out.

Calls of, "Sniper!" flooded the net. "Jax is down. Medic!"

The sniper had fired a magnetic coil rifle; Bukar could tell by the sharper report. Though a plasma bolt did more damage, their flash and heat signature gave away a shooter's position, so many snipers used slug-throwing weapons when range wasn't a major factor.

Troopers sprayed fire at every open window and doorway, while another trooper ran to the downed man and dragged him through a shattered storefront window. Men in second squad tossed a couple of smoke grenades that exploded with dull bangs. Thick clouds of gray smoke began filling the street. A medbot moved toward the storefront, passing soldiers crouched behind light poles and abandoned vehicles.

"Bravo team, on me," Bukar said, waving his arm. "We're moving up." They tramped blindly behind him through thick, chemically infused smoke toward the next building.

"White 1 Bravo, this is Black 4. We have the intersection ahead blocked off. That sniper's not going anywhere."

On HUD, the blue square of a Scorpion IFV along with several troopers were moving to the next intersection on the parallel street, cutting off a rear exit route for the sniper.

"Copy that, Black 4," Bukar said. "Hold your fire. We're entering the building."

Bukar's team stacked up against the office building's front wall before entering through remnants of glass doors. Shattered glass and broken floor tiles crunched beneath their boots as they fanned out and swept the vast lobby, paying particular attention to dark corners and rows of decorative columns. Ornate grillwork dividing the waiting area smoldered from previous bolt strikes.

They moved past out of service elevators and found the emergency stairs. "Dominguez, Reyes, take level two. Sims and I will take level three."

"Copy."

Splitting up, they began clearing the building from the bottom up. As they entered the stairwell, another shot cracked from above, the sniper still at work. The thump and report of an automatic grenade launcher answered, the explosion echoing in the stairwell.

"White elements, this is White 1 Bravo," Bukar called on proximity net as they approached the third floor. "Check your fire, check your fire."

"Copy, White 1 Bravo. Sensors show him on fifth floor now, north side," said Corporal Ellis from second squad.

"Bravo team, Sims and I are headed to five," Bukar said. "Sweep four and then link up with us. Report if you find anything."

Sims and Bukar climbed to the fifth floor. The door opened on a left-right intersection. A holographic sign straight ahead read Bradford Law Services, with an arrow pointing right. "Take the right hallway in case he tries to double back," Bukar said. He could tell that Sims didn't like the idea of splitting up, but he nodded and started down the opposite hallway.

Bukar inched forward and listened carefully as he methodically checked open offices along the way, peering through windows and swinging open doors. Many of the rooms appeared untouched, as if their occupants had simply vanished. He heard movement ahead and froze, listening. His visor registered movement a nanosecond behind what his senses already knew—a threat to the right.

He turned and fired reflexively toward a Repub soldier taking aim from the end of the hallway. Firing a long burst at the man—just a blur in the corner of his eye—he felt a sharp blow against his chest plate, as if someone had struck him above the sternum with a hammer and metal punch. His bolts shattered the floor-length window at the end of the hall with a tremendous crash and carved chunks of plaster from the wall. The sniper, wearing an active-camouflage poncho, turned to run, but one of Bukar's bolts caught him and spun him around in a spray of blood. Pieces of burning plaster floated to the ground like fluttering yellow butterflies as Bukar moved down the hall.

Looking over his weapon's holographic sights, Bukar advanced toward the body sprawled at the corner of the hallway. The sniper's poncho had turned a two-tone brown to match the carpeting. Bukar peered around the corner, found the hallway clear, then stepped toward the sniper. A heavy-caliber coil rifle with a holographic sight lay next to him, clutched in fingers at the end of a severed arm. Bukar kicked the arm and rifle away.

Just a boy. No older than fifteen, Bukar guessed. He lay on his back staring up at the ceiling, gasping for breath, pink froth coming from his mouth. The bolt had largely cauterized the wound, stopping most of the bleeding. Bukar stared into the right half of his chest cavity where his shoulder and pectoral muscles used to be. Looking like melting icicles, white ribs lay exposed over his collapsed lung.

"Bravo 1, this Bravo 2," Sims said. "You okay?"

"Yeah, I got the sniper. My side is secure," Bukar replied.

"Copy, almost done clearing my side. I'll work my way toward you."

Bukar raised his visor and knelt beside the dying boy, gazing into his frightened, agonized brown eyes. The kid's facial muscles relaxed in response to Bukar's compassion. *Just like me so long ago, one of God's lost children.*

Bukar held the boy's dark hand. "Don't be afraid," he said softly. "You will be in God's embrace soon."

The boy nodded slightly as a gust of icy wind blew through the shattered window.

Sims approached from Bukar's right and reported the floor secure.

Bukar nodded. "Roger that. Give me a moment, Sims."

Bukar laid his gloved hand on the boy's forehead and recited the last rites: "Through this holy anointing, may the Lord in his love and mercy help you with the grace of the Holy Spirit."

The boy gasped and gagged, convulsing slightly before his eyes turned into vacant brown pools.

"May the Lord grant peace for the fallen."

He rubbed his gloved hand over the deep groove in his chest plate. The cross he had affixed there was gone, blown away upon deflecting the sniper's bullet. He would have to attach a new one, but the loss did not disturb him. *It wasn't my time.* He prayed silently for himself and the boy, feeling a warming energy deep in his soul. *I am merely an instrument of the Lord, doing His work.*

Bukar stood, slapped down his visor and marked the building secured on his map. "Bravo team, let's move out."

21

CHAPTER

"DRIVER, HALT HERE," STAFF SERGEANT FAORA OR-
dered Aubrey.

"Roger that."

The tank slowed to a halt. *Dog Breath* paused a block behind
them. It had been stop-and-go all morning as the column of
tanks and infantry advanced through the streets of New Oslo.
First and second platoons were spread across several blocks while
supporting the grunts clearing the buildings.

Towering concrete buildings in every direction made Rutger
feel claustrophobic. He couldn't possibly monitor every window
and doorway in the angular concrete jungle. He scanned outside
with his visor's 360-degree panoramic system, but buildings and
abandoned vehicles on either side of the four-lane street limited
his field of vision. The jerking motion of constant starts and stops
had begun to fray his nerves.

He checked the tactical display for the hundredth time. They
had cleared nearly a quarter of the city since daybreak, but it felt
like they'd made little progress. Calls for fire support had been
few and far between. Rutger could do nothing but stare at the
exterior feeds and fight the urge to close his eyes. *They're out there,*

stay sharp. He'd seen medbots carrying several wounded troopers on stretchers, along with small groups of Repub prisoners being escorted to the rear.

"Okay, we're moving again," said Faora.

Aubrey eased *Bounty Hunter II* forward. Rutger traversed the turret back and forth, searching the windows. He checked the side streets as they entered an intersection. No movement to the right. To his left, tanks and troops from Anvil Company advanced a couple of blocks to the north, having linked up with Bruiser earlier that morning.

Ahead, infantry troopers from third platoon advanced in fire teams, sticking close to walls and abandoned vehicles for cover. They started disappearing into buildings to clear them.

Still looking ahead, Rutger increased magnification to 16X. A few blocks down, a man and a woman pushed a cart full of baggage down the sidewalk. They had encountered a handful of civilians while clearing this area, but most had departed. Those unwilling to take their chances as refugees sheltered in place and stayed off the streets.

Rutger kept watching the couple, more out of boredom than anything else. Increasing magnification to 32X, he could see the woman's wrinkled face, the gray stubble on the man's chin. They marched on with lowered heads but occasionally directed tense gazes toward the troopers and *Bounty Hunter II.* He watched them approach another thirty meters, then momentarily lost sight of them behind a light pole. He zoomed out slightly and caught them again as they stopped, partially obscured by a wrecked vehicle.

Behind the car, they appeared to be grabbing something from the cart. Rutger glimpsed the man shouldering an olive drab quad-tube missile launcher. *Oh shit!*

No time to warn the troopers advancing two blocks down. He then spied the woman on the other side of the car sighting in on *Bounty Hunter II* with a second launcher.

Presented with two targets, Rutger split the difference. He put the main gun's pipper on the vehicle and squeezed the trigger. A shaft of ionized cobalt struck the car and blasted it into fragments of glowing metal. The couple disappeared in a withering flash of white, but not before the man had fired one rocket at *Bounty Hunter II*.

With infantry in close proximity, Faora had set the automatic protection system to passive mode; it would only activate when presented with a direct threat to the vehicle. The automatic defense weapon swerved toward the incoming missile and engaged it with a burst of crimson bolts, detonating it in an orange flash as it passed through the next intersection. The concussive report reverberated through the fighting compartment.

"Report!" demanded Faora.

Though his reflexes and instincts had just saved them, Rutger froze under her query. "There was a civilian couple armed with missile launchers..." He paused and stared at the wreckage on screen. "I took them out."

"Okay," Faora replied. "Are you sure?"

"Yeah, I'm sure."

Faora keyed the command net. "Bruiser elements, this Bruiser 1 actual. Be advised, enemy forces reported to be dressed as civilians." She repeated the warning and then looked at Rutger. "Good work."

Yeah, thanks. He ruminated on all the *good work* he'd done with the Berserkers, and how he never felt good about it.

Lead elements of Task Force Marauder had reached the river and now closed on their final objective, a highway tunnel beneath the river that led to the city's other half. They'd started to encounter withdrawing Repub forces as they tightened the noose.

"Bruiser 2-1, this is Anvil 1-2. Enemy vehicle heading your way," said an Anvil Company tank commander over the battalion net.

Nicole's tank. On tactical display, Rutger saw Anvil 1-2, *Apocalypse*, three blocks to their north and a block further west, closer to the river.

The reported Repub vehicle shown as a red square traveled south on a perpendicular course to *Bounty Hunter II*. They would cross paths at the next intersection. The AI identified it as a six-wheeled lightly armored command vehicle. Flushed from hiding, it was traveling at over 80kph to escape the advancing net of Berserker vehicles. *Not happening.*

Rutger had the turret aligned already. "Stand by, Rutger," Faora said. "He's gonna fly through that intersection."

"Like hell." It raced into his sights a moment later, the gray and green camouflaged vehicle filling his screen. Rutger mashed the trigger for the dual 30mm autocannons, stitching the armored vehicle with fiery red bolts as it crossed in front of them. A dozen hits punched fist-sized holes into the vehicle's flank, igniting the fuel cells. Now a rolling inferno, the vehicle continued on inertia and plowed into the corner of a building. Thick black smoke from its burning tires blew into the intersection, obscuring vision.

The tactical display suddenly came alive as half a dozen enemy vehicles powered up and began moving several blocks ahead. The AI showed them as hollow symbols, indicating the computer had to extrapolate what the vehicles were from limited data due to the jamming and interference of the buildings. What the computer did show Rutger didn't like. One enemy hover tank and at least two armored combat drones were among the bogies. Seeing the mass of enemy firepower put Rutger on edge.

As always, Faora maintained her unflappable cool. "Driver, take a right up here. Get your game faces back on, guys. We're going tank hunting."

Rutger zoomed the gunnery screen out. Two red armor icons were traveling north along the avenue bordering the river, likely bound for the tunnel. A combat drone sat near an intersection two streets over covering their retreat.

"Bruiser 2-1, this is Anvil 1-2. We're taking a blocking position to your north if you want to have your elements sweep up from the south and flush them out."

"Copy 1-2, we're already on the move," Faora replied. She traced a path along the holographic map with her finger, showing Aubrey their route and giving Rutger a better idea of where to expect the enemy. "Break, Blue elements, continue to sweep east toward the river at best possible speed to close the door on these guys. Blue 1 will sweep north. Watch our six."

Blue 2 and Blue 3 acknowledged and maintained their easterly course.

Bounty Hunter II glided two blocks south before turning east. The covering combat drone sat in an intersection three blocks ahead. The AI pegged it as an ADV-71, a 50-ton armored autonomous combat vehicle armed with a pair of 100mm particle cannons. A rotating schematic of the vehicle appeared on an adjacent screen. It turned and moved toward *Bounty Hunter II* upon identifying the threat.

"Be ready for the shot, Rutger," Faora said.

What shot? He didn't have one yet. Too many wrecked vehicles were in the way. *We'll be damn near point-blank before I can target this thing.*

Rutger rotated the turret in the drone's general direction and kept his finger poised on the main gun's trigger.

"Driver, put us a few inches off the deck," Faora said. "Accelerate toward that pair of vehicles blocking the intersection."

"You want me to do *what?*" Aubrey asked.

"I want you to ram those vehicles. Now fucking do it!" Faora snarled.

What the fuck is she doing?

Bounty Hunter II accelerated rapidly.

Rutger ignored the other enemy vehicles on the tactical display, watching in rapt fascination as the drone approached the oncoming intersection. He tore his gaze from the exterior camera feed and focused on the sight picture as *Bounty Hunter II* flew down the street at 70kph, bearing down on the wrecked vehicles. He instinctively braced for impact.

The tank swerved slightly just before the jarring impact, its 120-ton mass acting as a colossal cue ball that sent the two downed air cars flying into the intersection ahead of them.

"Ground us! Now!" Faora yelled.

The air cars exploded in sun-bright flashes, hammered by the drone's particle cannons as they careened into the intersection.

Bounty Hunter II slammed down on the pavement and slid into the intersection in a shower of sparks. Pieces of the burning air cars rained down around them.

The drone burst into Rutger's sights. The bores of the twin particle cannons on its armored hull still glowed white. He squeezed the trigger before they could cycle for another burst. The drone disappeared in a flash of crimson. Its hull glowed white for a split second before it exploded in an angry fireball that sent its turret cartwheeling down the street.

Faora shouted, "Driver, gets us mov—"

Two 188mm bolts cut down the street from the left. The first flew high, fired before the gunner had proper sight picture, but the second only missed *Bounty Hunter II* by a meter.

"Targets left," Faora cried as Rutger swerved the turret to face them. The Repub tank had already slid from view through an intersection, but its trailing drone stopped and took up a firing position.

Without being ordered, Aubrey banked hard left and slammed into a pair of parked vehicles across the street. The crunching impact threw Rutger's aim off as he squeezed the trigger. The main gun bolt flew harmlessly past the drone and exploded on a distant building across the river front.

The drone fired in the same instant. Exterior holos blackened to save his retinas as the shockwave hit the tank like a hammer, raising a shower of sparks in the fighting compartment. The dual particle beams instantly vaporized centimeters of armor from *Bounty Hunter II's* right weapons pod.

Warning lights lit the console. A damage assessment schematic on the center multifunction display showed the right particle cannon disabled. Rutger ignored the warnings and swung the turret a couple of mils, centering it on the drone and fired. His first bolt penetrated the drone's thick glacis plate, the second rupturing its fusion bottle. It disappeared in an expanding white shockwave that left behind only a glowing husk and a raining storm of debris.

"Status report!" Faora yelled over the sound of drone pieces clanking on the hull.

"Driver up!"

"Gunner up, right particle cannon disabled."

"Driver, move us to the end of the block." Faora ordered.

"Copy that," Aubrey replied, accelerating toward the intersection.

Here we go again. Rutger rotated the turret all the way left, the barrel barely clearing light poles lining the sidewalk.

On tactical display, the Repub tank was turning east to escape. They would collar it at the next intersection.

Just before *Bounty Hunter II* entered the intersection, blue lightning flashed to their left and the bottom corner of a building exploded into permacrete chunks. Aubrey swerved around the rubble and turned the corner.

Rutger fired the main gun as *Bounty Hunter II* straightened out, cursing himself when the bolt shot high to the right and struck a building. Failing to destroy *Bounty Hunter II* when it turned the corner, the enemy tank now retreated, though its main gun still pointed at them. Rutger jerked the joystick down and left and put the glowing orange pipper on the massive gray and green tank. Before he could fire, the tank's stern exploded in a flaming fountain, and sparks flew as it ground to a screeching halt.

"We couldn't let you guys have all the fun," said *Apocalypse's* commander. *Apocalypse* was two blocks away and starting to move down the street.

"Copy that, Anvil 1-2," Faora said. "We owe you a beer."

The destroyed tank's 188mm gun still pointed ominously at them. Rutger put a follow-up bolt into the hull for good measure, the red-white flash temporarily darkening the vision feeds. Flames and black smoke poured from the hatches when the feed returned. *Nobody survives that.*

A threat warning sounded and flashed red on the screen. A Repub tank, powered down and hidden under rubble a block back, emerged to take *Apocalypse* from the rear, immediately firing a blue main gun bolt that carved into thin rear armor to destroy the aft power coupling. *Apocalypse* lost gravitational lift and dropped to the pavement as flames erupted from the rear access hatches.

Rutger caught a glimpse of the enemy tank as it slid from the rubble. *Son of a bitch!* It had a white and orange symbol painted on the frontal armor. He knew he'd seen the tank before, but he couldn't identify the symbol with *Apocalypse* partially obscuring his view.

"Target direct front," Faora said. Rutger panned the turret over but couldn't get a clear shot due to *Apocalypse* blocking the way.

Smoke rose from the turret and driver's hatches of *Apocalypse*. Twin *booms* erupted nanoseconds apart as the commander and gunner ejected, rocketing off to who knew where.

Unfortunately, the main gun barrel blocked the driver's hatch, preventing Nicole from ejecting. She emerged from the forward hatch dazed and coughing, and she started to scramble out when the Repub tank fired again.

Rutger watched in horror as *Apocalypse* exploded in a blue flash, consuming Nicole in an expanding orange bubble of gaseous metal. Her black silhouette danced against the devouring energy for an instant before she dissolved. The sphere then collapsed on itself, leaving behind a blackened turret lying askew on the sundered hull. Flames roared from the open hatches.

The shockwave from the close explosion shoved *Bounty Hunter II* sideways and backwards toward the adjacent building. Aubrey shouted over the intercom as the tank careened into the building, its left stern plunging deep into the wall, which crumbled beneath the tank's massive inertia as if struck by a wrecking ball. An avalanche of bricks and concrete crashed down on the tank and spilled into the street beyond. Rubble blocked the external camera feeds. Rows of emergency lighting on the ceiling activated, casting the crew in an eerie bluish hue.

Rutger's mind teetered on the verge of madness. Once again the fighting had become personal, yet another friend lost. He wanted to die himself, just so he could escape the grisly deaths and gruesome injuries that never ended. Only then would the tormented shrieks in his mind finally be silenced.

"Get us the fuck outta here, Aubrey!" Faora shouted over the intercom, snapping Rutger from his grim reverie.

The hull vibrated deeply as Aubrey redlined the repulsors and rocked the tank violently back and forth to escape the rubble. The massive amounts of waste heat generated by the repulsors couldn't be bled off; the intakes and exhausts for the heat sinks were blocked by rubble, along with those for the environmental control system. The fighting compartment—already hot and stale before the collision—resembled a convection oven within moments.

Rutger sat in shock for a moment, feeling like a lance had been shoved through his heart. The moment of stunned failure passed as he saw the Repub tank's red icon retreating east toward the tunnel. *Hell no!* A flash of rage popped in Rutger's brain like a blown circuit, and he jerked the turret control joystick violently to the right. The powerful turret drive motor whined in protest before finally moving the turret a few degrees clockwise. He then twisted the joystick hard to the left, repeating the process three more times, the turret traversing a few more degrees on each attempt. Rubble began to slide off the hull.

Aubrey gunned the repulsors one more time. *Bounty Hunter II* lurched free of the rubble like a lion uncaged. The outside world became visible again as static field emitters on the external optics cleansed most of the gray dust and grit from the lenses.

"Driver, hold here."

Hold? Rutger watched the Repub tank's red icon inch further toward the tunnel on tactical display; it turned orange as *Bounty Hunter II's* sensors started to lose track of the tank due to jamming. Rutger clenched his fists until his hands trembled. He looked to Faora, who remained businesslike while checking her displays. "What the hell are we waiting for?" Rutger asked.

"Our orders are to secure this intersection," she replied evenly.

"You're gonna let them get away with that? We can still get the bastard!"

She stared him down, both for questioning orders and his tone of voice. "Okay," she said curtly. "Driver, move us forward for a firing position on the tunnel mouth."

Aubrey eased *Bounty Hunter II* forward. Rutger slewed the turret right ninety degrees as they approached the next intersection. The righthand road sloped gradually downward for about eighty meters to the tunnel's gaping mouth. The targeting computer automatically switched thermal view when Rutger zoomed in on the dark tunnel. Abandoned vehicles choking the passage showed as gray silhouettes on screen. According to the map, the tunnel was about two hundred meters long.

"No target," Rutger said. The tank had also disappeared from tactical display.

"Driver, ease us forward slowly," Faora ordered.

Aubrey pivoted the tank and maneuvered down the center of the four-lane road, slaloming around several more burnt-out vehicles. Soon they approached the tunnel mouth.

There! Rutger spotted the tank's faint white heat signature accelerating away from them, partially obscured by vehicles. It had its turret trained to the rear, still searching for potential targets. Rutger tracked it with the targeting reticle, catching only slivers of view as it weaved around vehicles. *Come on, come on!* He waited for a clear shot between vehicles, or perhaps a better sight picture as it exited the tunnel, knowing he would get only one chance.

The tank had almost reached the exit. Rutger waited for his shot, finger poised over the trigger.

A chain of orange explosions flashed around the tunnel mouth, the concussions rocking *Bounty Hunter II* as Rutger pressed the trigger. The crimson bolt didn't get far, discharging against a mountain of falling debris that crashed down from the remote-detonated charges. Water began to cascade in from the river above. The tunnel filled rapidly, the waters rising and rushing toward *Bounty Hunter II*.

"Back us up, Aubrey," Faora said.

Rutger sat transfixed in stunned silence, staring at the center holo gunnery screen. His hand still clenched the joystick. He finally released the trigger. "Damn it!" He punched the gunnery console. The gunnery screen flickered momentarily before returning to a sharp three-dimensional image.

"Shake it off, Rutger," Faora said, sounding soothing for a change. "There's still plenty of fighting left."

CHAPTER 22

ON THE HOLO SCREENS, RUTGER WATCHED
Scandova's dim red sun sink below brooding purple clouds hanging low over the horizon. Two of the planet's small blue moons became visible as the curtain of night descended. *I might never see another sunset.*

A frigid breeze began to pick up, moaning wistfully through the open hatch overhead and swaying the towering firs surrounding the tank. *Bounty Hunter II* sat grounded on a rise, parked toward the front of the column. Behind Rutger, platoons of grounded tanks and armored support vehicles stretched down the four-lane road that bisected the forest, safe from direct observation and line-of-sight weapons. Logistics support vehicles and crews worked their way down the column, quietly and efficiently making last-minute repairs and topping the tanks off with ammo and fuel.

"You really think we're gonna attack?" Aubrey asked over the intercom. "One of the fuel truck jockeys said the Repubs are trying to negotiate another cease-fire. That's the rumor, anyway."

"Oh, we're gonna attack," Rutger said. "You think we got topped off with fuel and ammo just for show?"

"Well, we gotta be prepared, of course. But why are you so sure?"

"Because it's just my luck," Rutger muttered.

"I don't understand why they don't just give up. The entire city is surrounded. It seems like such a waste for them to fight on."

"Yeah, I don't get it either. But ours is not to wonder why; ours is just to do or die."

Rutger's last comment ended the conversation. He checked the tactical display again for an update as he waited for Staff Sergeant Faora to return from the battalion mission briefing. That she'd been ordered to attend in person made him even more nervous.

Rutger checked an external feed from a sensor pickup placed several hundred meters up the rise. Silhouetted against a backdrop of glowing stars, buildings at the spaceport appeared dark and deserted. He zoomed to 40X magnification with light-enhanced view and still saw nothing. Nevertheless, he knew the enemy awaited.

Circular in shape, New Oslo's sprawling spaceport covered nearly 3,400 hectares. Designed for around-the-clock operations, it would normally have been visible to the naked eye from tens of kilometers away, but it was blacked out and silent at present. Rutger could see a decent swath of the landing field, which currently held seven large freighters varying in size from 20,000 to 150,000 metric tons displacement. Warehouses, hangars, and other support buildings bordered the massive concrete landing pads. On the south side, a large mag-train railyard connected to the port through a network of above-ground railheads and underground tunnels. Rutger figured most of the Repub forces guarding the port were sheltering in the tunnels at present.

Faora hadn't been lying when she promised more fighting ahead. The Berserker-led task force had turned over mop-up operations in the liberated section of New Oslo to follow-on Fed forces less than two standard days before. Upon being relieved, Task Force Marauder had received orders to assemble on the northeast edge of the city to prepare for an armored assault on the spaceport. Additional Fed troops had encircled Repub forces still holding the eastern sector of New Oslo, but Rutger had no idea how that operation was going. *Probably dragging their feet and hoping for a surrender after we clear this spaceport.*

New Oslo's spaceport had been strategically bypassed in the initial assault to take the western half of the town. That accomplished, their orders were to clear the spaceport with as little collateral damage as possible. A successful assault would cut off the Republic's routes of resupply and escape, effectively ending the war, which was all Rutger wanted. He'd flatten the place singlehandedly for a cease-fire and a trip home.

Looking over the vast snow-covered fields, Rutger knew it was easier said than done. They would approach the spaceport over nine kilometers of pancake-flat ground, then assault through the rows of pillbox like buildings and warehouses that made up the terminal facilities. The distance seemed an infinite expanse to Rutger. *Nine klicks…it might as well be ninety light years.*

The idea of going home and seeing Callie—and his soon to be ex-wife, he supposed—seemed illusory. It felt like an eternity since he'd seen his daughter, so long that he had a hard time picturing her. *Will she even recognize me?*

Fatigue clouded his thoughts. He and Aubrey hadn't gotten much rest in the past 24 hours. Faora had made them re-boresight the main gun, clean debris from the intakes and vents, and conduct field maintenance on two repulsors upon arriving at their new position that afternoon. Unfortunately, they hadn't found a replacement for the disabled starboard particle cannon.

He fished out a stim capsule he'd gotten at FOB Vulture and pressed it against his wrist, injecting the cool liquid into his veins. It was the second he'd taken in little over an hour. He usually avoided such stimulants, tending to stick with caffeine, but right now he needed more powerful medicine to take the edge off his ragged nerves. The stim provided a moment of euphoria and a jolt of energy that quickly dissipated, doing little to eliminate his fatigue or quell his anxiety, but no drug could have done so under such ominous circumstances.

The rumble of fighter aircraft roared through the open hatch. Rutger watched their icons drift quickly across the radar screen, several squadrons of Fed JAF-42 Griffons and Berserker AF-23s flying final sorties on targets within the spaceport. He zoomed out and panned above, watching on external holos as they dropped ordnance or made spiraling strafing runs, particle cannons lashing out like lightning bolts until the birds pulled up at the last instant from their plunging dives. A few blue streams targeted them from the ground in token resistance. The enemy probably had more air defenses available, but they didn't want to reveal all of their A-A positions. Reports from the explosions sounded several seconds later, carrying over the field like distant thunderclaps.

A dazzling blue stream took out a fighter in an orange flash. Glowing tendrils of debris fluttered or plunged to the ground, but Rutger saw no sign of the pilot ejecting. The tactical display revealed it had been a Fed Griffon. *Hope he took out some targets before he splashed.*

It wasn't the first light show of the evening. A couple hours prior, Berserker artillery rockets had plastered the surrounding fields with submunitions, laying down long swaths of bomblets to clear antitank mines or troops that might be hiding in the flat expanse. Free of mines and resistance, tanks, IFVs and skimmers could attack at combat speed, limiting their exposure while crossing the field. Similar preparations had been made for Fed forces attacking from the north, but the tactic was far from foolproof, and the strikes also revealed potential avenues of attack to the enemy.

Intelligence estimates showed at least a regiment of Repub forces occupying the spaceport and surrounding terminal facilities. In their sector alone, Bruiser Company would face a battalion of about forty tanks and fighting vehicles along with supporting infantry. The initial warning order stated Berserker forces would form the main axis of attack, punching through the port terminal buildings from the west and advancing to the landing pads and rail terminal. Two supporting Federal divisions would launch coordinated attacks from the northeast and northwest to pin down or tie up large numbers of defenders in a pincer attack.

Rutger found the waiting as difficult as the preparation. Despite the growing chill in the tank, he kept the hatch open. After feeling like he'd been buried alive in rubble, and remembering the heat and fumes he'd endured, he now understood why Faora usually kept the hatch open. The tank felt like a metal tomb just as much as a fortress at times.

"Here she comes," Aubrey announced over the intercom.

Rutger watched Faora approach on the rear camera feed, several other commanders walking behind her. Her upright bearing was unmistakable, and Rutger noticed for the first time that she walked with a slight limp.

She quickly mounted the tank and slid inside, her expression and bearing revealing nothing.

"How did it go?" Rutger asked.

Faora stared off vacantly for a second. "How do you think?" she snapped, strapping herself in.

Her response didn't faze Rutger, who'd grown used to her icy demeanor. "Will we have eyes on target when we go in?"

"They're deploying several waves of surveillance drones for this mission," Faora said, adjusting her tactical display. "They'll be staggered, so we should have some eyes from above for a little while."

Rutger knew that anything flying above the spaceport would have a short life expectancy, perhaps a couple of minutes at best.

A data alert icon appeared on the tactical display. "Prepare to receive orders," Faora said. The data dump from battalion began. A map of the spaceport appeared on holo display, overlaid with target information, phase lines, and axes of advance. The operations order appeared on his righthand display.

Rutger scrolled through the information. The orders designated the eastern half of the port as the primary battalion objective, further divided into two sectors. Bruiser Company would take the southern half of the terminal buildings and railyard and Anvil would hit the northern sector and the landing pads. The download dissected the main objectives into individual assignments, and identified threats and targets. Rutger felt his body growing numb as he scrolled over clusters of enemy unit icons, red for known and orange for suspected, populating Bruiser's half of the objective. He checked the time: 1842. The attack would kick off in eighteen minutes. Fear began to mount in his mind like a turbine spooling up. His guts tightened and gurgled, starting to ache.

An incoming transmission alert appeared on the comm display. General John Breacher, CEO and Commander of the Berserker Corporation, appeared on the center holographic screen, staring down Rutger with diamond-hard gray eyes.

Holy shit! The old man himself.

"Troopers, I'm going to keep this short because I know you have a lot of last-minute planning and coordination to do, but I wanted to speak with you all briefly. We are on the final push of this long and bloody campaign. I know it hasn't been easy, and neither is the task before you. But if it were easy, the Scandovan Federation wouldn't have hired us. You have been chosen because you are the best—period—and I have full faith and confidence that you will accomplish this mission. I normally don't discuss financial incentives with troops in the field, but if we can secure this port in one piece, all hands will receive an extra victory dividend at the conclusion of hostilities."

Aubrey let out a hoot over the intercom.

"Listen up!" yelled Faora, silencing him.

"I wish each of you the best of luck. Godspeed, and give 'em hell out there. Breacher out." The holograph winked out.

Breacher's voice and image had been as clear as if he'd been sitting in the tank, but Rutger wondered if he was even on planet. Perhaps he'd broadcasted from the orbiting cruiser *Harbinger*. Scandova was considered a major operation—the Berserkers had committed an entire regiment—but the corps-sized fighting force had units of various sizes deployed all over the known galaxy, though most contracts called for battalion-sized elements or smaller.

Rutger knew the speech was supposed to be motivational, but it had an opposite effect on him. *We're in the meat grinder. God only knows where he is.* Breacher had a fearsome reputation as a warrior, known for leading from the front and being a soldier's soldier. Rutger didn't doubt the old man had paid his dues and seen some shit, but his neck wasn't on the chopping block tonight. *You should be down here leading us.*

"Fire her up, Aubrey," Faora said.

Bounty Hunter II's fusion reactor spun to life, followed by the throbbing hum of repulsors as the tank rose a dozen centimeters off the deck. Up and down the line, Patton tanks and Scorpion fighting vehicles followed suit, adding to the mechanical chorus of vehicles.

"Bruiser, this is Bruiser 6," Captain Hensley said over the company net. "Red and Blue elements will attack on axes indicated. White and Black will follow in trace with skimmers and

IFVs. Anvil company will be to our left. Cyclone will provide initial overwatch and then follow in trace as a mobile reserve. Be aware that heavy electronic jamming is being reported around the target area, so keep your visual scans up. Everyone set?"

Staff Sergeant keyed her affirmative along with the other commanders.

"All right, let's move out!"

Leading the column, tanks of first platoon began to ease forward toward the clearing. Following tanks moved out every few seconds to maintain proper spacing between vehicles. *Bounty Hunter II* began to glide forward, slowly at first but picking up speed as they turned and entered the field, snow whipping and eddying around them.

Rutger received notification on his tactical display of a battalion artillery strike commencing. Over seventy kilometers away, a Berserker battery of Taranis multiple-launch rocket systems loosed a thunderous barrage of stealth cruise missiles. Each tracked launcher carried twelve of the precision guided missiles that screamed toward the horizon.

"Accelerate to twenty-five klicks per hour until we form line abreast," Hensley said. "When all three companies are in position, accelerate to 120 kilometers per hour on my order. Watch your spacing. When we reach Phase line Susan, White and Black elements on skimmers will push ahead to assault the first set of objectives. We expect only moderate initial resistance initially. The enemy is concentrated at the center of the port. Any questions? Over." Hensley paused for a moment, no questions. "Okay, people, let's make it happen. Six out."

Bounty Hunter II accelerated down the slight rise and pulled into position about two hundred meters to the left of Hensley's tank, *Bad Medicine*. Hensley and the XO would lead the attack from the center. *Bounty Hunter II* would be the second vehicle from the far-left flank, with Blue 2 and Blue 3 to either side. Anvil company would tie in beside second platoon.

The two tank platoons spread line abreast, skimming over the ground like white ghosts. As they took their place in formation, Rutger saw Anvil Company's tanks accelerating in echelon to catch up to them, leaving contrails of snow in their wake. He wished *Apocalypse* were one of them.

The terminal buildings loomed uncomfortably like dark gray specs on the horizon. As Rutger watched them grow closer, his thoughts wandered and moments from his life swiftly passed before him: growing up with his mom and sister in the slums of Port City, meeting Serena, Callie's birth, graduating from Berserker boot camp, huddled masses of civilians, torn bodies along the roads, Staff Sergeant Duran's gruesome death, learning of his divorce, sleeping with Nicole…then watching her burn in a cauldron of flames. He tried to reconcile her death and the other countless lives lost in this godforsaken war. *Nothing…they all died for nothing.*

The Berserker missile barrage shrieking overhead jerked him back to the present. The missiles streaked east toward the terminal, skimming the ground and popping up at the last moment to deploy their deadly payloads. Each three-meter-long missile carried twelve smart submunitions that looked like black raptors with their wings deployed, which would home in on designated or self-identified targets and fire a depleted uranium, self-forging warhead from close range. Every tenth missile carried hundreds of decoys to saturate the air with objects to confuse enemy air defenses.

"Okay, boys," Captain Hensley said, "accelerate to attack speed."

The tank lurched forward and accelerated to 120 kph. Tactical display began to receive feeds from the reconnaissance drones, which Rutger could view in infrared, lowlight, and sensor-detection patterns. He could also see the targets and threats fed into the tactical display in standard symbol overlays. The AI processed the data in real time, acting as in-person intelligence analyst for the crew.

Ahead, the concrete canyons of buildings and streets began to emerge in greater clarity. They'd advanced far enough to identify windows and antennas on the buildings with minimal magnification. Several structures were already ablaze, along with several Repub vehicles destroyed by air strikes or earlier precision artillery missions.

How intact does this place need to be to get our dividend?

The fleeting thought vanished when Rutger spotted nearly a dozen Repub blower tanks emerging from an underground railhead on a recon drone feed. They turned west and fanned out toward the terminal buildings in Bruiser's sector.

Repub infantry poured from doorways of hardened buildings to occupy pre-dug fighting positions. They had known the Berserkers and Feds would want to seize the port intact, so they had cached their vehicles and personnel in the buildings and tunnels. The feed suddenly cut to static when an air-defense plasma bolt struck the drone.

Loitering overhead in a winking, writhing constellation, submunitions deployed by the cruise missiles began diving like hawks on Repub armor and infantry, their warheads exploding in strobing orange flashes. Rutger sneered sardonically as they pounded the enemy grunts in their holes. *Not quite as safe as you thought you were...*

"Target!" Faora said. The AI identified a team of Repub infantry manning shoulder-fired antitank missile launchers.

Rutger saw the careted point on screen some eight kilometers distant. He laid the main gun pipper on the red highlighted target box and zoomed in, trying not to fight the gyrostabilized weapon as the tank glided over the undulating terrain. The grunts appeared light gray against a darker gray landscape in the combination low-light and thermal-enhanced vision. The computer automatically added pastels of color to improve sharpness.

Upper torsos protruded from the trench, the troops beginning to shoulder their weapons and sight in on Berserker vehicles. Behind his visor, Rutgers's face showed no emotion, just focused concentration as he squeezed the trigger. The main gun flashed, dimming his displays. A glowing red shaft of pure plasma bolt struck and vaporized four soldiers in an expanding white ball of ionized fury, leaving behind a steaming crater five meters wide.

Up and down the line, Bruiser and Anvil tanks turned the night a hellish red as they hammered distant targets with their main guns. Aubrey kept *Bounty Hunter II* on the course Faora had outlined for him, making only minor corrections to maintain proper spacing. Rutger almost envied Aubrey, who only had to concentrate on driving. But lacking awareness of the larger picture, the unfolding battle, was both a blessing and a curse. Now a veteran gunner, Rutger didn't think he could ever return to driving. *Ignorance isn't always bliss.*

Rotary air-defense weapons on Repub vehicles emerging from hiding unleashed angry streaks of blue bolts at the smart munitions, plucking many from the sky. Some of the smart munitions found their mark, however, as evidenced by white flashes on the horizon and fountains of sparks and flames erupting from secondary explosions.

Bruiser and Anvil tanks maintained fifty-meter intervals, looking like a wave of white-clad knights charging across the snowy field. Behind them came the infantry spread out on skimmers, bobbing over the terrain while trying to avoid clouds of snow in the tanks' wake. The IFVs brought up the rear, carrying additional ammo and any troopers that didn't have skimmers.

Rutger felt for the grunts. They only had a lightly armored cowling to protect them, versus tens of centimeters of thick plasteel and composite armor of the tanks. He knew that the tanks were bolt magnets though and each of them would have their own battles to fight tonight.

Under heavy suppressive fire, several companies of Repub infantry had deployed in front of dozens of buildings. They unleashed scores of guided missiles at the Berserker tanks. The alert warning chimed persistently in Rutger's earpiece, and he double checked to ensure Faora had set the automatic defense weapon to air defense mode.

Rutger watched a wave of orange blips representing missiles on the threat detection screen streak toward *Bounty Hunter II* and the other tanks. The AI prioritized the threats, and the overhead cannon engaged, firing tight, controlled bursts at the incoming projectiles. A nearby tank's automatic protection system engaged with a loud flash and bang at a missile that had gotten through the web of annihilation.

The enemy had launched over seventy missiles in under a minute. It was a numbers game; Rutger knew some would get through. And then it happened. An Anvil tank far to his left sparked in a flash of orange flames as a missile struck just beneath the turret. It grounded hard in a billowing cloud of snow and frozen dirt, then spun away out of sight. Troopers on skimmers behind it maneuvered wildly to avoid the explosion that lit the field.

Rutger fired the 30mm autocannons at troops around the distant terminal buildings. Most of the glowing red plasma tore chunks from structures, not people, but he did get some satisfaction upon seeing an armored torso blasted into the air, followed by a secondary explosion on the rooftop.

The tank's AI identified additional threats ahead of them. Rutger sought out the targets—too many targets—as tracks of blue bolts and back blasts from missile launchers flashed hot on screen from rooftops, windows, and fighting holes in front of the terminal buildings. He alternated between the main gun and autocannons, attempting to manage their heat levels. He fired away at a seemingly endless supply of targets. He blasted them all, vaporizing men, severing limbs, and demolishing sections of buildings.

Despite the withering rain of incoming fire, the fanatical Repub troops held fast. Fiery missile tracks and sun-bright beams continued to create a chromatic maze across the field as the Berserker tanks howled over the snow covered plain, firing at targets.

The chain-link fence surrounding the spaceport raced into view. The wall of tanks crashed through it without slowing, sending poles and sections of fencing flying. Troopers on the trailing skimmers increased altitude and flew over the twisted debris.

"Phase line Julie," Captain Hensley announced. "Watch for enemy tanks. Keep your spacing, people."

Bounty Hunter II raced on at 120 kph despite a slight increase in gradient and heavily cratered ground, Aubrey's skill as a driver apparent as he kept the tank in formation despite the incoming fire and jockeying of other tanks taking evasive action.

Another salvo of Berserker missiles thundered overhead, the volleys timed to keep steady pressure on the enemy. They deployed their lethal cargo, and the submunitions streaked down in divergent trajectories toward targets scattered across the landing field and terminal buildings. Orange flashes rippled throughout the spaceport, sometimes accompanied by colorful secondary explosions. *Get those bastards!*

A brilliant blue bolt stabbed into the formation and struck Captain Hensley's tank just below the cupola. *Bad Medicine* grounded violently to a halt, smoke and flames shooting from around the hatches, which popped open a moment later to spew ejection seats. *Shit, only two!* Rutger thought, watching the seats rocket away on exterior view.

"We just lost Six," said the XO, Lieutenant Inkari. "I'm now in command. Keep up your visual scans. With all this energy flying around, your sensors might not read properly."

What little optimism Rutger had possessed perished along with Hensley. Blue bolts from Repub main guns sizzled through the onrushing formation. Rutger and his fellow gunners searched frantically for the firing tanks. A sense of panic filled him. Threats were everywhere, but the sensor equipment wasn't identifying targets he saw on exterior view. He caught a glimpse of a Repub tank covered in sensor-scatter netting, but it reversed behind a building after it fired, leaving Rutger without a target. Another main gun bolt flashed from a position to their left, just missing *Dog Breath* beside them.

"I don't see him!" Corporal Yurek shouted over the net. "Where the hell is he?"

"Rutger, 5-0-8-4 mils," Faora called out.

Rutger panned for the target as a blue bolt flashed by, just missing the front of *Bounty Hunter II*. Once again, no threat appeared on tactical display. *Our sensors are blind.* It was like being locked in a darkened room with a serial killer. He had to find the enemy tanks visually or not at all. Fear took the form of cold sweat that trickled down his body inside his combat suit. He kept his gun trained on the terminal buildings, saw a flash and searched for a target, but it disappeared in a heartbeat. *Fucking déjà vu!* A lot like the battle for Rolette when *Bounty Hunter* had been destroyed. He kept scanning, now in a state of near-panic, and tried to forget the ominous and obvious fact that they were only halfway to their objective.

23

CHAPTER

BUKAR LAY BEHIND THE ARMORED COWLING OF HIS skimmer, maneuvering through blowing snow behind the grav-tank formation as they bobbed over the terrain. His hands were becoming numb from the vibration and the cold. The frozen, cratered ground blurred beneath him at over 120 kph. *I hope there aren't any mines left.* If there were then he would probably die, either from the blast or being thrown from the skimmer at extreme speed.

He'd been sorely disappointed when the platoon received orders to attack the spaceport versus assaulting across the Klarven River. The center of the city had been so close. *It is simply God's will, but soon He will take me to Adeze.*

The lead tanks took evasive actions against missiles streaking toward them. Bukar banked his skimmer accordingly. Sims, Reyes, and Dominguez kept their spacing beside him. Bukar watched one tank and then another get hit and fall out of formation.

Ahead to the left, three hidden Mantis air defense platforms opened fire on the advancing companies. Bukar flattened himself on the skimmer as glowing chains of blue bolts cracked over and between the tanks. A Mantis gunner got a good lead on one tank and pounded it with a long burst. Sparks and pieces of hot slag splashed off its armored skirting until it finally grounded and corkscrewed wildly before flipping on its side.

Dominguez screamed for an instant over the net as a stream of bolts blasted him off his skimmer, which cartwheeled end over end before exploding in a shower of debris. LANCE CORPORAL DOMINGUEZ KIA scrolled in red letters on Bukar's HUD.

"This is no fucking good," Bukar shouted over the proximity net. "Move behind the tanks for cover."

Bukar fell in behind the armored bulk of a tank, displaced air buffeting his skimmer. Sims and Reyes accelerated in beside him. Bolts continued to sweep over the formation, then the firing ceased as quickly as it had started. Bukar didn't have time to ponder why.

"Phase line Susan," Lieutenant Palmer announced. "White elements, execute."

Bruiser Company infantry surged ahead of the tanks, accelerating to over 170 kph. The tanks fired main guns overhead at unseen targets, the sizzling bolts displacing the air in earsplitting cracks. Straight ahead, muzzle flashes dotted the landscape and buildings. Bukar waited for the bolt that would find and finish him. *Lord, be my guide and protector.*

Bukar fired periodic bursts from the skimmer's built-in 10mm plasma cannon to keep the enemy's heads down, but most of the long-range shots struck only snow and buildings.

The enemy's resolve began to erode under withering fire; many vacated their trenches and fled before the wall of steel charging toward them. Repub bodies and body parts flew into the night in flashes of death as more bolts from tanks and skimmers found their mark. Pools of scarlet blood shined in the snow, and the vile stench of burnt flesh permeated the air.

Two hundred meters out, Bukar flared the repulsors, causing the skimmer to decelerate rapidly. Three Repub troops bolted from a fighting position to his left. He stood up on the skimmer, balancing like he had so many times on his surfboard as a kid, and fired his rifle, the first burst missing high. His next burst sawed across the troops and cut them down screaming.

Bukar cut the skimmer's power. It grounded and slid over the snow, the momentum carrying him toward entrenched positions. He leaped into the first trench.

A Repub soldier huddled in the trench, mumbling a prayer. He looked up and flinched in surprise upon seeing Bukar's rifle pointed at him. He started to raise his rifle in slow motion, but Bukar snatched the weapon from him and flung it away. The man raised his hands and began to stand.

"Stay down and wait for the follow-on troops," Bukar barked.

The man nodded and sat back down, clutching his knees and shaking with fright.

Bukar peered out of the trench. The rest of the platoon were clearing other trenches, Reyes and Sims in the closest one. The tanks arrived and deployed into the streets between buildings. Getting his bearings, Bukar saw their first objective building ahead.

"Reyes, Sims, on me," Bukar said, springing from the trench. "Let's get to the first building."

"Copy," they replied.

Blue streaks of fire from a Repub machine gun lanced overhead from a rooftop window position on a building to the left. Bukar kneeled to fire on it, but the window exploded in a dazzling crimson flash before he could shoot, taken out by a tank's main gun. Several troopers cheered. "Get some!" someone bellowed.

An IFV pulled up before the building, and Lieutenant Palmer dismounted with a handful of troopers. They followed Bukar as he charged into the building, a large warehouse.

Rows of orange racks stacked with pallets of machine parts filled the huge room. Bukar headed for the offices on the left wall with Reyes and Sims following. Several other troopers, who had entered by blasting through a rolling overhead side door, swept the warehouse floor. Bukar found the offices empty.

He climbed a flight of metal stairs and found a Repub trooper splayed on the floor. Part of his lower jaw was missing. Steam rose from a ragged hole in his chest every time he moaned unintelligibly. Bukar kicked his weapon away. The man beckoned for help with an outstretched arm, but Bukar could do nothing for him. He marked the soldier on his HUD as a wounded POW for follow-on forces to deal with.

Peering from a shot-out window, Bukar saw tanks and IFVs from Cyclone Company pulling up. He loaded a fresh magazine into his rifle and headed downstairs to rejoin his fire team.

Sergeant Unger, a recent transfer to the platoon, strode over to them. "LT needs first squad to secure the control tower a half klick away. We need to get eyes on the airfield and the railyard. Let's move."

Unger led first squad from the warehouse into the street. Sharp reports of plasma weapons and thudding explosions filled the air as other elements of the task force met resistance, but the streets leading to the control tower were strangely quiet.

They bounded ahead, rifles sweeping over roof ledges and alleys as they moved toward the center of the terminal, finally arriving at the last row of maintenance hangars. The control tower stood across a wide taxiway. *Still no resistance here.* The closest action lay to the north across the landing field where the Feds attacked. Burning vehicles littered the landscape, and flashes of blue and red plasma bolts snapped across the expanse. To their right, row after row of mag train cars loaded with cargo and shipping containers filled the railyard.

An imposing structure, the permacrete control tower loomed like a lighthouse standing vigil in a sea of pavement. Broad and square at its base, the five-story tower narrowed as it rose and then widened at the top where smoked glass windows encircled the two control levels.

A sniper's bolt flashed just above Unger's helmet as he peered around the corner. He quickly ducked back. "Two hundred meters of open ground," Unger said over the proximity net. "I'm gonna pop smoke, then we'll run for it."

Unger launched two smoke grenades into the gap, then took two smoke hand grenades from another trooper and tossed them around the corner. He waited a few seconds for the red and yellow smoke to build before shouting, "Go! Go!"

Bukar sprinted through the smoke, catching glimpses of the control tower. The hand of fear clenched his stomach and twisted as glowing blue bolts snapped around him. His heart pounded as he chased shadows of his squad mates on HUD across the concrete expanse.

Muzzle flashes flared out from the tower windows high above. Bukar returned fire on the run, his rifle recoiling in his hands as he sprayed the windows with a long burst of bolts.

Suddenly he was flying, though it felt as if he were floating in slow motion. Normal time resumed when he crashed down on the pavement on his side, his weapon skidding away. Several dark figures pounded past through the haze.

He noticed Reyes lying on the ground behind him. Bukar staggered to his feet and retrieved his rifle, then he grabbed Reyes under the shoulders and tried to pull him up but found only the top half of his torso. The round of an automatic grenade launcher had blown away his bottom half.

PFC REYES KIA flashed on Bukar's HUD.

Bukar lurched back in grizzly surprise. He dropped Reyes and ran on toward the tower. Bolts sought him out, carving out chunks of molten pavement around him.

He burst into the bottom floor of the control tower, where other troopers had already swept the room, finding it clear. The room contained only thick concrete support pillars and blinking rows of servers and sophisticated comm equipment. Bundles of conduit snaked upward along the walls behind stacks of plastic ammo boxes and ration kits.

"Keep it tight, people. We're moving up," Unger said.

Bukar and Sims waited by the stairwell ready to follow the rest of the squad up.

"Reyes make it?" Sims asked, giving away that he already knew the answer to his own question.

Bukar shook his head. "No. He is with God."

Sims gave him a nod of acknowledgement as Bukar moved ahead and stacked up behind Unger and Corporal Zahn, with three more troopers bringing up the rear. Unger started pushing up the metal stairs, which turned at ninety-degree angles at every small landing, spiraling up to the top two floors. Bukar mentally prepped for the worst. The enemy had seen them coming and had plenty of time to make defensive preparations.

They ascended slowly and methodically, keeping their weapons trained upward. In the pitch-black stairwell, night vision cast everything in a gray hue. When Unger reached the bottom control level, he motioned Bukar and Sims to secure the stairway above while he and the other troopers swept the current level. Bukar nodded.

Unger kicked in the door. Gunfire erupted moments later, but Bukar couldn't see what was happening. The sharp crack of automatic plasma rifles echoed into the stairwell.

"Tangos down," Corporal Zahn reported over the proximity net.

Bukar and Sims waited tensely at the landing, covering the entrance to the floor above. Sweat began to trickle from Bukar's armpits. He thought about checking Unger's helmet camera feed but resisted the urge, keeping his eyes on the door above.

The door handle slowly began to turn. The door opened a crack, and a helmeted man peered through with a weapon at his shoulder. Bukar put a shot through the man's head, his visor blacking out the crimson bolt's blinding flash. Pieces of armor, bone, and brain matter decorated the door, and his body slumped forward onto the threshold, propping the door partially open. Blood started to trickle down the stairs.

"Tango down," Bukar whispered. LET'S GO WE CAN'T WAIT ANY LONGER, he thought-texted to Sims before cautiously starting up the stairs, keeping his holographic sights trained on the doorway.

Bukar stepped over the body and peered into the room, immediately sensing motion. He squeezed a three-round burst into a Repub soldier's torso. The woman wore power armor, but it couldn't save her from the immense energy a 10mm bolt packed at close range. She crumpled to the floor, the holes in her armor still glowing orange.

Frenzied shouts came from the room. Bukar kept his rifle trained on the door with one hand as he retrieved a plasma grenade from his webbing and thumbed the safety off. He set it for a two-second delay and tossed it far into the room, then he stood back against the wall and fired a blind string of bolts through the doorway to discourage anyone from trying to toss the grenade back at him.

The explosion rattled the metal stairs and shook the wall. Bukar peered inside. Everything flammable in the room was ablaze. "Follow me!" Bukar shouted to Sims as he rushed into the gray haze.

Bukar entered the room and swept it with holographic sights. The grenade had eviscerated two men behind the door, and several other soldiers further into the room lay dead or dying. Sims entered a step behind him and unloaded half a magazine into the rear of the room, shattering the floor-length windows and tearing apart computer consoles. Smoke curled from their glowing barrels. A chorus of moans and screams arose from the wounded.

Three terraced rows of air traffic control stations facing outward ringed the open room. Bukar quickly moved to check the next row down, flushing out a man who sprang up firing a submachine gun, his bolts flying high and wide. Bukar and Sims cut him into convulsing shreds. Still holding the submachine gun, his severed arm flew several feet, yet his twitching finger kept mashing the trigger and firing bursts until the weapon's bolt locked back empty.

Despite his helmet's filters, Bukar tasted acrid smoke and smelled charred flesh as he checked the rest of the room, staying back from the angled floor-to-ceiling windows.

"Top floor secure," Bukar reported to Sergeant Unger over the squad net.

"All clear down here," Unger replied. "We're coming up."

"Water..." a Repub soldier moaned from the floor. Bukar kneeled beside the dying man, a charred and gruesome mess of dangling intestines and severed limbs, his right leg and hand blown away by the grenade.

Unger and the rest of the squad entered and fanned out, stepping carefully over the windrow of bodies near the door. Bukar fished out his condenser bottle and put it to the man's lips, knowing it would quicken his death, but he wanted to provide what comfort he could in the man's final moments.

"Okay, let's get eyes on the field and start identifying targets," Unger commanded. The troopers moved to the windows, staying well apart. "Preacher, quit dicking around with that prisoner and give us a hand."

"Yes, Sergeant." Bukar put away his condenser bottle and began to stand.

A tempest of blue plasma bolts seemed to come from everywhere at once—across the landing field, the hangars past the taxiway, the railyard. The remaining glass windows shattered as bolts stitched the top floor, gouging out chunks of the concrete support walls.

Bukar hit the deck as troopers at the windows returned fire. Flaming chunks of ceiling tile fell throughout the room like hell's rain. Bukar crawled rapidly toward Sims, who crouched between two consoles firing rapids bursts with his light machine gun.

Sergeant Unger peered over a nearby console with electrobinoculars and started marking targets.

Bukar crawled a few more centimeters, almost abreast with Sims. "Shit!" Sims cried. Then Bukar saw it down in the railyard—a Repub blower tank leveling its main gun toward them.

"Get ba—" Sims began to say, turning to grab Bukar.

A blinding blue-white flash that stuck like a wrecking ball cut off Sims' warning. Bukar's visor opaqued to maximum darkness to block the flash. Excruciating pain radiated through his body as he tumbled through the air across the room, landing on a console that crumpled beneath his weight.

When he came to seconds later, Bukar felt pain that pulsated with every beat of his heart. He saw only darkness and panicked, thinking that he might have been blinded, but then realized his eyes were reflexively clamped shut. He took a moment reopening them, dreading what he would see.

He forgot where he was for a moment as he staggered to his feet and tried to make sense of his surroundings. Flames licked from every console and piece of furniture that hadn't been destroyed outright. A huge chunk of the control tower had disappeared, as if bitten off by a massive beast. Bukar's power armor was scorched black and covered in a dark, sticky substance—the melted remains of Sims, he realized in horror, whose body had shielded him from the main gun's blast.

Wind howled through the ragged hole in the tower, doing nothing to clear the smells of burnt ozone and barbequed flesh. Bukar looked around for survivors but only saw remains of bodies blown across the room and piled against the wall like dead leaves. Some of the men had vanished completely, vaporized in a heartbeat. Two smoking boots were all that remained of Sergeant Unger.

Overcome by it all, Bukar threw open his face shield and vomited, then wiped his face with the back of his armored hand. He stumbled forward and peered from the smoldering chasm.

The tank's barrel still sighted on the tower, dropping slightly as the gunner adjusted his aim to finish the job. The muzzle looked like a dark tunnel to an infinite abyss. *My time has come. God, have mercy on my soul.*

A dark streak plummeting to earth caught Bukar's eye. A depleted uranium self-forging warhead detonated over the tank in an orange flash, and a white finger of light pierced the turret. The submunition's needle-like shaft penetrated the thin top armor and ignited the ammo stores within. Jets of white-hot plasma shot skyward from blown access hatches. The conflagration quickly dissipated, leaving only a scooped-out hull.

Bukar collapsed to his knees and wept.

CHAPTER 24

BOUNTY HUNTER II CLOSED FAST ON THE TERMINAL buildings a little over two klicks away. Rutger's tactical display remained blank, though he knew that at least two tanks were actively targeting them. Infantry threats cluttered his holos, however, situated in windows and on rooftops. He ignored them and watched the streets warily for tanks as Faora engaged infantry targets with the automatic defense weapon.

A trio of Mantis air defense guns engaged from the left. Rivers of 40mm blue bolts slashed across the Berserker formation, blasting several infantry troopers off their skimmers. Pieces of metal and men scattered into the snow.

The Mantises turned their fire on Anvil Company tanks angling toward the landing field. One tank's side armor skirting got plastered by the incoming fire. Energy from the pulsing blue bolts glanced skyward as they pecked into the armor in a shower of sparks. Smoke and flames poured from its side as it grounded hard, kicking up a blanket of snow.

"Target 10 o'clock, 3500 meters," Faora said.

Rutger reluctantly abandoned his tank hunt. His holo screen already directed him toward the threat, not in his primary designated fire zone, but the AI had given it to him since he had the proper angle. He spotted three of the four-barreled Mantis weapons systems, only their turrets visible above the ground. They were dug in beside a thick concrete landing pad that supported one of the giant starships moored at port. The vessel's massive sponsons overhung their positions to provide overhead cover from artillery.

Rutger stroked the trigger and sent a main gun bolt into the far-left Mantis, vaporizing the turret in a white flash. A blue-tinged shockwave like a miniature supernova erupted a second later when the ammo stores exploded.

The second Mantis crew fled as Rutger swerved the pipper onto their gun, but it exploded before he could squeeze the trigger, falling victim to another tank. The third Mantis already burned, its crew fled or vaporized.

Berserker main gun bolts, particle cannon streams and bursts of 30mm autocannon fire slashed across the apron, lighting up vehicles and buildings that hadn't been destroyed in the initial artillery strike. Strobing flashes illuminated the colossal starships parked across the field. Now and then an errant bolt would strike a ship, raising a fountain of sparks.

As they passed Phase Line Susan, the infantry rocketed ahead and fanned out on their skimmers. Bruiser tanks started veering off on their assigned axes through the terminal buildings, while Anvil tanks made for the landing pads.

A bolt struck the ground to the right of *Bounty Hunter II* sending a geyser of snow skyward. The expanding shockwave of energy buffeted the tank, causing it to fishtail slightly. Rutger's restraints dug into his shoulders as Aubrey fought to get them back on course.

Still nothing on tactical display. In the right holo, Rutger finally caught a glimpse of an enemy tank as it pulled out from behind a building. *It's him!* At this range he clearly saw the sigil on its frontal armor—a skull wearing a flaming crown. He'd almost put the glowing targeting pipper on it when an enemy APC pulled up in front of it and blocked his aim. *Damn it!* Losing sight of the tank, he settled for the APC as its 90mm plasma cannon traversed toward grunts on skimmers. Rutger stroked the trigger and watched it explode into flames. His view remained blocked in the aftermath, unfortunately.

He checked the tactical display again out of desperation and picked up a faint reading, the tank's red icon fading away behind the buildings. With no line of sight, Rutger decided to launch two hypersonic Javelin missiles from the rear launchers. He watched them tracking rapidly across the display, homing in on the tank. The tank's icon suddenly flashed and then disappeared. The missile tracks vanished a second later with no confirmation of them locking onto a target.

With no sign of the tank, he targeted windows on the terminal buildings as the infantry on skimmers made their final approach. He gave each window a two-second burst from the 30mm autocannons, letting the tank's forward momentum slew them across the targets while he kept an eye on the streets. Glass and concrete disintegrated under his hail of fire, and a thick haze began to obscure the target area.

Rutger switched the holos to thermal viewing. Through the curtain of smoke, he spied an enemy tank pulling forward from the end of the street, its commander apparently thinking he was safe from view. Rutger made out the faint heat signature from the tank's muzzle as it peeked out to fire, only the front half visible. He slid the pipper onto the tank's turret ring and stroked the trigger, then smiled with grim satisfaction as the tank disappeared in an expanding white bubble. *Got you, motherfucker!*

Rutger quickly returned to the tactical display, hoping to get a read on the skull tank, but it remained elusive, and there were plenty of other threats to deal with.

"Black and White elements, continue advance," Lieutenant Inkari directed over the command net. "Red and Blue elements, hold positions and cover the grunts as they hit the first objectives."

Rutger felt vulnerable as they sat with the main gun trained down one of the secondary streets. Infantry troopers entered buildings to take their objectives. Cyclone Company tanks started pulling in behind Bruiser Company.

"Ensure the APS is set to passive mode," Faora said.

Rutger had set the APS to passive when they'd moved in close to support the grunts; the switch remained in passive mode. Electromagnetic emissions sensors remained scrambled. Only a few threats populated the tactical display, mostly gleaned from other passive sensors or identified by friendly elements. A couple of recon drones remained aloft to provide overhead views of the spaceport. Rutger watched one of the drone feeds for a few moments. The battle appeared to be progressing roughly as planned. Fed units to the north were having a rough go of it, but they appeared to be making steady progress toward the landing field.

Minutes seemed to drag by as they sat waiting. Lieutenant Inkari finally relayed orders: "It appears the enemy is trying to mount a counterattack to the north. Red and Blue elements, advance to the center of the port. Black and White vehicles will follow in trace, over."

Faora keyed acknowledgement and then ordered Aubrey to move *Bounty Hunter II* ahead into an alley. *Blood Shed* and *Dog Breath* traveled down the paralleling alleys. Rutger kept a watchful eye on the rooftops as they advanced at 25 kph. The trailing IFVs watched their six. Rutger hoped they were paying attention to the numerous spots where enemies might be hiding.

They moved into an open concrete expanse, *Bounty Hunter II* in the lead. The railyard lay directly in front of them. The three tanks of second platoon fanned out as the XO and first platoon continued along the southern row of warehouses, protecting their right and rear flanks. Each tank covered a sector of the railyard, a vast maze of stacked conex boxes, mag railcars, and overhead cranes.

The threat warning beeped annoyingly in Rutger's ear. Two enemy tanks had appeared at the edge of his threat display, to the rear on the starboard side. Rutger savagely pushed the joystick hard right to swing the turret toward them.

"Enemy tanks four o'clock!" Faora yelled.

Fear gripped Rutger like a vice. He hoped the turret would traverse fast enough to bring his gun to bear first. Two enemy tanks slid from behind a row of storage containers. *Dog Breath* was already turning its main gun on them. Crimson flashed an instant later, followed by showering sparks when *Dog Breath* struck the lead tank.

A split second later the second tank fired over the rear deck of its destroyed wingman, its blue bolt finding *Dog Breath*, which grounded hard in a pall of black smoke. *Dog Breath's* crew punched out, their ejection seats lifting on columns of orange flames and whisking them up and out of sight.

Rutger didn't have time to consider their fate as he brought the main gun to bear on tank number two. *You're mine*, he thought as the tank began to slide into his sights. He'd almost slewed the pipper onto it, then the tank began to reverse into the containers. The flaming skull was plainly visible on its prow. *Shit, shit, SHIT!* He watched the faint electromagnetic signal start to accelerate away to the east.

"He's displacing!" Rutger yelled into his mic.

"Aubrey, take us around the corner," Faora said over the intercom. Then she keyed the platoon net. "Blue 2, advance down the tracks. We'll try to flush him out."

Bounty Hunter II advanced toward the labyrinth of multicolored containers, which reminded Rutger of children's wooden blocks. A pair of enemy soldiers shouldering quad missile launchers popped out from behind a railcar fifty meters to their left. They fired all their missiles nearly simultaneously, lighting up the row of graffiti-covered railcars behind them, the missiles' backblasts clearly outlining their bodies.

Rutger spun the turret toward them. In less than half a second, the automatic defense weapon spun to life and intercepted three of the incoming missiles in dirty orange flashes. The APS defense pods discharged and swatted away three more.

Two missiles made it through the defenses. One had been damaged in flight; it glanced off the turret face with a deep clang and wobbled skyward. The final missile struck the main gun barrel with an explosive flash, puncturing a jagged hole through the bore.

When the missile exploded, electronics inside the turret sparked, and a massive heat surge washed over the fighting compartment, but the gun's electromagnetic containment field had prevented the cobalt polymer round in the chamber from cooking off.

Where exposed, Rutger's skin burned as if he'd baked for hours on a tropical beach. The holo screens flashed over for a second as he swung the targeting reticle onto the retreating figures and squeezed the trigger, hosing the area with roaring autocannons. Searing red bolts splattered the two retreating men against the side of a railcar and gouged out gobbets of glowing slag from the metal side walls.

Rutger had expected to see the red warning light blinking on his console. "Main gun is offline," he reported as they approached the corner. *Shit! What are we going to do now?*

"Do you want me to halt?" Aubrey asked.

"Continue to advance, Aubrey," Faora said. "Take us around that corner."

Rutger watched the Repub tank's electromagnetic signal accelerate down the rows of containers. It turned left about 400 meters down the row, its stern disappearing around the corner just as *Bounty Hunter II* entered the row.

The skull tank's commander wasn't running, just relocating to an optimum firing position, waiting to strike like a cobra when the odds were again in his favor. Rutger could almost sense it waiting around the corner, despite no trace of a signal on tactical display. *He's one crafty son-of-a-bitch. I'll give him that.*

"He's waiting for us at the intersection," Rutger shouted.

"Aubrey, accelerate to 120 klicks," Faora said.

Rutger stared in disbelief at the approaching intersection. "Didn't you hear me? The main gun is—"

"Shut up," Faora snarled, cutting him off. "When we turn that corner, you'll have one shot at this guy with the remaining particle cannon. Make it count."

The tank raced down the row. Rutger traversed the turret left in anticipation, knowing that hundredths of seconds would determine their fates, but he could only rotate to a 40-degree angle in the narrow confines. Containers flashed by in a multicolored blur. With the intersection rapidly approaching, he kept shifting his gaze between the tactical display and external holos, his mind trapped in a cycle of terror, unable to free itself from memories of past encounters with the skull tank, and the moment yet to come. *This vendetta's about to end…one way or another.*

"Driver, I have the controls," Faora said.

"You have the controls," Aubrey replied.

A square red icon appeared on tactical display, glowing brightly: the skull tank waiting to spring an ambush on them at the intersection, just as he'd suspected. They approached the intersection moving too fast to safely turn. *What the hell is this crazy bitch doing?*

"Be ready," Faora shouted over the intercom. She adjusted the collective control dial and raised the tank to five meters in elevation, exposing its vulnerable underside. She proved surprisingly adept at the controls and obviously had extensive experience as a driver.

Rutger couldn't see the ground now, only a blur of containers as they whipped past. He flipped off the safety override for the particle cannon's field inhibitor. The shot was going to be dangerously close. His heart thundered as they approached the intersection.

Rutger's stomach lurched as Faora banked hard around the corner, dipping the left side thirty degrees while reversing forward repulsor thrust. Massive inertia fishtailed the tank's stern to the right as it turned, drifting through the intersection.

The huge, bulbous mass of the Repub tank slid into view at the corner of Rutger's targeting screen. A blinding blue flash and a thunderclap of energy erupted ahead, but the blue bolt crackled harmlessly underneath *Bounty Hunter II*, the gunner expecting them to be at ground level.

Rutger flung the turret over, trying to get the particle cannon pipper to settle on the skull tank as *Bounty Hunter II* moved on three axes. The enemy tank's main gun was already traversing and elevating to get a bead on them.

Rutger operated on pure, frantic adrenaline now. Events seemed to move in slow motion as he manipulated the pipper onto the upper hull just below the turret ring. He reflexively squeezed the trigger. A white-hot lightning bolt of concentrated protons stabbed through the turret armor with a thunderous crack and eruption of sparks.

"Good hit!" Faora shouted as she brought the tank around.

Flames and smoke billowed from several access panels and the glowing hole in the turret armor. Rutger waited, finger poised over the trigger as the particle cannon power cycled to fire again. Faora rotated *Bounty Hunter II* to face the skull tank. As she lowered the tank into a standard hover, a figure emerged from the skull tank through the commander's hatch. Black smoke roiled around the man as he rolled off the turret and then slid from the hull. No one else emerged, the driver and gunner apparently dead.

The enemy commander pulled himself to his feet and faced *Bounty Hunter II*. He wore a long field coat of black leather over his tanker uniform. He removed his helmet and stuck it in the crook of his arm. Wearing a solemn expression, he came to attention and executed a crisp salute.

Rutger slid the pipper onto him, center mass.

Every muscle in the commander's face fell slack. His eyes widened in astonished fear.

"Rutger, don't!"

He ignored Faora. Nicole's body engulfed in flames flashed through his mind as he pulled the trigger.

The protonic current struck the tanker, the massive transfer of energy superheating his bodily fluids in an infinitesimal part of a second. He exploded, splattering blood, organs, and bone shards over shipping containers and the prow of *Bounty Hunter II*. All that remained of the commander was a red and black stain on the pavement.

An unexpected silence descended as the cannon cooled. Lieutenant Colonel Tyree, the battalion commander, broke the silence over the command net. "All Berserker and Federation Forces, this is Marauder Six. Cease fire, cease fire! The local Repub commander has surrendered. *Do not fire* unless fired upon! Over."

Rutger finally released his death grip on the gunnery joystick. A wave of fatigue immediately washed over him. Feeling hollow and spent, he finally turned to face Staff Sergeant Faora. She stared daggers at him for a moment, then stood and popped her hatch open. Rutger didn't give a shit. *Maybe this war is finally over.* He leaned back in the gunner's seat and pondered the thought of finally going home.

AFTER THE BATTLE, BUKAR HAD JOINED THE RE-
mains of third platoon, now consolidated into two squads. Most
of the Repub army had surrendered when the spaceport had been
captured, but a substantial force of diehard Repub holdouts still
occupied downtown New Oslo, where his sister lived.

Bukar grew impatient as they loaded the IFVs with ammo
and equipment in preparation for the final assault into the city.
Lieutenant Palmer approached as he finished strapping a box of
rations onto the vehicle's bustle rack.

"Sir, any word on when we'll be attacking?" Bukar asked.

"We aren't," Lieutenant Palmer said. "We've just received
orders to pull back."

Bukar's steadfast bearing melted away to a look of concern.
"Pull back? But we haven't secured the city yet."

"Don't worry, those Repub bastards will get what's coming
to them. We're gonna hit them with a tactical nuke. The Feds
have had their fill of fighting, they want to set an example to
discourage any future rebellions and convince the other holdouts
to surrender."

No! Adeze... "How soon?" Bukar asked, dreading the answer.

"This stays within the unit, but time on target is noon."

"I have to get to her," Bukar announced with finality.

Comprehension dawned on Palmer's face. "That's right, your sister lives there. Sorry, Preacher, I forgot. They're gonna broadcast a warning fifteen minutes before the attack. Hopefully she can reach one of the bomb shelters in time." He shook his head. "I'm sorry…I really am. I wish there was something we could do." He paused, at a loss for more words of consolation. "We're moving out in fifteen minutes. You'd better be on that IFV."

"Sir, I have to go to her. She's my sister—I can't leave her."

Palmer studied him. "I'm gonna pretend I didn't hear that. I hope to hell you make it out, just realize your ass will be on the carpet if you do."

"I understand, sir."

"You should really reconsider, though. Downtown is crawling with hostiles. You might not even reach her."

"I have to try. Thank you, sir."

Palmer clasped his hand on Bukar's shoulder. "Preacher, you're the finest soldier I've ever known. It's been an honor. Godspeed."

Light snow had turned to steady rain by the time Bukar departed the assembly area on the outskirts of New Oslo. He walked quickly down the street, feeling energized at being on his own. No squad to watch over, his mission a single objective. He checked the time on HUD: 0908. *Faster! There isn't much time.*

A flock of gray carrion birds with red eyes feasted on a bloated civilian corpse at the next corner. The body seemed too big for its clothes, but he guessed it was an older woman. Bukar broke into a jog, boots pounding over the cracked and blistered street. He passed crumbling apartment blocks and deserted shops, cut through parking lots choked with abandoned vehicles and crossed snow-covered playgrounds pocked with shell craters. Burnt-out military vehicles, mostly Repub, had been stripped of any usable parts down to their titanium hulls.

Bukar slowed to check every intersection before crossing and ran wary eyes over windows and alleys. Sometimes he felt eyes upon him, but he encountered no living civilians or soldiers. The streets were ghostly quiet.

After detouring for a block around a collapsed building, Bukar arrived at a pedestrian bridge that crossed the Klarven River into the downtown area. Twisted and sagging toward the water, it had been hit with munitions in several places, and a five-meter section in the center of the span was missing. He scanned the opposite bank, noticing no observation posts or checkpoints. He quickly crossed, easily jumping the center gap with aid from his power armor.

Streets here were likewise empty at the moment. Two blocks further, however, a pair of female civilians turned the corner ahead. *Shit!* They spotted him, stopped in their tracks, and then quickly disappeared back around the corner.

Bukar glanced around, then took cover inside a storefront with a shattered window. Once a clothing store, the place had been looted and the racks overturned. Scattered garments lay on the floor, many of them charred in spots. He didn't want to ditch his uniform, but wearing it would draw too much attention. The war hadn't ended yet down here.

After several frustrating minutes, he found pants, a shirt, and a jacket that would fit his large frame. He stripped off his armor and shimmied out of his skintight powered suit. He felt exposed and vulnerable. Cold.

He donned the civilian clothes. Unable to find shoes that fit, he put his combat boots back on. Looking in a mirror, he laughed at himself. He realized he would pass only a cursory inspection at best. His boots were a dead giveaway, and his clothes just seemed all wrong. He hadn't been a civilian for a long time. He stashed his rifle under a pile of clothes, knowing he would never return to pick it up, and strapped his M-9 service pistol around his waist, concealing it beneath his shirttail.

Getting dressed had eaten up precious time. *Go now...keep moving.*

He walked quickly toward the city center. The humid air began to thicken with a gray haze from burning buildings nearby. The basso rumble of distant artillery drifted through the streets. He came across an older man and woman pushing a cart, apparently scrounging for items. Their tired eyes barely noticed him. *Maybe the clothes are working.* All of the civilians he'd encountered wore ragged clothing as well.

The streets remained largely empty but for the debris of war. He didn't see any lights burning, though he assumed people still had solar generators. Intel reports stated that thousands of civilians remained trapped in the city center. *I can't save them. Only the Lord's grace can.*

An air-cushioned military truck turned onto the street behind him. Bukar stayed calm, resisting the urge to bolt around the upcoming corner. The truck buffeted him with air as it passed, but it didn't stop. He assumed the women he'd seen a few blocks back had reported him, but he doubted the Repub forces would put much effort into searching for a lone enemy soldier.

Highrise buildings, parking garages, and multilevel shopping centers marked the edge of the city center. Bukar had memorized the address and route to his sister's place, but any detours would eat up more precious time. *Only a couple of hours left now at the most.* But he couldn't be sure, since he had no watch or HUD to check the time.

Bukar walked for roughly three kilometers, shivering in the rain and cold despite his exertions. He could see the skyscrapers rising into the haze as the address numbers counted slowly upward, signaling that he was getting closer.

Military traffic began to increase. A convoy of air-cushioned APCs led by a wheeled truck approached. Repub soldiers sat atop all of the overloaded vehicles. Bukar waited on a corner for at least a couple of minutes as the convoy passed, keeping his eyes down. He felt the troops staring at him, but the convoy moved on.

He walked a few more blocks and reached the heart of New Oslo. The buildings loomed impossibly tall and imposing, rising in tiers of reflective glass and polished facades. Soon he spotted what he thought to be his sister's building. He increased pace as he considered her fate. *Maybe she left.* She might have relocated with a friend, or been forced to evacuate. He did not think, however, that she'd been forced into a camp or killed. He could almost sense her now as he covered the final few blocks. *She will be there—I know it.* His intuition rarely failed him.

Several white signs lettered in red greeted Bukar as he turned a corner: ENTERING MILITARY CONTROLLED ZONE. ALL VEHICLES AND PERSONNEL SUBJECT TO SEARCH. DEADLY FORCE AUTHORIZED.

Past the signs, a pair of wheeled armored vehicles blocked the next intersection. Several Repub soldiers to either side checked IDs as people filed past. Two more soldiers manned heavy plasma machine guns atop each vehicle.

Shit! He felt a coolness creep into his gut. He still felt the cold steel of his pistol and his stun grenade in his pockets. He was so fricking close, but he had no ID and couldn't possibly force his way through the checkpoint.

Bukar turned around. A man stood nonchalantly at the corner, a cigarette hanging from his mouth. Their eyes met. Bukar averted his gaze. He hadn't been standing there a moment ago.

Is he following me? Bukar realized his nerves were probably getting the better of him. He crossed the street and walked two more blocks, searching for an alternate route. Another checkpoint blocked the way. Despair and frustration seized his thoughts. The sun had risen higher behind the gray clouds. He hadn't much time left.

Bukar backtracked, wracking his brain for a solution. The sound of running water grabbed his attention. He stopped and watched rainwater flowing down a gutter into a storm drain at the curb. *The sewer!*

Bukar looked both ways. He waited for someone to cross the intersection a block behind. Then, finding the street empty, he gripped the cold grate and heaved it upward. He stood it upright on the lip of the opening, then lowered himself in. The cold water from the melting snow on the street flowed over him, chilling him to the bone. He couldn't see the bottom of the channel. He used his arms to lower himself further in the hole, supporting himself while he probed with his feet to find some sort of ledge or purchase.

Men shouted in the distance up the street, accompanied by the whining engine of an approaching vehicle. Bukar dropped. The grate slammed down above him and clanged on the concrete.

He landed with a splash two and half meters below. His legs slipped out from under him on slick concrete, sending him falling hard on his tailbone in half a meter of frigid, stinking water. A steady current flowed around him. The air reeked of dirty water and the grate above provided little light, and he could barely see even after his eyes adjusted.

Bukar tried to get his bearings. He faced a drainage pipe that slanted slightly downward in the direction he thought he needed to go. Bukar groped around the opening. *A meter wide, give or take.* A sense of claustrophobia began to creep into him. He would have to crawl through water up to his chin. *So be it. Adeze would do it for me.*

He shivered from the cold and a terrible sense of urgency. Pushing and clawing forward, he could barely fit his head above the surface breathe. He began thinking of sewer gases and realized he could easily pass out and drown down here, but he didn't feel lightheaded or any other symptoms of hypoxia. He wished he had his helmet. *Yeah, how about an entire environmental suit and a flashlight while you're at it...*

The drainage pipe came to a four-way intersection. He looked back at the dim shaft of light where he'd entered, unable to tell if he'd traveled far enough. *This was a bad idea.*

He took several deep, calming breaths before turning into the left-hand pipe. He couldn't get used to the darkness. *C'mon you've been through worse. Only a couple hundred more meters, then you'll be past the checkpoint.* He kept telling himself that, over and over between prayers. *Lord, give me strength.*

He thought he heard shouting and the clang of metal, but knew it was probably his imagination. Churning water filled his ears and deadened his senses, yet made him feel trapped at the same time.

He crawled rhythmically through the muck. A cross-current entering from a larger pipe to his left formed a vortex that caught him briefly and sunk his head below the water. Bukar braced against the tunnel wall, got his head back above the surface, and moved on.

Soon he lost all sense of time and distance. His clothes clung to him, and his hands occasionally squished into unseen things in the muck that made him cringe. His mind ran wild as he pondered what might live down here. He remembered stories about giant reptiles and rabid rats living in the sewers back on Beninia.

He paused upon hearing a squeak—not his imagination this time. An instant later, several thick, furry creatures scurried onto his shoulders and upper back, clawing at his clothes and exposed skin as he wriggled forward. *Fuck! Fuck!* Were these just rats, or were there worse things living in the sewers on this planet? He frantically scrabbled forward, swatting at the rats and occasionally rising to try scraping them off on the tunnel ceiling. Neither method proved successful.

Bukar wanted to scream, but that might attract more rats. *Oh God, I'm going to die down here.* He thrashed forward, feeling them bite and claw at his skin, tasting their filth in his mouth from the water. Finally, his mind teetering on the brink of insanity, he screamed, then plunged forward madly into the circling swarm. Rats swam past his face and screeched into his ears. He banged his head against the top of the pipe trying to breathe, sucked in some water and coughed it out. Bile filled his throat. He floundered forward and managed not to vomit.

A shaft of light pierced the tunnel ahead. Bukar lurched toward it and came to another storm drain. Able to stand now, he hysterically swatted the creatures off his legs and back. He felt a rat climbing up the inside of his pant leg and crushed it, feeling it squirm and claw as its bones broke. He shook his leg, and the dead rodent fell into the water.

No ladder, just the like the drain he'd entered through. He tried to brace his arms and legs on the vertical pipe and inch his way up, but he kept sliding back down, scraping his back and arms on the wet concrete. Rats kept trying to ascend his legs.

He finally found decent purchase on the pipe and inched upward to the grating. He paused, back bent beneath the grate, one boot sole on each side of the pipe. He stopped, panting, his face streaked with slime and filth, the skin on his lower back abraded. *One try...you won't make this climb again.* He flexed his legs and lower back, grunting through clenched teeth as he attempted to lift the grate, which barely moved with a faint clank. Then one of his boots slipped. Bukar plummeted back to the water and hit his head against the wall. White pain filled his skull, but quickly dissipated into panic as rats started climbing him again.

Looking around as he swatted rats from his legs, Bukar realized what he had to do. *She would do it for you.* He dropped to hands and knees, took a massive gulp of air and submerged, swimming blindly ahead and hoping to ditch the rats.

Bukar plunged ahead until he could hold his breath no longer. His head banged the pipe when he emerged with barely enough room to catch a breath, but he'd shaken the rats for now.

He moved on, just able to breathe with his nose above the water. An almost imperceptible current flowed over him from the left, then it was gone. He backed up, felt around the left wall and located a pipe, slightly smaller and completely submerged. *It goes in the right direction.*

Bukar hesitated to enter, however, with no way of knowing how far the pipe lay submerged. Ever conscious of time ticking away, he steeled his nerve, took a deep breath, and entered the pipe.

His lungs burned as he crawled forward, and he banged his head several times. *Shit, maybe I should go back.* But he'd already gone too far, so he pressed ahead, pulse pounding at his temples, lungs aching with the instinct to breathe. Perhaps his appointment with the Lord had come. If so, then he would go gratefully, but he wasn't quite ready to submit just yet. He took a few more crawling steps, ready to unleash his pent-up breath at any moment. He lurched violently upward and smashed his head again. Still no air.

Raw panic filled every fiber of his being as Bukar clawed at mystery muck on the bottom of the pipe, moving about two more meters before he could take no more. He shot upward and hit his head again...but this time his mouth and nose were clear of the water. *The tunnel must have ascended. Praise God!*

Bukar greedily sucked in dank air for a couple of minutes, enjoying the act of breathing, before moving on.

A concrete barrier stopped him. Bukar felt around and found he'd reached a left-right intersection, the pipes leading away too small to crawl through. He probed overhead and reached for the sky—he'd discovered a vertical shaft. Further probing revealed the bottommost metal rung. The touch of metal, a chance to stand upright and another shot to escape this dank, soaking hell pumped adrenaline into his veins. *You aren't out of this yet.*

Feeling weaker than he had in years, he grabbed the rung and pulled himself up, boots scrabbling on the slippery tunnel wall. His left hand found the next rung. Panting from exertion, he grabbed another rung and then the next until he finally got a boot on the ladder. He started to climb in earnest.

A manhole cover stopped his progress. He listened for a moment—no voices or traffic noise. *Clock is ticking.* Bracing himself on the steps, he pushed up with his arms, but the cover didn't budge. He began to panic. Maybe he hadn't found a way out; maybe the cover was secured somehow. He climbed a step higher, put his back beneath the steel, and pushed up with his legs. The cover finally gave way. Overcast daylight blinded him as he slid the manhole cover aside.

A cold breeze blasted into his face. Bukar shivered violently, knowing he needed to get moving and generate body heat. Barely peering above the opening, he scanned the street and found it vacant, the distant sound of vehicles the only indication of people nearby.

Bukar emerged from the hole and rolled onto slush-covered pavement. He struggled to his feet, wet clothes hampering his movement as he jogged toward a corner. *Only a block away!* he realized, noticing a building address. He rounded the corner and jogged down the street, numb feet sloshing inside his boots.

He soon reached the proper address. The glass front doors were shattered. Someone had boarded up the entrance, and someone else had torn down the polymer sheets and cast them onto the sidewalk. Bukar drew his pistol, ensuring it was clear of water. *I hope she's okay up there.*

He entered the foyer, the area dark beyond the scant daylight shining through the doors. It felt good to be out of the wind. He scanned the room as he approached the bank of elevators. The space had been thoroughly ransacked: mirrors smashed, furniture upended, front desk computer terminals ripped out, only their wiring harnesses remaining.

To his right, he glimpsed a dark figure. Bukar swiveled toward it, his finger taking up slack on the trigger. Then he lowered the pistol, recognizing the dark man covered in filth was his reflection in one of the few intact mirrors. *Good God, you're a mess.*

Not surprisingly, the elevators were out of order. He found the stairway door propped open with a chunk of concrete and began the long ascent to the sixty-eighth floor. His legs burned from fatigue when he finally reached the top.

Bukar emerged into a short left-right hallway terminating at opposite doors. *They must be penthouse suites.* Adeze had done quite well for herself, which did not surprise Bukar. His heart hammered as he approached the door. He knocked three times, paused, then knocked twice more. He heard movement inside. Instinct and habit told him to stand clear of the door, but he didn't want to alarm her.

"Who is it?" Adeze called, her voice unmistakable.

"It's me, sis. Joseph."

Several electronic deadbolts and locks clacked. Adeze flung the door open and stared at him. Her synthetic eyes, a dazzling green, studied him, then she stepped forward into an embrace that lasted several moments. Her warmth felt intoxicating, and Bukar suddenly felt self-conscious of looking and smelling so awful.

"I'm sorry it took so long to get here," Bukar said. "And that I stink like a sewer."

She laughed. "You made it, little brother. And yes, you most certainly need a change of clothes. Come, follow me."

The apartment was beautifully furnished in a minimalistic style. Several solar-powered heaters in one corner worked overtime to heat the place. She handed him a blanket off the couch, and he wrapped himself in it.

"Sit down. Make yourself comfortable."

It didn't seem real seeing her in front of him. She had aged, but so had he. He resisted the urge to follow her, to not let her out of his sight. She returned with a fresh change of clothes.

"Whose clothes are these?" Bukar asked.

"They are...they were Eddie's."

"Eddie?"

"He was my boyfriend, killed by the security police. They said he was caught looting a grocery store..." Her words drifted off.

"I'm sorry to hear that. I didn't know."

"I know. I guess neither of us did a great job of keeping in touch." She went into the kitchen to retrieve something.

"Yes, and again I am sorry. But I'm here with you now."

"Little brother has come to rescue me?" she said, returning with two steaming cups of tea.

Bukar didn't reply. He took a sip of the hot tea, savoring it. His mom had made it the same way.

"You knew I wouldn't leave," Adeze said. "Why have you risked your life coming here?"

"I needed to see you."

She studied his expression, and she knew. "How much time do we have?"

Bukar glanced at the holo-clock on the wall. "Not long, I'm afraid."

"Oh..." Sadness flashed across her face, but her smile quickly returned. "Come, I want to show you something."

He followed Adeze to her studio in a spacious back room. A floor-to-ceiling neural painting covered the far wall, almost five meters across. He'd neither seen nor heard of one so large.

Neural paintings worked via holographic projection interface. Every person saw slightly different things in the projected art, for the paintings interacted with an individual's unique neural patterns, though each usually had a general theme. For the projections to elicit the proper psychic interface, the artist had to be an expert programmer and a master in using nano-synthetic paints. Some claimed that only artists with true psychic abilities could paint them. They were wildly popular, extremely rare, and outrageously expensive, each the product of several thousand hours of work. Bukar figured this one had taken tens of thousands of hours to create.

"It is...miraculous," Bukar said.

"Do want to experience it?"

He nodded. "Yes."

She picked up a remote and keyed a button that closed the curtains and dimmed the lights. The holographic projectors cast light toward the wall, and the colors and shapes came to life in Bukar's mind like a psychedelic hallucination, only far more vivid and crisp.

The image was more powerful than anything he had ever seen. They were together along with their parents, back on Beninia. He could smell the ocean and taste the salty air, the experience like a time machine, a journey through his most vivid childhood memories. The painting symbolized their family's love, their love for one another, and all the pain and heartache they had endured. It took him to emotional depths and highs he had never felt before, and for a few moments he felt truly complete, totally connected to Adeze, the universe, to God. It was pure love. Tears streamed down his face.

After the holo went dark, she turned the lights on and opened the curtains.

"What is it called?" Bukar asked.

"*Family.* I made it for you, for us. What do you think?"

He took a moment before speaking, at a loss for words. "It is incredible. Perfect." Looking at his sister, Bukar suddenly felt inadequate, a failure. "You saved my life. I wanted to save you, but I have come too late."

"You already saved me, Joseph. I could never have done all of this without you. If not for you, I would still be on Beninia doing lord knows what. You allowed me to pursue my ambitions—to travel, to paint, to live a life I only dreamed about. Your strength and support showed me the way. Your sacrifice made it possible."

"But your eyes—"

"Being blind taught me to really see, and I can see you now, little brother. The strong and good man you have become. Mom and Dad would have been proud."

"But I'm not a good man," he said, tears in his eyes, baritone voice trembling. "I have done terrible things…"

She took his hands. "Necessary things. You did what you had to do, as did I. I know you, Joseph. You are a good man."

He nodded.

"Thank you for being here with me."

He regained his composure, drawing strength from her words, her presence. "The Lord has brought us together, and he shall carry us away as he did Elijah."

She hugged him.

He held her tight against him as a second sun blossomed outside the window and cast the room in brilliant, blinding light. A searing orange blast wave followed. In a glare brighter than a thousand suns, Bukar felt his sister's love and God's burning embrace.

EPILOGUE

★ ★ ★

"ALL ARRIVING PASSENGERS FROM PAN GALACTIC flight 207, luggage pickup is at carousel G43," a synthesized female voice announced over the loudspeaker in Port City's space terminal.

I'm finally home. Rutger found it hard to believe. Hostilities on Scandova had ended a month ago. In the aftermath, the Berserkers had assumed the duties of an occupying force as their contract drew to a close, in addition to the mundane tasks of cleaning and repairing their equipment. As the time dragged on, Rutger had thought of little but going home for good and patching the remnants of his old life together. *Things will be right again, for the first time in a long time.*

Staff Sergeant Faora hadn't reported him for killing the tank commander, which surprised Rutger. She had done the opposite, in fact, recommending him for promotion to sergeant and reluctantly approving his leave request.

"You'll have a tank of your own when you come back," Faora had said during their final conversation.

"Yes, I know."

"You are coming back, aren't you?" She stared at him as though she knew. "You do know that if you go AWOL you'll lose the escrow in your holding account and be out for good."

"Yeah, I know, Staff Sergeant."

And I don't give a shit. He was finally home, and no one could convince him to rejoin the Berserkers.

Rutger's sister Brianna picked him up at the spaceport terminal. She gave him a hug, and Rutger shook hands with her husband, Darrell. Rutger stared at the streets as they drove in a ground car to his sister's apartment on the outskirts of town.

"Did you see any action?" Darrell asked as they drove.

Rutger kept staring out the window. The question made him angry, though it wasn't unreasonable to ask. He was a mercenary who had just come from a war-torn planet. Darrell was just making conversation, but Rutger didn't answer right away.

He caught Brianna shooting Darrel a "Why would you ask that?" look.

"Yeah, I saw some action," Rutger finally said. "But that's over. It's good to be home."

A lie—he'd been home for half an hour and already felt like a stranger in his hometown, unable to relax, his senses on alert. Nothing had changed here; he saw the same old grimy apartment blocks, fume-belching industries, and worn-out people walking the streets. Everyone just went about their meager daily existence, oblivious to the fighting and carnage he had witnessed lightyears away.

Thankfully, Darrel asked no further questions.

Rutger stayed at his sister's place. Exhausted, he mainly slept and ate, rarely going outside. His sister asked when he planned to see Serena and Callie. He said he would soon. He thought about calling Serena before stopping by, but he couldn't bring himself to do it, fearful he might say something rash about the divorce. He decided to check out where she lived first. *A recon of the area,* he caught himself thinking.

He took a ground taxi across town to her address in an upscale block of high-rise condos. Serena appeared to be living quite well. *Thanks to my blood money, bitch.*

Rutger sat down the street at a hover bus stop for several hours until they emerged: Callie, Serena, and her new man. *One big happy family.* He only caught a glimpse of them before they got in a car, but he couldn't believe how big Callie had gotten.

Seeing the interloper who'd hijacked his family made Rutger's blood boil. He found a bar and got drunk, then stumbled for several klicks back to his sister's house. He'd lost his access card and had to pound on the door for Brianna to let him in.

The next morning, he realized that Brianna and Darrell pitied him and seemed to walk on eggshells in his presence, regarding him as one would a wild animal. So Rutger thanked them for their hospitality and departed to rent a hotel room. He spent several hours drinking beers from the overpriced minibar while scheming on how to get his family back. Serena wouldn't consider coming back if he couldn't support them. *I need a job.*

He found a listing on his holo-pad for a security job at an industrial plant that produced precision components for the Planetary Federation's military. OPEN INTERVIEWS BEGINNING AT 9 AM, IN PERSON ONLY read the listing. Rutger remembered how that worked. The unemployment rate on New Helena hovered at around 25%, and he would be competing with several hundred other applicants. *Get there early.*

Dressed in a newly purchased business suit, he arrived at 5 am. *What the fuck?* Unemployment must have been worse than he remembered. Men and women had camped out overnight for spots in line along the plant's perimeter fence. At least two hundred people were ahead of Rutger. *Suck it up. You knew it was coming.*

Applicants ahead of him talked about the latest pelota matches and violent reality holo shows. *Is that all you people have to worry about?* Rutger had once followed them too, but now he didn't understand how people could worship rich athletes and stars while barely being able to provide for themselves.

"I think I've got a pretty good shot at this job," said a short, sandy-haired man behind Rutger, who found his plastic smile immediately annoying.

"Yeah, me too," Rutger said.

"What's your experience?" he asked with a chuckle.

"Military. I've got a lot of experience with local and remote security. Cameras, recon drones—"

The asshole cut him off with gut-busting laughter. "You don't have a chance, pal! At least half of this line are university-trained industrial security specialists, myself included."

"I guess we'll see," Rutger said, turning his back on the little prick.

As it turned out, they didn't see. Around noon, with hundreds of applicants still in line, the loudspeakers made an announcement. "The security position has been filled. We thank you for your interest. Please disperse." A collective groan erupted from the line, which broke up as the message repeated.

Rutger turned to the short man. "Wow, that surveillance degree really helped you."

"Go to hell!"

"Already been there." He went off to find a bar and a bottle of synthos.

Rutger spent two more days watching Serena's building. Her boyfriend left every weekday morning at eight and didn't return until six or so.

He formulated a plan and bought a pistol illegally from one of his old underworld contacts. He wasn't really sure why he'd purchased it, perhaps a sense of security, but it felt good in his hands, familiar.

Rutger headed to Serena's the next morning and sat at the bus stop, drinking synthos as heavy rain lashed the plexiglass shelter. He looked like a typical derelict, albeit a little cleaner, and no one paid him any mind. The building had a doorman armed with a shock baton to keep out the riffraff. The entrance had a biometric lock. Visitors had to be buzzed in by a resident.

He took another pull from the bottle, the cold liquid burning his throat. A couple of hours later, the doorman forsook his duties momentarily to shoot the shit with a cabby he obviously knew. Rutger seized the opportunity and followed the next resident inside. Worried that his shabby appearance might alarm someone, he bypassed the elevators and took the stairs up to Serena's floor.

Rutger pulled his hat down and knocked on her door. "Delivery," he said, pitching his voice low.

Serena opened the door. Her bottomless brown eyes bugged when she saw him. "Sam... What are you doing here?"

"Surprised to see me?"

"You should have called before you came."

"Why, would you have answered? You didn't answer any of my holo messages."

"We aren't ready for you. How long are you in town?"

"I'm back for good," he said, slurring his words slightly. "You don't seem very excited."

"You need to go," she said, starting to close the door.

Rutger stuck his foot in the jamb and pushed inside. "Whoa, whoa, hold on. I just got here."

"Have you been drinking?"

"Perhaps I have," Rutger said, eyeing the spacious, well-furnished living room. "Quite the fancy setup you got here. Our entire apartment could have fit in your living room."

"It's ten-thirty in the morning. What the hell's wrong with you?"

"Where's Callie? I want to see her."

"Well, you're not going to. You've obviously been drinking, and she's sleeping right now. Call me and we'll set up a visit."

"A visit? She's my fricken daughter, and I'm gonna see her right now." He looked down the hall past Serena, then began to push past her.

"I said no, Sam." Serena blocked his path and put a hand on his chest. "Look, I'm glad you're home in one piece, but you just can't drop by and force your way into our place." Rutger took another step. "I said no!"

The front door behind Rutger beeped as it slid open.

"Hey, Serena, I forgot my data pad," said a tall man with black hair. He then noticed Rutger. "What the hell's going on here? Who are you?"

"Oh, I'm sorry. We haven't been properly introduced," Rutger said, stepping toward him. "I'm Sam."

The man's dark eyes flashed anger. "Right, I know who you are, buddy. You're the piece of shit who left your family to go play merc. Don't worry, I've taken good care of Serena and Callie."

"Jerome, don't," Serena said, trying to squirm between the two men.

Rutger swung. Anticipating the punch, Jerome partially blocked it and swung for Rutger, who sidestepped and parried with a downward strike of his left arm. Rutger followed up with a chop across the bridge of Jerome's nose, which broke with a sickening crunch.

Jerome crumpled to the floor in a daze, tears in his eyes and blood gushing from his nose. "You broke my fucking nose!" he cried nasally.

Rutger loomed over him, ready to strike again. Pressure built in his ears in time with his pounding pulse. Serena shoved Rutger aside and knelt beside Jerome, then she looked up at Rutger with tears and venom in her eyes. "You fucking bastard! What the hell is wrong with you?"

Rutger stared at her for a moment, then turned to go find Callie. "No!" Serena screamed. She slipped past and blocked Rutger's path.

"I want to see my fucking daughter," Rutger growled, trying to move around her. She slapped him. Rutger scowled and stared her down, knowing he couldn't strike back at her.

A big hand suddenly grabbed him from behind and threw him against the wall. Before Rutger could react, a meaty fist pumped into his stomach, knocking the wind out of him. Rutger barely managed to block the next punch as he groped for the pistol in his jacket pocket.

Rutger got hold of the pistol as Jerome tried to wrestle him toward the door. He smacked the butt of the weapon across the top of Jerome's head with a crack, opening up a deep gash. Jerome's grip loosened. Rutger shouldered him into the wall, knocking over some holo pictures on a small table, and shoved the pistol under his chin.

"You think you can just take over my family?" Rutger said, staring into fearful eyes. "I should end you right now. I've killed better men than you for far less."

"No!" Serena screamed.

Rutger saw movement in his peripheral vision and ducked just in time. The heavy food purator Serena swung at him barely grazed his head. He turned and shoved her hard against the wall. She stared at him in shocked, wide-eyed surprise that turned to pure terror when he trained the pistol on her. She froze like a cornered animal. In that instant, he hated her with all his being. His finger tensed on the trigger.

Rutger heard Jerome staggering to his feet. He turned and leveled the pistol at him. "Get the fuck outta here!"

Jerome raised his hands and slowly backed to the front door. He hit the open button and bolted out. Rutger locked the door behind him and electronically engaged the deadbolt.

Rutger turned to Serena, who had collapsed to the floor sobbing. He staggered past and dropped into a kitchen chair. The pistol limp in his lap.

Rutger stared at the pistol—*What the fuck have I done?*—then pocketed it. "I'm sorry. I didn't mean for this to—"

"Shut up! I fucking hate you." Sobs wracked her body. Rutger knelt and tried to hold her. She jolted as if electrocuted, then began raining punches on him, pounding her fists against his chest. He let Serena punch herself to exhaustion. Moments later, her anger spent, she fell into his arms and sobbed.

"Why did you leave us? I didn't want to raise our daughter alone."

"I'm sorry," Rutger finally said. "It seemed like the only option at the time."

"I missed you…I'm sorry I wasn't strong enough." She cried some more.

Tears stung his eyes. "It's all right," Rutger said, holding her close and smelling her hair again.

"Mommy," a soft voice said. "What's going on?"

Rutger turned. Callie stood in her pajamas, looking pale and weak. Recognition dawned on her face. "Daddy!"

"Yeah, sweetheart, it's me," he said, choking back tears.

She ran over and hugged him, and his heart melted. "Daddy, you're back!" *God, she's changed so much!*

"Come check out my room, Daddy." Rutger helped Serena to her feet. They followed Callie to a room full of dolls and teddy bears. A medical monitor stood next to her bed, incongruous and ominous.

He looked at Serena. "Is she…?"

Serena nodded.

"What about the gene therapy treatments?"

"Jerome lost his job a couple months ago when the plant was bought out in a merger. He lost his benefits, and since you took us off yours—"

"Because you said you didn't need them."

"I know. We may have to move if he doesn't find work soon. He's a good man, Sam, and well educated. He's out every day looking for work. You know it just takes time. It's hard—"

"I'll put her back on my plan, and I'll start sending some money again."

"I thought you were done."

So did I. Was he or wasn't he? Rutger grappled with indecision as he watched Callie play with her toys. She had a nice room and a good life here. *Better than I ever had.* And that settled his inner argument. "Look...just don't keep her from me. Have her send me vids and show her mine. Don't let her forget about me. I'll finish out my contract and we can figure something out long-term."

As his words trailed off he heard sirens in the distance. He looked at Serena.

"Sam, I'm sorry. I was scared. I hit the emergency alert when you were fighting with Jerome. They're going to arrest you."

Rutger sighed. "It's not your fault. You were protecting Callie. I need to do the same." He kneeled, and stroked Callie's hair. "Baby girl, I need to go."

Tears welled in her eyes. "But you just got here, Daddy. Don't go. Stay and play with me. I missed you."

"I know, sweetheart. I missed you every day."

"Please don't go, Daddy. Please, please stay." She grabbed his legs. He heard the sirens on the street below. Police would be coming up any moment now.

"Baby, I'm sorry," Rutger said, tears streaming down his face. "I'll be back soon, and I'll stay longer, I promise."

"Daddy, I love you."

"I love you too, sweetheart. You have no idea."

He turned and looked at Serena. She hugged him. "I'm sorry...I hurt you," Rutger said. "I thought I could handle coming home, that things would be like they used to be." He kissed her on the forehead, his hate gone now. "We were young and dumb, but I did love you. I still love you…Take care of yourself and our baby girl."

Tears streamed down her face. "I will."

Rutger wiped away tears with his sleeve as he ran for the door. He sprinted to the elevators and pressed the call button. A car was already ascending. *Shit, the police might be on it.* No time to run though. It had already arrived. The door opened on an empty car. He stepped inside and shook his head, trying to clear his mind. *There'll be cops waiting in the lobby.* He pressed the button for the roof.

The elevator opened onto the building's rooftop landing pad. A security guard sitting in a plexiglass booth by the elevator didn't look up as Rutger stepped out, too busy scrolling on his data pad.

Good, he hasn't been alerted…yet.

Rutger stepped into drizzling rain. Building lights and holographic billboards glowed on surrounding rooftops beneath the overcast sky. He looked toward the queue of air cars approaching and saw only one rider waited ahead of him for an air taxi, but he remained nervous. He breathed the wet, sulfur-tainted air. It felt better to be outside, but he knew he didn't have much time before the police arrived looking for him. He glanced back nervously when the elevator doors opened, but it was just an older woman waiting for a ride as well.

Rutger discretely dropped the pistol into a trash barrel.

A yellow and black checkered air taxi pulled up. Rutger climbed in the back, feeling the car sink slightly from his weight. *Probably a bad repulsor.*

He'd hoped that the holo screen in the back seat would be out of order, as they often were, but this one worked. He stared bleakly at the latest news vids, hoping to not see himself. *You're being paranoid now.* The heat wouldn't be after him that bad for a domestic assault. *But I did have a weapon. I need to get the fuck outta here.*

"Where to, buddy?" the cabby asked without turning around.

"Spaceport." It was all the way across town.

"That's thirty credits."

Rutger inserted his credit chip into the reader, then looked back at the roof through rain-streaked windows. No cops yet, but they would figure out where he'd gone and pull the rooftop security vids.

The taxi's turbofans wined perceptibly as the car accelerated, rising steeply toward one of the major air lanes. Rutger slumped back against the seat and searched departing flights on his data pad. He needed a quick departure and found one, an expensive direct flight, but he had enough credits. He completed the transaction and downloaded the ticket information onto his data pad.

They'll run my name. They might get me at the spaceport. The flight left in an hour, and if the cab made good time he would probably be okay. His personal effects back at the hotel could be easily replaced.

The driver merged into an air lane. Towering buildings below seemed small and insignificant to Rutger. New Helena and Port City were no longer his home. The place hadn't changed while he'd been gone, but he had. His heart already ached for Callie, and Rutger fought back another wave of tears. He would miss her, but he knew what he had to do—all for her. The thought renewed his sense of purpose.

"Where you heading?" the cabby asked, looking in the mirror.

"What?" Rutger said, lost in thought.

"You're going to the spaceport. You headed somewhere or do you work there?"

"Oh, I'm going to..." He hesitated, thinking of the police, but they could pull his travel itinerary easily enough. "I'm going to Scandova."

"Traveling awful light, aren't you?"

The nosy driver annoyed Rutger, but he decided to play it cool. "I sent my personal effects ahead."

"Ah, you moving there?"

"Nah, just work."

He checked his watch. The cab would make it in time for his departure. If there were no issues with terminal security or the flight, he would arrive on Scandova in time to link up with Bruiser Company before they departed for the next assignment.

Time to go home.

ABOUT THE AUTHOR

RYAN ASLESEN IS A BESTSELLING AUTHOR BASED out of Las Vegas, NV. He is a former Marine officer, a veteran of the War on Terror, and a graduate of Presentation College and American Military University. His military and work experience have made him one of the premier writers of military science fiction. His bestselling Crucible and War's Edge series are highly regarded for their authenticity, explosive action, and military realism. When not writing or lost in his imagination, you will find him spending quality time with his family. He is currently working on his next novel. He can be reached at <u>ryan.w.aslesen@</u> <u>gmail.com</u>.

Go to www.ryanaslesen.com to check out more great military science fiction books.

Made in the USA
Las Vegas, NV
10 September 2021